Best of Friends?

Hayley Coulson

authorHOUSE®

AuthorHouse™ UK Ltd.
500 Avebury Boulevard
Central Milton Keynes, MK9 2BE
www.authorhouse.co.uk
Phone: 08001974150

© 2009 Hayley Coulson. All rights reserved.

No part of this book may be reproduced, stored in a retrieval system, or transmitted by any means without the written permission of the author.

First published by AuthorHouse 7/2/2009

ISBN: 978-1-4389-6391-4 (sc)

This book is printed on acid-free paper.

Acknowledgements

Thank you first and foremost to the Rix/Hawkes and Phillips clans, my surrogate families, for your unconditional support and always a floor to sleep on!

To Alg, Jude & Jules for encouraging me to put pen to paper (or hand to keyboard) all those years ago to write something amusing about one of the most difficult subjects!

Thank you to Nic, Bex, Jax and Russell for some great ideas, Lina for design inspiration and my oldest friend Teen for your consistently valuable feedback and finally, a big thank you to AuthorHouse for giving me a home.

For Susie

Chapter 1

It was like a slow-mo moment as he walked across the dance floor through the coloured lights. He was like a Greek God and I couldn't believe he was coming to talk to me. I had spent two hours getting ready for this night and he must have noticed. He told me I was beautiful, spun me around the dance floor and then kissed me passionately... What a night!

As I struggled to open my eyes, the room seemed to be moving slightly, like the aftermath of an earthquake. My mouth felt like it was stuck together and that a small sewer-dwelling rodent had crawled in at some point in the night. I tried to move my head and it was pounding like a bass drum in a White Stripes song. There was something stuck to my forehead; it was a fake eyelash. I felt in a fog and very nauseous, then I heard the snort from behind me... I had brought the God home.

The ten seconds that it took to decide whether to turn over and remind myself of what he looked like, seemed like an eternity. Could I still sneak to the bathroom and freshen up without waking him? I did *not* feel good, what an earth did I look like? On a good day, I looked pretty normal, blonde hair (well, sometimes), brown eyes, average size and a smile. I was more cutesy than a looker but this morning, I had a sneaking suspicion that I mostly resembled Lily Savage after a typhoon. I slipped out of the bed at the side and crawled like Spiderman (after some bug spray) to the bathroom. As predicted, I needed some work; about four showers and a car wash should do it but the shower would be too noisy and would wake my guest. I did the best patch up job I could but there was no hiding the dark circles or the fact that due to extreme dehydration, if I moved my skin, it stayed there. I was fighting the waves of nausea and having to breathe deeply and I was unsure of my next move; do I attempt to sneak back into bed with my Greek God? Another round with the Adonis would surely tip me over the edge but then I don't want him to think I've run out on him, if he's as gorgeous as I remember, I really don't want to let this one get away.

Sniper crawling back across the room like Charlie Sheen in Platoon, seemed even more indignant than when I left the bedroom but it had to be done. Luckily he was facing the other way, I could just see the back of his head. Wow, I hadn't noticed that he was slightly balding before; oh well, nobody's perfect. I snuck back in bed and was immediately overwhelmed by the smell of onion, which I'd thought was me before the bathroom break but no. I was leaning over trying to get a look when I noticed the hair and spots on his back and then he farted; bloody charming. The smell kicked up so bad that I thought my eyes were melting and the nausea was suddenly back with a vengeance, as I tried not to gag. It was fair to say that my Adonis was losing some of his sheen right about now. He started to move, I started to panic... the slow-mo happened all over again and as he started to turn, memories began to flood my brain, as I suddenly remembered the night before!

The stark truth hit me like a bitch slap from a 300lb heifer. He didn't walk over the dance floor in a manly strut towards my statuesque figure cutting a move, looking like a demure Kylie in the Spinning Around video... No. The harsh reality was, I'd been absolutely plastered, looking like a crack addict drag queen and dancing like I had a club foot. He did the one-legged pissed walk and practically fell on to me during 'Club Tropicana', spilling half a pint of cheap lager down my front. He grabbed me, mumbled something about my breasts and we started going at it like a couple of crazed teenagers. I went to the men's bathroom (the queue for the women's was *far* too long), made some lewd comments as I walked past the men at the urinals, then threw up. We stopped at the burger van, I ended up wearing most of my snack as a necklace and then we made our way back to mine, where we stripped off, fumbled our way through two very excruciating minutes before the drink took it's inevitable toll on his anatomy and we both passed out. Not exactly my finest hour.

Right at this moment, I really wish I could say that *wasn't* me; that I had been kidnapped and replaced by slutty aliens or been the victim of some vicious mind control experiment. I'd even settle for a misspent youth; that it happened years ago, that I was in my teens or early 20's. Sadly not. I wish I could tell you I've grown up but I fear my friends might disagree, after all this wasn't my first. Don't get me wrong, I wasn't in the habit of bringing home a vast array of swamp donkeys but it wasn't exactly headline news in my household either. I remember my first minger, it's not something a girl forgets. It was the summer of '96; Olympic fever was abound as they kick started the Atlanta games, the Spice Girls were telling us what they wanted, what they really, really wanted and it was a year filled with unexplained disasters. Unfortunately, it sticks in my mind for a different reason. I was 17 and he was a good thirty years my senior, he had teeth like a retired racehorse, a slight limp from a gimpy leg, his hairline had receded back so much it started on his shoulder blades and he had such bad acne scars on his face that it could well have been the place that they faked the moon landings; no-one could deny I was doing my bit for care in the community. Thanks to my friends, our drunken liaison ended in the club.

I had *tried* to be more mature, now that I, Nicola Thompson, was about to reach the golden age of 30; this was just a minor slip that's all. I had cut down on my drinking for one, I only drank at weekends. Well, I had a glass of wine or two most nights but that was medicinal, so it doesn't count. Anyway, I live a long mile away from my folks, with my best friend Marcus and our roommate Sadie and a bottle of red whilst watching American trash TV was obligatory. We were lucky enough to live a pretty care-free existence which suited my penchant for not taking life too seriously. Besides, we couldn't be blamed, it wasn't *our* fault. Marcus and I grew up in a large crowd, in a very small village, we were just two of *many* kooky personalities struggling to get noticed. We all went to the same schools, our parents lived nearby and it was one of those places, where everybody knew everybody and everybody's business.

All through our school years, we were inseparable but over time, the group had sadly diminished and many of our friends began to move away and take different paths. That's why this year is significant, in four weeks time Marcus and I are having a joint 30th birthday party and thanks to Marcus, *everyone* is invited. It will be the first occasion in a long time that we will occupy the same space and share the same room together and I feel very,

very nervous. Why? Well, when you're younger, an eclectic mix of personalities is a sure fire recipe for fun but as time marches on, the only thing that's sure to fire is a temper (or six). Our track record wasn't great because between us, past and present, we covered all the bases with every possible character trait.

Take Jenna, for example. Although a previous alcoholic nymphomaniac, she's now married to the most boring man that ever walked the earth; David. He's a Police Officer, who she met after a drunken binge when she got caught stealing ceramic animals off someone's rather decorative front lawn. She stopped coming out, as she knew David and his colleagues could follow her all over town with the help of CCTV and even shops from the comfort of her habitat home; they only get excited now when John Lewis has a sale.

Then on the opposite end of the scale, there was Carly. My partner in crime throughout most of the 80's, 90's and early naughty 0's, she was funny and smart and could add naturally pretty to her list of attributes. Don't worry; we dealt with this like adults, by telling good-looking members of the opposite sex that she used to be a man called Reg. However, she only had eyes for Pete, an all round top bloke, who also grew up in our circle. I haven't seen them for three years after they moved away and thanks to my own stupidity, we don't talk now and I *really* miss them.

Somewhere in the middle were Emma and Alice. Emma is an organiser by nature and always takes things too far. She's an emotional volcano waiting to erupt and it's wise to keep some flat shoes about your person because when she blows, you'll need to run quicker than Linford. I used to think it was a ginger persecution complex but for scale, you'd need to think Halle Berry at the Oscars (or indeed Halle Berry at *any* awards ceremony). She's married to a guy called Justin and she has two kids… No, really, she's a mum and her children scare therapists. Alice is a timid creature and an inoffensive walkover who's managed to go through most of her life without a single thought of her own, just latching on to other people's fads. She's engaged to another childhood friend, Greg, who has made his way around half the village, so naturally Alice had to try him out as well. He cheats on her of course and she happily turns a blind eye.

Just a small selection to prove my point and maybe explain why I had tried to persuade Marcus not to invite our *entire* childhood entourage, as I was sure it would all kick off but he seemed intent on bringing everyone back together, rationalising that enough time had passed to eradicate any bad feeling. I wasn't convinced but I did however, have to listen, as Marcus was always the voice of reason but unfortunately for me, he was also the voice of pure scorn which I was *not* looking forward to today…

I still had to get Hairy Kebab Man out of the house without Marcus and Sadie seeing him. He seemed to think that our two minute consummation was the start of a beautiful relationship and all I could think was I needed to eat some crap, drink some coffee and some full fat coke and then throw up again; or maybe the other way round, I hadn't quite decided yet. Either way, Hairy Kebab Man was adding to my nausea and he *had* to leave only he wasn't catching on to my subtle hints and was trying to impress by telling me that his father does actually own a kebab van, so he can score me a free one, whenever I want. Oh God, yep, there was actually a little bit of sick in my mouth. He moved in for a kiss and I managed to duck and pat him condescendingly on the arm in one swift move and say, "Errr, thanks. I'll see you around". He seemed a little dejected but I also suspected that this wasn't his *first* arm pat. He muttered something illegible and finally left.

The second the front door slammed shut, Sadie was in the hallway with arms folded and eyebrow raised. Her stare was interrupted by Marcus yelling from the front room, "Has it left yet?" I was officially mortified but the worst part was that I *knew* my humiliation was far from complete. Marcus shouted out again, "Well...?"

Sadie began to laugh and all I could manage was, "Don't... I think I'm gonna be sick", as I ran towards the bathroom.

Chapter 2

Sitting down with Marcus to discuss every disgusting, gory detail of a night out was common-place. We'd head over to the local café 'Babe Ruth's', order up some serious hang-over food and *literally* chew the fat over the embarrassing antics of the night before. OK, so it was nearly always *my* embarrassing antics but he seemed to enjoy the feeling of superiority and the opportunity to mock the apparently shameless, such as myself.

Marcus and I go way back to pre-school and we'd stayed such great friends because he made me laugh, I mean *really* laugh. He loved to take the mick and I had never failed to be a constant source of material; it was a match made in heaven. Although it wasn't all swift kicking while the other was down, being the person Marcus was, he would never mock and run, he would always take the time to pick me up and dust me off. He would do this really cute thing where he'd tell me that I'm better than this and I deserved to find a nice guy and settle down. Of course, I would always laugh my ass off. Here endeth the moment.

Marcus Benjamin came from impressive parentage; Samuel and Neil were a gay couple who were intelligent, fun and refreshingly honest. My mum had told me the story a million times of when they first came to the village, the shock and horror that there were two men nearby who shared the same bed. They stopped traffic, quietened pubs and almost formed congas in the local supermarkets, where people were desperate to see what they were up to and how they lived their life. They persevered, joining in all the activities and committees and after a while the locals began to leave the comfort of their caves and Samuel and Neil became a popular addition to the village. They decided to start a family, using Samuel's swimmers with a surrogate mum and the result was baby Marcus. I guess he was good-looking, I'd never really thought about it, he had really shiny, black hair, like he'd coated it in boot polish, dark eyes and skin and he dressed immaculately. His general demeanour, to anyone who wasn't me, was sweet and charming and he could schmooze his way out of any conflict. If I stopped to think about it, he was the perfect guy; so naturally, he was gay.

He was also my harshest critic and today was no different. "Get showered, get changed, we're going to Ruth's. And for Christ's sake, wash that mustard out of your hair, you skanky cow".

"What mustard?" I tried to hide it but had no idea where the offending condiment was.

"You have congealed bright yellow gunk in your hair". Marcus stood there looking at me incredulously. I failed to find it, mainly due to the fact that every time I turned my head it took five seconds for the world to catch me up. I shrugged my shoulders indicating that he must be mistaken and with a raised eyebrow, he pointed to what had caused his revolt and added, "Also, I called in forensics and they found breadcrumbs and three bits of lettuce in the hallway this morning, they sent them off for testing but they suspect burger". I wanted to bow to his superior mocking but figured I might not make it back up again.

I did as I was told and made my way slowly but surely to the bathroom, for the third time that morning. The shower at first felt like needles on my skin but after a few minutes, the hot water hugged me and it felt really good, I needed to clear the haze. I noticed there were a couple of pieces of lettuce in the plughole... and I'm still single? Shocker! I cleared the mist from the mirror and the horrific reflection made me jump. The hairdryer was too loud and really hot, so I decided to just tie up my wet hair. I found a few UDI's ('unidentified drinking injuries' to the t-total), which looked pretty nasty but luckily they were out of sight, so I wouldn't have to explain them. I took more time to dress myself than an arthritic pensioner, partly due to bending down not being an option today, as I still didn't have full control over my reflux system. I threw on a hoodie, completing the look of 'proud Chav, with very first ASBO' and peeked my head round my bedroom door. Marcus was waiting patiently in the hallway but I suspected his restraint was purely down to the fact that he knew this was going to be a good yarn.

We left the house and Marcus even helped me down the front step like an invalid and I could see him trying not to laugh as I breathed heavily. The air out was cool and crisp which felt really nice on my head, like a soothing cold flannel but aesthetically, it just made my eyes even *more* bloodshot, like a basset hound on pot. We made our way very, very, slowly over to our favourite haunt, knowing the arduous journey of half a mile would ultimately be worth the sacrifice.

Babe Ruth's was a café that was done out like an American diner but served traditional English breakfast's, with pictures of Hollywood starlets on the wall, next to posters promoting the Best of British, to say it had an identity crisis was an understatement but it's what gave it it's unique charm. The name was supposed to be a clever play on words for its owner Ruth, which would be fine, except Ruth… well, she's about 412 years old and looks like a Shar-Pei dog that stayed in the bath too long.

"Hey kids, what'll it be today?" Everyone under the age of 50 was a kid to Ruth.

"Ooh, a brew, two sugars please, Ruth. I'll have a full English as well, with tinned toms but hold the beans".

"Good night, was it treacle?" Oh, she knew me so well. I just nodded in mock shame and she smiled.

"I'll have a tea, no sugar and two poached eggs on two toast, please". I just glared at Marcus for a second. He was putting me to shame with his pretentiously healthy eggs. When using my vocal chords above a certain sound register no longer hurts, I *will* be having words.

"You kids sit yourself down; I'll bring it over in a jiffy". It was always a jiffy, I had never worked out the exact length of time a jiffy was but it was always a jiffy.

Marcus didn't hang about. "So what happened?"

"Whoa, straight in there with the questions, Kojak".

Marcus had waited all morning for this. "Well…?"

I was momentarily distracted by Ruth's special diner music in the background; it was 'Elvis' singing 'Hound Dog' – someone, somewhere, was sending me a sign. I took a deep breath (actually, it was half a deep breath, a full one and I would have passed out this morning). "Well... We started off in Dribbler's, then we went to Job's, then on to Crusty's, then we ended up in Vom's".

OK, so it was like talking in code, we had nickname's for everywhere we'd drank over the years. They were terms of endearments really; reminders of the roads well travelled. Dribbler's got its nickname from Greg's 20th Birthday; Pete got so drunk, he actually started dribbling. Job's was so named because Jenna, fully loaded, took it upon herself to perform a usually private act under one of the tables. Crusty's was delightfully immortalised as despite the tasty cocktails (or maybe because of them), the carpet was so minging, your feet always got stuck to it and then of course, there was the infamous Club 'Vom'; I *just* don't think this needs an explanation.

I was biting my lip, dreading telling him the next part which Marcus picked up on and leaned in with a wry smile. Oh crap. I took another half deep breath, ready to get the words out quickly. Here goes, "It was all going great, we had a good laugh in Dribbler's and Job's *and* I even abstained from a round of shots". I paused for effect. Sure, Marcus liked me in his own special way but thinking highly of me was *not* something I suspected he did, so I didn't want to ruin the moment. "*They* were all over the shop but me? No sirree. You'd have been *so* proud".

"I am, I am". Marcus was nodding his obvious approval but then I remembered that much like watching the film 'Titanic', he knew how this story ended, so it was pointless dragging out the subplot.

Best of Friends?

I really didn't want to fess up to the next part, so like the grown up that I am, I looked down at the table and muttered, hoping he wouldn't hear, "Then Luke came in".

"Riiiigghhht". Marcus could be such a drama queen.

So I guess at this point, I should tell you about Luke. Luke Frost was also one of the original group, you know, same school, parents knew each other, all that stuff. What's he like? Well, if I were to honestly describe Luke, he's outrageously good looking, he's stunning in fact, a blonde and blue-eyed, biological marvel and damn, didn't he know it. I wish I could say that he used his natural God given talents for good but the truth was, he used it to acquire anything or anybody he wanted. He was a Salesman by trade and every time I saw him, he nearly always had a new job. He had his own, very unique brand of bullshit but I hadn't been inoculated, so unfortunately, was not immune and so Luke and I had what you might call, history…

I began to relate the next part of the evening to Marcus as quickly as I could, hoping to display my indifference but where I was struggling to salvage my oxygen this morning, it actually just made me sound slightly demented. "Well, he came in with another girl. Which was fine, doesn't bother me. It's not like *I'm* dating him". I was playing with my cutlery. "I'm *not* bothered". The constant repetition was not helping me to convince, either him or myself.

"Of course not". Marcus was good at disdain, he had the voice (and the eyebrow's) for it.

"I'm not!"

Marcus reached out his hand across the table and patted mine. "Let it go, Captain Ahab, let it go".

I was pouting, trying to limp off that last remark. "Anyway, I was standing there with my work buddies, having a laugh when he just struts in, so I ignored him and carried on laughing…" Marcus sat there open mouthed. What did I say?

"Oh no, you didn't….?" Marcus searched my face for answers and apparently found them. "Oh God, you did! You fake laughed!" Marcus held his head in his hands to hide his vicarious shame.

"No!" I glared at him but he was laughing now. I let out a big sigh and bit the inside of my mouth, waiting for him to stop howling at my expense. "Fine…" I conceded, shaking my head. "…maybe a little". He gloated and I ignored. "*Anyway.* He pretended not to notice me and then started putting his hands *all* over her, whispering in her ear and all that. It was obscene!"

"Obscene? In Job's? Trust me luv, they've seen worse". He wasn't wrong but he was supposed to be on *my* side.

"AND she'd just eaten a packet of cheese and onion crisps, her breath must have been hanging!" OK, so I was seriously grasping at straws and I quickly lowered my tone, before only dogs could hear me, "It was obvious he was only doing it to make me jealous". I was kicking my feet under the table like a petulant child. "Like *I'd* care!" Me thinks I doth protesteth too mucheth.

He feigned boredom now, breathing out the word, "Indeed".

I moved on with the story and confessed my next move. "So then I ordered a tequila". Marcus condescendingly nodded and smiled. God, I might as well tell the whole truth and nothing but the truth. "Then I ordered another".

"Way to go Georgie Best!" He was laughing aloud now.

I then spoke the next sentence so quickly, I almost expected a puff of comedy smoke to come out of my mouth when I finished. "Then my earlyish night went out the window, we ended up in Vom's, I got soaked by Hairy Kebab Man during 'Club Tropicana' and... you know the rest". I looked around, making sure no-one else was hearing my shame, before I put my head in my hands.

"Wow! You *have* been busy, haven't you?" He was placing his serviette on his lap and clearing a space in front of him, ready for his breakfast, whilst biting his top lip. "You know, I've never tried the 'throw your drink' chat up line before? It sounds like a winner".

"Yeah, what can I say? It won me over". Hell, if you can't beat them, get a bigger bat... or join them. "I'm pretty sure he spilt his beer on me just as George Michael said 'drinks are free'. You just can't ignore that kind of timing". I managed a genuine smile for the first time that morning while Ruth served up our breakfasts.

Marcus tucked in to his traitorous eggs. "This is what happens when you go out without me". He was really enjoying the sober superiority and I let him have his moment.

"Alcohol used to be my friend, you know?" I crossed my fingers. "Me and alcohol were like that, we go way back alcohol and me, we have a beautiful history; why would alcohol do this to me?"

Marcus let out a big sigh, put down his knife and fork and looked pained. "*You* do this to yourself. Every time you run into him, you either end up going home with him or you retaliate by hooking up with the first bloke that you come in to contact with. If you're not careful, you'll get a name, you know".

"What? Ethel?"

He rolled his eyes as he picked up his cutlery and started slicing the rest of his toast. "Why do you always let him get to you like that?"

"I dunno. It's like I'm totally over him you know, I'm like together, I'm having fun and then wham!"

"What the Club Tropicana song again?" He couldn't hide his obvious amusement at that one.

"No! I mean wham, as in, you know, 'whoa there', it hits me like a train and then I realise I'm hooked or something. It's totally pathetic and if it were someone else, I would be mocking that patheticness right now but I can't help it". I felt like a total loser, which was confirmed, when I looked round and saw the man on the next table shake his head at me. I shifted down in my seat and tried to hide my face, I was going to have to use my hand to cover my shame and I was really wishing that I'd left my hair down, I was now going to have to finish my breakfast one handed.

So it took Marcus a little longer than normal but... "You're better than this, you know?"

I laughed for a good minute, nearly choking on a hash brown. I eventually stopped laughing, he stopped frowning and we held up our forks and clinked them together. I felt exhausted now; it was definitely time to change the subject.

"So what did you get up to last night? Did you go to that bar?" I was glad to let him do the talking for a second, so I could shovel in my forkful of fatty goodness.

"Hmm, I did". Marcus was displaying the same amount of enthusiasm that I would normally reserve for a dental appointment.

"Oh dear, doesn't sound good. Gaydar on the fritz again?" I had to ask, he wasn't always that great at spotting other gay men, despite his impressive pedigree.

Marcus let out a wistful laugh and reflectively nodded, he took a moment to acknowledge his own lack of skill. "No, believe it or not, that was fine; it really *was* a gay bar this time. Wall-to-wall gay men".

"Wall-to-wall gay men? Wow! What do you call that a plethora? A flock? A *gaggle* of gay men?" I was feeling much better already, oh the power of a good mock.

Marcus sat there staring at me, waiting for me to shut up. I smiled, dutifully closed mouth and gestured that he should proceed with his tale of woe. "It wasn't like any of the clubs in London; it was proper cheesy and a total cliché".

"I see, more camp than a scout jamboree, huh?" I'd been waiting to use that line, for some time.

Marcus spoke into his brew, "Exactly".

"Bummer..." Sometimes, I wish I thought before I spoke. "Sorry, no pun intended". I desperately tried not to laugh while Marcus manufactured a faux scowl.

We chatted some more about Marcus' evening and how he'd thought about escaping through the bathroom window and then he reprimanded me for not answering a help text he'd sent. We finished our food and after a good thirty minutes to let the stuff get past my oesophagus, we made our way back outside and gingerly back home.

Sunday evening came around quickly as Marcus, Sadie and I just lazed around on the sofas, eating crap and watching classic hang-over films like The Goonies and Top Gun. I was thoroughly exhausted after my cringe-worthy confessions at Ruth's. We came back; I got into my trackie bottoms and totally slobbed out. I was a wounded soldier, so the troops rallied round. Marcus had been on tea duty all day and Sadie had whipped up a dinner time feast of toasties to keep my strength up (although there was a dicey moment, when I got a whiff of Sadie's personal creation of banana and bacon). They kept the volume down, kept the junk food coming and kept the lights dimmed; they were pretty darn good friends.

Our roomie, Sadie Wood, was a 25 year old waif, who was at times perhaps, not the sharpest tool in the box. She was however, a total sweetie and her naivety actually made her all the more fun. When we were looking for a new housemate, Marcus and I conducted interviews and during our thorough and sometimes brutal investigations, we asked all the essential questions; what's your credit rating? Any outstanding loans? What's your favourite tipple? What are your views on reality TV? And if we didn't like them, we asked how they felt about watching The Walton's re-runs on a Sunday? That usually sent them packing. When Sadie came for her interview, she had impressed us with her superior knowledge of 80's films and music; so naturally her credit rating went out the window.

Every Sunday, Sadie made us watch the Antiques Roadshow, personally I'd prefer to put liquid paper in my eyes but Sadie loved it, she would sit there and try and guess the value of each object, "Fifty quid!"

Cue pompous, bow tied, tidy-moustached, Sir John Gielgud sound-alike, "It's from the Ming Dynasty and in today's market would fetch around £50,000".

Sadie argued her case, "Well, I wouldn't pay that for it".

Marcus and I shared a quick glance and a smiled; it had become a beloved Sunday tradition.

Sadie let out a huge sigh and then uttered the immortal words that should have been included as the 11th Commandment, as the words that shoult *never* be spoken on a Sunday, "Ahh man, I really don't wanna go to work tomorrow".

My reactions had been slowed by the Sambuca the night before or maybe it was the Tequila or the vodka... so Marcus jumped in quicker than I could. "You said the 'W' word! You *know* the rule about the 'W' word on Sunday's! Quick chuck on another film, I need to recover!"

"I second that motion!" I was backing my man, with a mouthful of peanut M & M's and one fell out... attractive.

Sadie pleaded, "But Antiques Roadshow hasn't finished!"

"No sympathy's Sade, you should've thought about that before!" He can be my wingman any time.

Chapter 3

I turfed up to work ten minutes late, which to be fair was quite good for me on a Monday morning. My work was at a Travel Agent in town and my colleagues were ready and waiting for the quick fire round of 'Who's your minger?'

It was my friend Sally who chimed in first, "Morning!" She was always really annoyingly chirpy, we often called her Sunshine Sally and suspected Prozac. "So, who *was* that chimp?" I was going to have to review the friendship. I sat there with a questioning look as she continued, "Well, he was sort of short and hairy... but you could *see through* his hair, like a chimp! In fact, in that stripy shirt he belonged in one of those old PG Tips commercials". Couldn't fault her keen observation skills and attention to detail, I suppose, she'd obviously focussed on him better than I had. I chose not to answer, hoping she'd let it go. I was wrong. "Sooo..." The pause seemed to go on forever. "Who *was* he?"

I looked around the room, hoping that no one else was paying any attention to our exchange. Unfortunately for me, everyone seemed to have stopped what they were doing and were staring in my direction, smiling in unison, it was like a scene from Stepford Wives. "Erm, he was errr... Steve". I was drowning. "Yeah, that's right, Steve and his dad owns a... restaurant in London". I was slowly but surely booking my place in hell.

"Steve? He didn't look like a Steve".

You've gotta love that logic. I searched her face then looked around again at the others who weren't even remotely phased by her stunning deduction and responded, "Well, we can't all look like our names".

She looked pensive, actually weighing up my comment. "I guess not". Then she shook her head, as if to remove the unwanted element from her brain. I thought that I had rather cleverly, thrown her off her momentum but it would appear that she had *plenty* of pep in reserve. "So did you and Steve...?" She gestured something with her eyebrows.

"No! What do you think I am?!" I took a moment to reflect on my own question and then thought better of it. "We got some food and said our goodnights". I was trying to hide my face now, I was really crap at lying and I thought they'd see it.

"So are you gonna see him again?" She was poorly stifling a giggle.

I shrugged my shoulders and shook my head as if I were playing it cool and walked back to my desk but the truth was unless he came up and re-introduced himself, I *wouldn't* see him again. Despite the fact that I couldn't remember his name, I wasn't sure I could pick him out of a line up.

My boss came in the room and said her usual Monday morning comment, "Afternoon, Nicky".

I did my best smile through gritted teeth. "Good morning, Amanda".

Amanda was one of those people who was obviously bullied at school and wanted to get her revenge in later life. "The girls inform me you all went out for drinks on Saturday". The room went quiet and for a moment, you could hear the wind whistle through the door.

I threw them a glare, wondering why on earth they'd told her. "Err, yes… it, err, it was a bit last minute".

"I was busy anyway. Family commitments and Michael Jackson needed a bath".

Don't worry, they weren't practising any weird water rituals on the King of Pop; Michael Jackson was their dog. Amanda's husband Brian had been a lifelong fan, so Amanda was grateful for the dog, it could have been the kid's names *and* they were girls. I'd seen pictures of the infamous dog and it looked miserable but I suppose it can't be easy being named Michael Jackson. The sniggers and the jeers from the other dogs at the park, all of them hiding their puppies away, when he walks by... I wouldn't be surprised if Brian had made him outfits as well, like little doggy sunglasses, a red leather jacket and a white, diamond encrusted sock to go over just one of his paws. It was clear I'd given this *way* too much thought.

Amanda cut into my daydream. "Some new brochures came in today, I need you to sort them out, if you think you can manage that?" Oh, it was fully loaded and dripping with sarcasm but it was not the appropriate time to use the 'lowest form of wit' quote, so I smiled through clenched teeth and told her it wasn't a problem. Today, I would be her number one target, topping the list for all the crappy jobs.

I dutifully did as I was told, gracing customers with my best smile. I was struggling a bit with loading up the bottom shelf as the skirt from my god awful uniform was a little tight today and was cutting in to my intestines, probably making them look like a row of sausages whenever I bent down. The weekend's antics had definitely left me carrying a few extra pounds. On top of the calorific alcoholic beverages I had consumed, I had also done the 2:00am rat burger, named so, for its suspected content. Not good. It's not my fault of course, I blame the English language, it's the names of these offending items. I mean, bur-ger, ke-bab, both with just the two syllables, if either were more difficult to say under the influence, I would be sliding in to a nice size 10 right about now. If ever a court of law needed physical proof of the damaging effects of alcohol, it was the 2:00am, two syllable food item that would never be consumed during a period of unimpaired judgement. I was wondering if it would be inappropriate for me to lie on the floor to fill the bottom shelf. I looked round at Amanda who was watching my every move and concluded that perhaps it was not one of my better ideas.

Sunshine Sally, also has the patience of a Saint, as she waited all morning for Amanda to go to lunch, to land the next one on me. "Oh, I meant to say earlier, I got some cracking photos from Saturday".

I looked up from the brochures and glared at her for a second, hoping I didn't hear what I thought I had just heard. "What?"

"Saturday. I got some really good pics". She repeated her treacherous statement, even more zesty than the first time. My heart was beating at a ridiculous pace and I felt a pain in my arm, was it a heart attack? "And what pics would those be?" I had tried to compose myself but I couldn't hide my voice breaking, like a 13 year old boy going through puberty.

She continued her smiling torture and I half expected to hear 'Stuck in the Middle with You', while she sliced my ear off. "Well, I got some nice one's of us in The Rat & Parrot, like the *before* photo's, you know? What do you call that place again?"

"Dribbler's". My tone was flat and my manner wary.

She ignored my wary and raised me a perky, "*That's* the one! Then I got some good ones of us doing those shots in The White Hart... sorry, Job's. And there's a great one of Tamsin in Crusty's". It was executed with such dramatic villainy that I was thinking she must have a talking mirror at home.

"Yeah?" I waited a moment. I was rapidly looking from eye to eye, waiting for a flinch. It was like a scene in a Western, my eyes narrowed. I waited a moment more. The imaginary pain in my arm was subsiding; relief was beginning to wash over me, was that it? Nothing. My eyes widened again. No more photographs. I could feel myself smiling and I finally breathed. That was all the photos she had, thank you lord! The reprieve allowed me to inject some actual enthusiasm into my next sentence. "Sounds good, Sal. You'll have to download them on to Facebook, so we can *all* have a proper look".

"I intend to". She smiled and I walked back over to my desk feeling so much lighter than just a moment ago but still needing to sit down and gather myself. Phew! That was a close one! The relief was immense. My breathing had become rhythmical again and my heart was just returning to its normal pace when suddenly she said, "Oh, and there's those photo's I took in Vom's..."

I felt the hairs on the back of my neck raise and a cold shiver slowly crept over me. The sound went out the room for a minute as I looked over towards her and she had the same big, beaming smile. She knew she had me and she was enjoying every last, evil minute. I slowly leaned forward and looked down the line of desks, all the girls suddenly looked down at their keyboards and were really trying not to laugh; Tamsin on the end was failing miserably.

I finally managed to speak. I desperately tried to sound disinterested, whilst fighting the urge to throw up. "So... um... what photos did you take in Vom's?"

Sally's smile widened, leaving me to wonder, just how big was her mouth? "Ooh, let me see. Well, there was that one of Julie on the dancefloor. There was that one of you and, errr..." The pause was unnecessary and just damn right mean. "Tamsin on the dancefloor". Tamsin practically fell off her chair at this point. Suddenly, Sally speeded up, pointing at her fingers like she was counting. "A few good pics of us at the bar, more of the dancefloor, a couple of you and the Chimp and there's one of the loos, which was totally weird, 'cause I don't remember taking that!" She was facing her computer and biting her top lip now, trying not to laugh.

I narrowed my eyes at her again. My tongue was paralysed in my cheek and all I could manage was an all-knowing "Huuuh". I was staring into space. On the outside, I looked like an extra in 'One Flew Over the Cuckoo's Nest', on the inside, my brain was racing so fast at the possible images she could have captured that I thought I might pass out.

She managed to compose herself again for a brief moment and almost like my thoughts had been projected on to the nearest wall, she stated, "Don't worry, like you said, I'll download them on to Facebook, so you can see them all next week".

She was still looking away but I could see her shoulders shaking. It was an unexpected aerial assault and my communication skills were down, so I was unable to get in my last pathetic plea, before Amanda walked back into the office with her sandwich. God damn her work ethic!

This was payback. Two months beforehand, we had all gone out after work for Julie's birthday and that night it was Tamsin who got drunk, pulled a swill swimmer and I happily took pictures and posted them online for all to see. It was cruel and to be fair, I had this coming, I had to take it with good grace. Silently, I was vowing never to put compromising pictures of friends into the public domain again but luckily, my tongue was still paralysed so I didn't verbalise this statement. Although I felt I had learnt a harsh lesson, it was not a vow I was likely to uphold until my dying day.

Amanda broke the silence, "Are you just going to leave the rest of those brochures on the floor, Nicky, where some poor customer could trip?"

"No, Amanda". I smiled with all the saccharin I could muster. "I'll move them right away."

It was the longest day. The only thing that broke it up was three texts from Marcus about how Monday's totally sucked. I finally sent him one back and told him all about my own hellish day at the office and he sent a message back with about ten Ha's in a row, with a few smiley face's thrown in for good measure, he told me to thank Sally for making his day and then spouted something about Karma. I guess asking for sympathy on this one, was a step too far. The day was nearly over, thank god, when my phone vibrated again. I thought it might be Marcus, with a few more Ha's and a LOL that he might have forgotten but instead it was an extremely unexpected message from Jenna. *"Hey babe, how u doin? Been long time. Fancy a drink sumtime this wk? Love ya. Jen x"*

I wouldn't have batted an eyelid normally but I hadn't heard a peep from Jenna for about four months. I sat staring into space for a moment, wondering what she wanted then replied back confirming a date and time. Maybe it was because Marcus and I had sent out our party invites a couple of weeks before and it reminded her that we hadn't spoken in a while? Maybe...

Chapter 4

Wednesday night arrived and I was spruced and ready for drinks with Jenna at Stumpy's. It was a Wine Bar in town and of course, that wasn't it's real name, it fell into our affectionately nicknamed places to go. The owner was a really nice guy but he was… what's the politically correct term? Somewhat vertically challenged. Marcus kindly gave me a lift there but spent the brief car journey warning me not to drink too much and bring back anything that wasn't mine, I think that included men. I wasn't holding out much hope of an action-packed night, I reminded him that Jenna was boring now and he came out with some sentence about pikeys never changing their socks and I parted with him, promising to leave decorative lawn animals alone.

Jenna Jones (she kept her own name) was already at the bar, you could spot her obviously dyed, blonde hair a mile off and a chest that with one swift turn of the chair, could wipe out the bar in seconds. She was sat with a near empty glass. "Crikey luv, leave some for me!"

"Babes! Fabulous to see you!" She gave me a massive hug that nearly crushed me. Jenna was always a little OTT.

"You too, hon". I *had* missed her, I might not have seen her for a while but I often thought about her. She was always the person I ran to when I wanted to a no holds barred night out and vice versa. Jenna was the ringleader on many a night out that started as an innocent tipple in a quiet pub to waking up with a temporary traffic sign in your bedroom. She was unpredictable, highly strung, oversexed and a bottomless pit when it came to alcohol. She was the only person I knew, who could drink me under the table but then of course, when she was under the table... I'm not going to finish that sentence.

Let's just say, back in the 'good old days', it was rare that she ever went home alone. I used to applaud her bedpost notches but by the time we hit our mid-20's her bedpost already looked like it had been half-eaten by woodworm. It had to be said, when it came to men, she was impressive; what Jenna wanted, Jenna got. I even saw her pull from a club balcony once, not a feat easily achieved. However, underneath my congratulatory back-slaps, I wasn't always 100% behind Jenna's lack of... I was going to say self-respect but it seems a tad pretentious, so I'll go with inhibitions... but with my own behaviour of late, I would hardly stand up in court as a decent character witness.

I guess I was the Hardy to her Laurel or maybe more the Stimpy to her Ren, as we generally left a trail of destruction behind us. When she settled down with David, I hoped it would be a good thing, a grown up thing, a stable influence. I thought it might be good for me, as being a part of the tornado that was Jenna was exhausting. I still craved the fun but not in the same extremity or frequency anymore or indeed the consequences, legal ramifications or hangovers that followed. Obviously, I didn't always adhere to this profound new philosophy.

Unfortunately, Jenna's marriage to David has not turned out to be what *any* of us expected. The scales had been quickly tipped so far on to the other side, they'd fallen on their arse. See, David thought he knew about Jenna's past indiscretions and was no longer, even slightly, amused. He didn't even laugh at the ceramics story any more, and that's one of my favourite anecdotes. He told her that her behaviour could affect his job and as a consequence, when Jenna did have a night out, he had her (not very discreetly) watched. Truth was, her life before? He didn't know the half of it, which was probably just as well but due to David's spies, our nights out dwindled and then gradually came to a crashing halt. Most of the time now, I only saw her when she had a problem she wanted to talk about. God knows why she came to me; I normally just took the piss out of her. I still kept the hope that whenever I received a message from her asking to meet up, that it could still be for a good drink up and not just me playing a cross between Doctors Seuss and Freud. I wondered which one this was going to be; talk and mend or drink and destroy? As homage to our past, I put on my drinking shoes. Just in case.

She looked OK, a little tired maybe but hair done, dress on, one drink down already, it could've been a call to arms. It was time to find out. "So. How've you been?"

"Oh, you know same old, same old". Hmm, non-descriptive and evasive, I guess that meant problem time; damn it. I ordered drinks and Jenna came out with something straight from the mum book of questions which she must have borrowed from the library, what am I saying? Stole from a shop. "So how are you? Still living like you're in college?"

"Ha ha, yeah. Beats growing up, right?" Right back at ya sister.

"Yeah".

There was an uncomfortable pause; small-talk never was my forte. "Err... yeah. So, what is the same old, same old, for you these days? I haven't seen you since Emma's latest kid, what's its name again?"

"Jessica". Jenna looked disapproving at my lack of memory.

"Yeah, Jessica's christening. You and David left early, right?" Social chit chat could be a painful thing but from her body language, I'm not sure that I wasn't on to something.

"David had the late shift that week". She looked really uneasy, so like an over-eager reporter, I wouldn't let it lie. Only problem is, I'm shit at investigating. "Oh right. So... he works a lot at errr... work, with his..." I was looking around for help now but I wasn't going to find it. "...workmates". Columbo needn't worry about his job.

A few moments passed as she just sat there, nodding slightly and staring at the optics behind the bar. OK, so I *was* on to something but I lost her to the fairies with my opening line of interrogation. I needed to get a grip. What would Horatio Caine do? I'm not sure quippy one-liners and putting on my sunglasses was going to coax the truth out of her. I went with simple. "So". I had her attention again as she looked towards me. "What do you do when David's on late's?" Good, a complete sentence. I even crossed my legs and put my thumb to my chin. Now I looked the part.

Wait a minute; don't tell me I hit the jackpot already? She quickly turned to face the bar again while the colour literally drained from her face. Shit, I take it back, I'm good! "Jen...? What's up?" She turned on her stool to face me again; she looked like she was going to cry. I suddenly felt a twinge of guilt; my superior detective work had made her teary. Bad friend, *bad* friend! "Jen? What is it?"

She looked back to see if the bartender could hear us and when she comfortable he was out of earshot, "I cheated on David".

She shoots, she scores! "What?! When?! You never leave the house! Do you keep a spare in the basement?" OK, so my bedside manner needed a little work. I needed to put on my sincere face; damn it, I think I left it at home.

"I'm serious Nic; I've been having an affair".

It was like a 1940's drama. She did everything shy of putting the back of her hand to her forehead, feigning a swoon, so I treated it with the flippancy it deserved. "I hear you. You've stepped out on your man. The question is, did you *pop* down the shops or did you go on a month long all inclusive holiday?" It was clear I'd lost her at 'I hear you' but I carried on regardless. "Well, obviously I was just messing with you, luv. I mean, as *if* you'd step out of the house!" I was laughing at my own joke, I was laughing alone, I didn't laugh for long. She wasn't picking up on my not so subtle hints, so I figured honesty is the best policy. "I'm just wondering where you could have met someone, is all? Because, I've gotta be honest with ya hon, you've become a total hermit".

She looked up with a start, wide eyed, like I'd accused her of stealing a liver off a transplant patient. "I have not! I go out!"

"Where?" My eyebrows practically jumped off my face.

She tried to keep indignant but she was stammering. "Places. You know... out". Well, that cleared that up. "I do! You *know* I do!" I still sat in silence. "Well, you know I *want* to". She slumped on to the bar and looked forlorn into her drink. "But he's always watching, you know?"

I actually felt sorry for her for a moment. "I do know, hon. That's why I'm asking where you could've possibly met this guy?" I stopped in my tracks for just a second, while I decided not to make any assumptions, "I mean, it *is* a man, right?" Plus, it was worth it just to see the look on her face.

"Of course it's a man!" She checked the barman's location and lowered her voice again. "He's the catalogue delivery guy". Light dawns! "He comes twice a week".

"*Does he?!*" I rubbed my thighs suggestively and made big gestures with my eyebrows, before I realised that wasn't *actually* very impressive. I frowned and took a sip of drink.

"He comes *round* twice a week!"

Consider me chastised; well, at least for a second. "So the question is, *does* he deliver? What services does he provide? Super fast? Recorded?" I pursed my lips and held my finger to my mouth in my best mock saucy postcard pose.

She let out a small laugh and then finished off her wine and I tried to catch up. "So, David's not suspicious about your increased catalogue activity? Or the new toasters, alarm clocks and stylish free pens that you've acquired for being a loyal customer?" It was like mocking tourette's, I just couldn't stop it coming out. She sat there, smiling and shaking her head, while I continued on. "Tell me you at least get a discount?!"

The barman came back and we ordered another two glasses of rosé, we made ridiculous fake small-talk while he poured the drinks. He wasn't fooled as Jenna was talking about her new curtains and I was nearly nodding off. Once he handed over the change and was out of earshot again, Jenna continued. "He doesn't notice a thing, Nic. I take care of the bills and house stuff and he brings in the money, that's our arrangement".

Did I hear that correctly? "Arrangement? You make it sound like a business deal".

She looked at me like I'd hit the nail on the head or pinned the tail on the donkey, whatever was more appropriate for David. "That's how it feels. I hardly ever see him anymore and when I do, it's all politeness; he treats me like I'm his mum or something. He hasn't touched me in months".

"Well, I'm glad. If he thinks you're his mum, that'd be pretty sick there, hon". I let out a big laugh, noticed I was on my own, quickly turned it into a cough and tried my best to look contrite. Note to self, must suppress humorous outbursts. "Sorry".

It seemed to have worked as she continued on in confidence. "I don't know what to do. Barry wants me to leave him but I don't know if I can".

"Barry?!" Oh no, too late, I'm laughing.

Jenna looked pissed off. "Yes, Barry. Stop it!" Oh God, now she looks wistful. "He's great if you must know. He's kind, caring…"

"Available...?" Must control interjections, must control interjections.

"That's not it, he loves me and I think I love him".

"You think? Look mate, I can't tell you what to do here but I wouldn't be rushing to end your marriage on a maybe". Was I really encouraging her to stay in this God awful marriage? "Although, if you're looking elsewhere then there's obviously some bigger problems". That was better. I was so far back on the fence that I think I got splinters in my arse. "You and David really need to talk". See, sterling advice! I was getting better at this, I think it could be the start of my evolution into someone infinitely more sensible, "And until you sort this out, you should get Barry to keep his package in his van". Maybe not.

"I don't know what I'm doing". Jenna looked dejected. "David and I used to be fun, he couldn't get enough of me but now he has me till death do us part, he's become one of those guys, who like... orders his food and... the grass is greener on the other side, you know". After a few beverages, Jenna's grasp of proverbs, left a lot to be desired.

Jenna had been like a machine when it came to men, a vacuum, no, maybe a shredder? She chewed them up and spat them out but I guessed she'd changed; she appeared to have a conscience now. The Jenna I once knew wouldn't have cared about cheating on David. Which begged the question, did she love Barry? Ha ha! Sorry, couldn't help it, I'm going to have to find a way *not* to say his name. Maybe she *did* love... what's-his-name, maybe this *was* different? Or maybe, she just needed the attention. Jenna did crave the spotlight, I often fell into it quite unwittingly and then ducked down and crawled out again but

Jenna could bathe in it all night long. Maybe this was her warped way of reminding me she was still very much around.

Over the next few hours we managed another six or seven glasses of Rosé each, we agreed that she and David would talk about his controlling behaviour and his recent apparent disinterest in her. I nodded studiously, I found my sincere face (it was in the bottom of my bag after all) and I managed to bite my tongue during some golden comedy opportunities when she talked about Ujamaflips special delivery and prompt dispatch. We then put the world to rights, aggravated the barman with jokes about his peanuts and stumbled off into a very cold night, prompting Jenna to leave me with a final gem. "Corrr, it's cold enough to freeze the balls off a grass donkey". I didn't feel it needed a reply, as we climbed in to cabs promising to get together again next week. I wanted to believe her.

Chapter 5

The next day, I rocked up to work thirty minutes late feeling like a truck had driven over my head. "Afternoon, Nicky".

"Morning, Amanda". I wasn't sure if I could hold the fake smile today, my jaw was aching. My phone vibrated in my pocket and I waited until Amanda left the room to check it. It was Jenna texting to tell me how she spent the night talking into the big white telephone and that David would be home in an hour. Bless her, she *was* out of practice. I replied, giving her some handy 'hide your hangover' tips and wished her well with her husband.

Sally approached and predictably was annoyingly chirpy. "Morning! Ooh, you look rough... and crikey!" She backed off, holding her hands up, "You smell like a vineyard!"

OK, so maybe I should've taken more time to hide my *own* hangover. "Errr, thanks! I went out with an old friend last night". I was weirdly trying to smell myself, when she wasn't looking.

"On a school night? You must be mental. Bloke or girl?" Oh God, here she goes with the eyebrow gestures again. I managed a pathetic little hung-over laugh and didn't bother to answer, I just couldn't be arsed.

Sally then spent the next hour giving a thorough analysis of her favourite TV programmes, while Amanda was out the back, sorting out some currency. I sat there, got up and made a coffee, sat back down in silence and didn't even pretend to listen while Sunshine Sally waffled on. I was slowly dying, hoping the injection of Nescafé and paracetamol would soon kick in.

My phone shook again but this time it was Marcus, he only worked half a mile up the road from me and was asking if I wanted to meet for lunch; the perfect antidote to a rough morning. I asked if he could come and pick me up, as in literally, as my legs had stopped working an hour ago and he replied something I'd rather not repeat, I asked him if he kissed his fathers with that mouth and then counted the minutes until lunch.

Foolishly, we'd agreed to meet in a local pub and the smell of stale ale nearly knocked me on my arse and for a moment, I thought I might recreate the Mr Creosote 'better get a bucket' scene. Luckily, I was able to contain my innards and managed to order a pint of full fat coke before we sat down. I needed to soak up the vino that was sloshing around in my stomach and so unsurprisingly, opted for stodge but Marcus on the other hand, healthily sat there and healthily complained about their lack of salad choice, whilst drinking his healthy orange juice, which just made me feel worse. I'm sure he did it on purpose, just to rub my nose in it. Thinking about it, he probably chose the pub just to watch which shade of green I'd turn today. You couldn't deny his evil genius.

Apparently it was my turn to order and pay but before I could, Marcus was straight in with the real reason why he'd arranged the luncheon. "So, I was thinking, after the party, we should go on holiday".

I couldn't quite hide my surprise, "Holiday?"

"Yeah, you know, you get on a plane, lie on a beach, hit cockroaches with your shoes. I was wondering if you knew anyone that worked in your office who could sort it out for us?" He was on form, today.

"Ha ha. I'm laughing on the inside".

I was holding my head and he was smiling at me. "You still feel rough? You and Jenna must've sunk a few. What did she want anyway?"

"Between you, me and the condiments... marital problems". I should've kept Jenna's confidence but I didn't like keeping secrets from Marcus if I could help it, besides, this was just *too* good to stay shtum.

"Yeah, no shit. Knew they wouldn't last; not after the Best Man had already taken the bride for a test drive". Sadly, he wasn't joking. Years before, Jenna and Nate (the Best Man) had a drunken tryst and David was the only living person that didn't know, which certainly made the speeches worth listening to.

"Yes, my friend, you did". I nodded and then thought better of any sudden, sharp head movements. I looked around, very slowly after lessons learned from the nodding incident, to check that there wasn't any barmen, CCTV camera's, crack team SAS guys hanging upside down from the beams, listening in. "Well, it turns out she's having an affair. Leopards, spots, you make up the sentence". I flicked my hand toward him, letting him know that I didn't have the energy for another round of 'I told you so'. Instead, my friend came up trumps with a round of jokes about how she never leaves the house; my soul mate. We both laughed and I dramatically paused for effect when I told him the guys name and Marcus laughed for a full five minutes while I went up to place our order.

I returned to my seat and Marcus was wiping a tear from his eye after his big after-laugh sigh. "Ahh, that was good. Nothing like a good laugh to get you going in the morning".

I looked thoughtful for a moment. "Well, that and prunes".

He seemed disgusted and pleased at the same time, he secretly enjoyed my toilet humour. Marcus looked around the room, much as I had a few minutes ago but with a lot more mystery than I had been able to muster. He leaned in and lowered his voice, "I take it she hasn't told David?"

"No. I told her she needed to talk to him about how controlling he is and that he hasn't been paying her any err... physical attention". I gave Marcus that knowing look.

"Ooh, school boy error".

"Quite. I told her that I'm not sure whether she should come all out with the whole affair saga just yet. She needs to see if there's anything worth salvaging from her marriage first". I was feeling quite proud of how grown up I sounded.

"Why?!"

"Why what?" I was playing with the salt and so didn't see that Marcus was horrified.

"Why would she lie? She's cheated on her husband, she has to tell him". I now caught his tone and looked up. He was staring at me as if I'd kicked his dog.

"Well, I… erm". I nervously spilt the salt. "I just thought that maybe, she should deal with one thing at a time. I mean, I'm not saying she should *never* tell David about Barry". I let out an inappropriate laugh and then quickly tried to cover it. Fortunately, Marcus knew me well and laughed with me, shaking his head. Feeling like I needed all the luck I could get, I collected the spilled salt from the table and threw it over my left shoulder; unfortunately a couple had just sat down behind me. Marcus put his head in his hand and hid his face. Oops.

We sat in silence for a minute or two, hoping that the salty couple behind didn't suddenly pull a Godfather and go and get a gun out of the toilet and make me sleep with the fishes. Finally, Marcus broke the hush, he'd obviously been getting quietly excited on his own, bless him, about his previous holiday suggestion and so with added verve, he said, "So what do you think? A bit of sun, sand, Speedo's and Sangria?"

I was fishing out my slice of lemon from my drink; the citrus was just too much today. "You can leave your Speedo, second skin's at home mate. Who's going?"

I was looking for somewhere to dump the lemon and Marcus was looking at me with disgust, wondering what I was going to do and no doubt praying I didn't throw *that* over my shoulder. Then he asked, "What do you mean?"

I unwrapped my knife and fork from its serviette and wrapped the lemon in it instead, much to Marcus' chagrin. "Well, we need to choose carefully after last year". I was preaching to the choir but I needed to make the point and he nodded his acceptance.

The previous year we had gone away to Ibiza with two gay couples that Marcus knew and I had met a few times and really liked, and Sadie and one of her friends. A seemingly nice, inoffensive crowd but oh boy, was it a big mistake. One of the couples went off and did their own thing, so we didn't see them the entire holiday, the other couple bickered from the second we got on the plane, not stopping until we landed back at Stansted and only drawing breath occasionally to criticise Marcus and his recent single status (which according to them, was down to his friendship with me!) It only took two days before Sadie's friend found herself a young studly, so Sadie felt she had to pull and ended up with a spotty, Red Bull-obsessed Mancunian who still did the big-fish, little fish dance and smelt of sweaty socks. Marcus, as well as the flak from his mates, was getting hit on by every Tom, Dick and Tranny within a five mile radius and *I* had a stomach upset for days from a dodgy kebab… oh, and ten shots of After Shock on the first night.

"You're right. I hadn't really thought about that". Marcus looked weirdly nervous and hesitated before he said, "I suppose we could go on our own?"

"On our own? What, like, just you and me?" It was that last glass of Rosé that was impeding my ability to grasp the principle of sensitivity.

Marcus responded abruptly, "Well, yes, that's generally what that means".

"Oh… I err, I guess so".

We'd never been away just the two of us before, I was so used to going in a crowd. I wasn't sure how this would play out. I was obviously displaying my thought process on my face because Marcus was now pouting. "Don't get too excited, will you".

"No. I think it's a great idea. I do! Really!" I tried to inject some enthusiasm, only it came across as annoyingly fake. So I told him exactly what I'd been thinking.

The waitress brought our food over just in time. It gave me a bit of space to think before I put my foot in it again. Marcus began slicing up his lettuce leaves and I began filling the gaps on my plate with sauces. Marcus stopped what he was doing to smile at me as I squirted on the mayonnaise, near the ketchup and just over from the salad cream.

I decided to change tact. "So where did you have in mind? Shagalluf? Faliraki?" You just can't buy class.

He looked very uncomfortable. "What about the Dominican Republic or Bahamas or somewhere like that?" I searched his face for a hint of a smile. Was he serious? He actually looked it, he wasn't laughing. I looked around to see if a modern day Beadle was going to jump out from behind the jukebox. A good few seconds had passed and not even a smile.

"Bahamas? What are we, 50 or on a honeymoon?" I ignored his wounded look and gained an unexpected burst of energy. "I know it's all white sands and blue seas and stuff but what else is there to do?" I was dipping a chip in the salad cream and was suddenly off in my own little world. "I mean, they have all those fancy cocktails and you can drink out of a coconut shell, which I'm not denying is pretty damn cool but they don't do a pitcher of vodka and Redbull for under 10 Euro's, do they?" I was dipping another chip in the mayo now, and ignoring one of my mother's golden rules about not talking with your mouthful. "No, they don't". Not to mention, my one-way conversation. Poor Marcus just sat there, cutting up his tomato, knowing there was no point speaking until I'd worn myself out. "There's some pretty impressive spa's at some of those resorts and the accommodation is second to none, I grant you but it wouldn't surprise me if you have to take your bank statements with you before they'll even let you buy dinner, plus it's full of smug couples and the elasticated waist brigade", aaand breathe.

Marcus sat there with a fixed expression, for a good ten seconds without blinking. He took me picking up the chicken burger and filling my face with it as a sign that I had indeed kicked the soap box into touch and ended my little moment. His head flinched, like his ear was still hurting from where I'd practically chewed it off. "It was just a suggestion".

It took about five minutes to finish one mouthful and even then I had to wash it down with the coke. Marcus sat eating in silence and I felt bad, he was so excited about going away when we came in. I put down my burger but didn't have anywhere to wipe my hands as I'd used my serviette to wrap up the lemon. I looked around to see if anyone was watching, unwrapped the fruit and hid it under my plate, Marcus looked up momentarily and just shook his head. I wiped my hands on my lemony napkin and quietly said, "I think it's a great idea to go away after the party".

He slowly raised his head and a wry smile came back to his face. "I just thought it would be nice for your actual birthday. You know, sitting on white sands, near bright blue seas, drinking out of coconut shells".

I let out a little laugh and nodded, "Yes, it would but so would sitting on yellow sands, near bluey-green seas, drinking ice cold San Miguels... out of a bottle".

I had learnt from the master and he acknowledged my efforts. "You have done well, my Padawan learner".

We were back to normal. Just as well, walking on eggshells (or coconut shells in this case) was not really my thing. I dunked another chip in the ketchup and returned to my usual bullish self. "*Anyway*, why not Shagalluf? Who doesn't love watching the male dancers at BCM's in their tiny, tiny hot pants and who knows, you *did* meet Wes at the Waterpark. As I recall, your eyes met over the Rapids".

Wes was Marcus' one serious boyfriend. He was fabulous, funny and fit as you like and he was happy for me and my *then* boyfriend, Rob, to tag along. It was 2002, the year that Rudolph Giuliani gained an honorary knighthood, the Queen Mum did her final royal wave, the Peseta was replaced with the Euro and we were in Shaggalluf yet again with our friends, spending said Euro with abundance. We'd dropped away from the rest of the group and spent every waking moment with Wes; drinking, dancing and having a fabulous time. Well, Marcus, Wes and I did, I think Rob came home with a strong desire to watch Rugby, drink ale and beat his chest. It was Wes who made all the effort to keep in touch when we came home as anyone could see, he was mad about Marcus. They stayed together for nearly four years until Wes broke it off a couple of years ago, citing Marcus' indifference. I was gutted, I loved Wes but obviously more than Marcus did. Despite many late nights up talking with Marcus about what went wrong, I never *did* get to the truth about why he lost interest in Wes. Sometimes, when he didn't want to let on about something, he could be as hard to read as assembly instructions for flat-pack furniture.

Marcus took a mouthful of green stuff, quietly chewed and swallowed before he said the blasphemous, "Aren't we a little too old for Magalluf?"

I simply smiled and said, "You're *never* too old for Shagalluf, my friend".

Chapter 6

For the rest of the week, I got my head down at work, tried not to engage in too much small-talk with colleagues and pulled my weight. I knew I was skating on thin ice and the looks that Amanda kept throwing my way were melting that ice at a rapid rate. Two days this week had been consumed purely with recovery from revelry and professionally, that wasn't funny. I had been promoted last year because despite my timekeeping, I was actually *good* at my job,. My job required social skills and although my small-talk deftness left a lot to be desired at times, I was there to make suggestions about what people should do and aide in decisions, I was *paid* to give my opinion; and casting judgement on a situation (whether people wanted my views or not), was definitely right up my street. However, I was not proving this week that I was worth the extra pennies I'd been given.

Fortunately, the weekend came around very quickly. Marcus and I had a quiet one lined up involving pizza and party planning, not that there was a lot for us to do, we had managed to delegate the main tasks, we just needed to finalise our guest list and collate our RSVP's. The decision to have a joint birthday was easy; the guest list on the other hand, had been a problem. Marcus seemed intent on getting the old crowd back together but I was uneasy, like Tower Bridge, a lot of water had passed under and quite a lot of shit! At some point or other, most of us had rowed, bickered and fallen out; except Marcus. Marcus stayed friends with anybody and everybody, even if he didn't like them; it was an innate skill. I thought about all my friends growing up and I wondered what all of us could possibly have in common anymore? Sure, there were some great memories but all probably best remembered from a distance now. It seemed that as we got older, when you threw us all together it *always* ended in tears. Case in point, Carly and Pete's leaving do was the last big gathering of all our friends, which was over three years ago, the night of the 'big fight'.

Marcus seemed anxious to get the party planning part of the evening out of the way, so we could just chill out.

"Carly and Pete will be coming but they'll be a bit late, Emma's bringing 'That' Justin and the kids and Mitchell and Daniel want to bring a flan". Marcus always called Emma's boyfriend 'That' Justin ever since he dissed the 'X Factor' one night. Marcus was a closet devotee.

"A flan?" My eyebrow was heftily raised.

"Yeah, remember Mitchell went on one of those week long cooking holidays? Well apparently, he is now the flan Queen". Marcus was shaking his head and shrugging his shoulders.

"A flan?" The other eyebrow joined it.

"I'm told he makes a mean Pavlova as well".

"A flan?" aaannnd add some dimples.

"I know..." He gave in way too easily. "So what do we do about Jenna and David?" Marcus grabbed a couple of beers from the fridge and shouted from the kitchen. "Do we send Jenna another invite for just her and then order a few pairs of slacks from catalogue man, so they can meet in secret over a vol-au-vent?" He was laughing at his own funny.

I shouted back. "Don't even joke about it! If he shows up in his little uniform, everyone'll think he's a stripper!"

Marcus came back in the room and handed me my beer. He was singing along to the 'Kings of Leon' and I sat there, desperately wanting to ask him. Oh, what the hell. "Did you say that Carly and Pete are coming?" I was trying to pick up the pizza without burning my fingers, forgetting of course, that it was a takeaway pizza, had only just been delivered and therefore my beer was likely to be warmer. Instead, I just made a mess.

"Yeah, they're coming down the day before". Marcus was tapping his feet and handed me a piece of kitchen roll without looking up.

"Thanks". I was wondering if my newly acquired detective skills that had emerged during my chat with Jenna, would help me navigate this next conversation. "Did Carly email or phone you?"

"What?" Marcus was not really paying attention as he was trying to break apart the pizza slices.

"When she contacted you, did Carly email or phone you?"

"She phoned me at work." He was now struggling with some stringy cheese and was way too involved in the task to look up but cautiously asked, "Why?"

At work? She knows his work number. Then again, Marcus has worked for the same firm for twelve years, his number hadn't changed. "Oh, I was just wondering". I was watching him make more of a mess than me. "Does she phone you at work a lot?"

"We probably speak about twice a month". This was the first I'd heard about it. Marcus had the good grace to look a little guilty or was it nerves? I couldn't quite make it out. He seemed quite astute in his assessment of my reactions though. "You're upset". He was looking directly at me, warily awaiting my response.

I tried to lie, "No! Of course I'm not. Why would I be upset?" I knew it was silly to be upset. I was happy that Marcus had kept in contact with Carly; she was a great mate once. "I'm glad; I think it's nice that you've stayed friends". I smiled over at Marcus and he smiled back. He picked up his beer and went to take a sip, while I sat there, *way* too involved in my own thoughts. "You've stayed friends all this time. That's great. You know, that you still talk to them, that you're still in the know and finding out what's going on. Even though you didn't tell *me* how she's doing... I mean, you've been finding out all this time if she's OK and what she's been up to and not telling me..." I got up quickly and switched off the iPod. "Cock it, you're right, I *am* upset! Twice a month?! Why didn't you tell me?" I'd gone from quiet to yelling in under five seconds, I was surprised Marcus didn't fish out his copy of the Guiness Book of Records. I hadn't meant to yell and I was trying to promise myself that I wouldn't do it again.

Marcus looked very sheepish and a little scared. "I didn't think you'd want to know."

That promise didn't last very long. "WHAT?! Bullshit! Of course I'd want to know! You knew I'd want to know! You know me, you know I'd want to know".

Marcus looked stunned for a second then shrugged. "Well, I didn't know that you knew that I'd know that you'd want to know…" He was desperately trying to lighten the mood and no doubt hoping that I would take a moment to gain some much needed perspective. I breathed a huge sigh and did just that.

"I just really miss her". I *had* really missed Carly and Marcus was fully aware of it. Despite the fact that I always implied I didn't care I'd lost her friendship, he knew better than anyone, so I felt a little betrayed. "I can't believe you lied to me".

"I *didn't* lie, hon. I just I omitted certain facts because I thought it might upset you and for some... I don't know, *outrageously* silly reason, I thought you might yell at me". His smile widened, then he added more sombrely. "I know you miss her".

I stared at him for a couple of seconds, he was genuinely sincere and he looked like a deprived dog in need of a good home on one of those emotionally blackmailing adverts. "I'm sorry I yelled... and I'm sorry I've become so predictable that you *knew* I'd yell".

He smiled back. "No worries, luv. I bought some new earplugs after LOTR-gate". He stared wide-eyed towards the TV and nodded his head in a trance, like he was reliving the incident.

See, I'd gotten on my high horse a couple of months beforehand regarding the final instalment of Lord of the Rings. Marcus had finally talked me in to watching all the films, including all the DVD extras (all nine hundred hours of it) and having not read the works of Tolkien (well, I figure time management, if there's a film, why read the book? Plus, there's always some smart arse down the pub who's read something that's then been committed to celluloid, who will tell you all the bit's the film missed out from the book anyway), I had sat myself down, over the course of a week to visually partake in the delights of the Hobbits and friends. I admit, I *had* really enjoyed the films, they *were* classics… until that is, the last scenes of 'Return of the King'. I mean, as if it weren't enough that eagles happened to swing by and pick up the wee fellas from a certain lava death at Mordor (which of course begged the question why the fecking eagles couldn't have dropped the ring in themselves on a fly-by, thus saving the fellowship all the death and hardship? Marcus suggested that maybe Mordor's air traffic control was run by the French and they were on strike again that day) but oh no! Then they added in those God awful saccharin scenes when Frodo finally wakes up with everyone running in to the room one by one in super slow mo, looking like Goldie Hawn on acid! Instead, I went on an hour long (yes, *hour* long) rant about how I'd invested all that time and how my butt cheeks had gone numb, only to be let down by a shocking plot line and a stomach churning cliché. So I could forgive Marcus some imaginary ear-plugs.

"Sensible". I nodded my encouragement.

"Thanks". He held out his beer bottle for a celebratory clink.

Marcus jumped up from the sofa quickly. "So, tonight's films are Armageddon, Dogma and Good Will Hunting?" It was Ben Affleck night.

"Splendid, although could we do it the other way round? Ben, Owen and Bruce at the end? It'll make sure I don't nod off, 'cause I don't wanna close my eyes, I don't wanna fall asleep, 'cause I miss you baby, and I don't wanna miss a thing…" Marcus looked like he's sucked a lemon, my dulcet tones weren't impressing. Note to self; don't sing.

Best of Friends?

Marcus and I had almost exhausted the party planning; we just needed to agree the food. Mitchell and Daniel had offered to take over the decorations and chose the theme of 'Black & White'. It was very grown up of us, which is why of course; everyone knew I had bugger all to do with the decision. It was probably just as well, I'd probably exhausted every fancy dress costume there was over the years. I had been; Noddy, a Leprechaun, a Canadian Mountie (don't ask), the arse end of a comedy camel (not a wise move on any account but especially not with a flatulent boyfriend) and Wonder Woman to name but a few. However, this was a party to celebrate reaching a momentous age and I was thinking there was no harm in at least *attempting* to have a little class.

We finished talking about the party and argued about what film to put on next, prompting a reminder from Marcus of my chosen order, so I told him it was a girls prerogative to change her mind, he threw a cushion at me and told me I was full of shit. We finished the last of the pizza, had a meaningful conversation about George Lucas using potatoes for special effects and then we argued about who's turn it was to get the next beers as neither of us could be bothered to move. It was our usual thing. I lost out on 'Rock, Paper, Scissors', got the drinks in and we settled down quietly for our final film.

It was about an hour in when, out of nowhere, Marcus started pissing himself laughing. That's the marvellous thing about alcohol; if administered correctly, can activate ones funny genes and anyone who cracks under it's highly amusing pressure and begins to titter, can pass on said titter in an infectious wave to those within close proximity. This is why, I'm now laughing too, only I've absolutely no idea why. It turns out a scene on a train had reminded him of a story about Emma's birthday in the West End after a show, where we all got the vomit comet home and some poor drunken sap tried to chat up Carly (probably thinking that being underground in a small train carriage would improve his chances), Carly pretended to be Reg and poor sap went running at the next stop. Marcus was giggling and his eyes looked a little glazed; it was actually very cute. He totally let his guard down after a few drinks, it was refreshing to see the veneer slide, plus he started to swear like a tradesman which always cracked me up. I now joined him with the uncontrollable laughter, when I reminded Marcus of the other gem that evening. "That was the night Pork and Cheese Freddie picked us up from the station and we knocked out that Queen medley".

Pork and Cheese Freddie was the little Portuguese cab driver that really *did* believe he was Freddie Mercury; it was pure comedy gold. He had perfected the Freddie pout, the Freddie air punch, had the Freddie tash and sang loudly to all the songs, encouraging his fare's to do the same. Greg even reckoned he picked him up from town one night wearing a yellow jacket and white vest top; we couldn't prove this though as Greg wasn't the most reliable source. Marcus leant forward laughing, spilt some beer on his jeans and didn't care. "Ha! Yeah! Freddie had the right arse because we kept getting the words wrong to 'We Will Rock You'!"

It was sadly true, we only knew about seven random, non-succession words of the first verse; Buddy, boy, day, mud, face, can, place. In-between were just incoherent mumbles which in the world according to Pork and Cheese Freddie was simple blasphemy and I'm surprised he didn't turf us out at high speed.

Marcus and I sat there crying with laughter for most of the rest of the night, until I eventually fell asleep on Marcus' lap on the couch. Actually, what I should say is that we both passed out on the couch and didn't even hear Sadie come in. The next morning, we both woke up with crook necks and shocking headaches, so there was only one thing for it, we shook Sadie awake and headed down to Ruth's for some well needed sustenance.

Chapter 7

Things were really slow at work this week, so I spent the first two days trawling through the holiday deals, as per Marcus' request. Two weeks all inclusive in Lanzagrotty, some week long specials in Tener-grief, and countless packages to the Costa del Hole, where they'll even throw in a free stabbing. Cheap last-minute deals, the holidays no-one else wants, the holidays you *just* can't sell.

    I still needed to convince Marcus to go back to Magalluf. Over the years, I'd had some fantastic memories there; not just the holiday where Marcus met Wes but Shagalluf (as it's more affectionately known) was also the place of my first holiday abroad without my parents. See, most of my childhood holidays were spent at Caravan Parks across the UK but always near some coast or other, where it pissed it down continuously for two weeks. You got covered in mud, it was cold and damp and you went to bed with a roll neck and thermal socks under your jammies, fighting the frost bite. It was like trekking the Himalayas, only with Bingo and the Chuckle Brothers. The first time mum & dad took me and my younger sister abroad, we just worshipped the ground they walked on and we were nice to them for at least a week. Who knew sea could be blue and beaches were made of sand? It threw me for a long time that if you went down to the sea front, you didn't have to take a wind-break or wear a ski jacket and our European counterparts, it would seem, don't feel the need for piers and waltzers on every coast. I fell in love with the idea of a proper sun-filled summer holiday after that and it's a love affair that's lived on. That's probably why I became a Travel Agent, I spent so much time scanning holiday brochures as a kid that I knew exactly what was on offer. Although booking everyone else on their dream holidays instead of going myself could sometimes be torture.

My first holiday abroad, *without* the folks, was in 1995 with Carly, Emma, Jenna & Alice. The song of the year was 'This Is How We Do It' and with five girls on Pleasure Island, it was like our mantra. We dabbled, we drank, we danced and we almost drowned. (Well, OK, so I'm over-exaggerating a little with the drowning but there *was* an embarrassing incident with a pedalo). It took some convincing of our parents to let us go, Carly more than most, so in the end she blatantly lied to her mother, telling her she was going on a two week study course in Wales (she would have to explain the tan later). A taxi picked us up from Alice's house and the second we pulled away from the driveway, our holiday started. A sneaky tipple at the airport, followed by a few cheeky ones on the plane, we landed in style and our first night was memorable. Well, the first two hours were, I don't remember much after that but I know it was a great night! We quickly got into a routine, not getting up until lunchtime, spending the afternoons and early evenings, feeling the sun on our faces down on the beach, washing the previous night away in the warm blue azure of the Med. A few games of bat and ball (extra points if you could hit the person with the dodgiest hairdo), a cold one... or two, read the latest Jackie Collins and then head back for a power nap and a shower. We'd get ready to go out to dinner about 10.30pm and then move from bar to bar, dancing, singing, laughing and drinking. While OJ was facing the most public murder trial *ever* known, we were enjoying a freedom that none of us had experienced before, a total escape from rules and boundaries for two whole weeks. We met some fabulous men and we partied till the sun came up. It was truly magical.

Not forgetting of course, that a summer holiday abroad wouldn't be complete without a visit to the Waterpark and our day on the slides was definitely one to remember. We'd been there for about five minutes before we met a big group of lads and so me, the girls and our newly acquired friends queued to go on the latest ride, the 'Black Hole'. When we got to the top, the lifeguard said it was a ride for two, so one of us girls would have to share with one of the blokes. I volunteered, in an effort to save the nice men from close proximity to Jenna, a confined space and nowhere to run; my only stipulation being that I went at the back, as me and pitch-black darkness were not good friends. The lifeguard shushed us along, the girls went first, leaving me and a pretty big muscley fella whose nickname was Arnie (!) holding on to our inflatable double doughnut. Now there's a reason why they normally request the biggest of the duo to go at the back, as I found out when we pushed off from the top and with all the weight at the front, shot down the tube like a bullet. My face was being pushed back so far from the g-force that I was sure the edges of my mouth were touching my ears. When we reached the end of the tube, I could hear the water rushing and we shot out like a human cannonball but being top-heavy, we quickly nose-dived and hit the water almost vertically which of course, caused the back end of the doughnut to act like a catapult... My friends were lined up waiting for me at the edge of the pool at the end of the ride, along with all the people waiting to collect the inflatable's for their turn, so the memory of me flying through the air in a frog pose, will live on way longer than I ever will.

Of course, despite my amphibian impressions, I'm no fool, I'm aware that I look back on it all now with rose-tinted specs. It wasn't all funny jokes and lovely blokes, we did have quite a few arguments as well. For example; there was the night that we drank nothing but shots and Alice's peach schnapps wasn't quite finished with the world and made a special comeback appearance right on to Emma's foot; she was wearing open-toed sandals. Then there was the row over Paulo the local lothario, between Jenna and Carly; normally my money would've been on Carly but Jenna was willing to go the 'extra mile' to secure her man. There was the issue of five girls in one apartment, with one bathroom; I don't think I need to explain the logistics and resultant bickering that followed *that*. Last but of course, not least, was the incident, where Jenna downed far too many ice-cold San Miguel's, walked straight out into the afternoon sun, passed out on her beach towel, woke up, threw up in the sand next to her and so we carried her down the beach and dropped in the cool sea in an attempt to sober her up. It worked; well, after an hour and a half in the sea clinging on to a li-lo for dear life, two coffees, a litre of water, four paracetamol and a long shower when she got back. Special times!

Luckily, time was being kind to me this week as before I knew it, it was Wednesday again. Marcus (the only one that can cook out of the three of us), was in the kitchen whipping up a little chicken number, so I went out to join him. "I found a few deals in Majorca".

Marcus looked up with a wry smile from stirring some kind of sauce thing. "Majorca? Is that all there was?"

I saw a carrot on the side and nabbed it before he could notice and then jumped up on to the counter, swinging my legs like a 4 year old. Loudly crunching on the carrot had alerted him to my theft and my defiling of the kitchen surface and he was staring, so I tried to stop the leg swinging. "Why? Don't you want to go back there?"

His eyebrows were now making weird shapes at my vegetable kleptomania but he continued on, "It's not that I don't want to go back there, there's parts of the island that are stunning but I'm guessing, you're thinking of just the one resort and well, it's just… don't you think it's time we tried something different?"

I rapidly blinked my eyes and feigned a nervous tick. "Different? What you mean, like, change?"

Marcus rolled his eyes. "Yes, I know you've already made your thoughts clear on my suggestions; I just thought it would be nice to go check out some *new* places". He hesitated before he said, "You decided who you want to come yet?"

"I thought you wanted to go with just us?" I was eyeing up another carrot that was laying on its own next to the runner beans, daring to be nabbed. I stealthily got down from the worktop and crept over. Hang on, I just realised. "We're having vegetables?!"

I'd foolishly announced my presence and he intercepted my carrot grabbing with a firm slap of the hand. "Well, all I was thinking when I said that was, Sadie's away this year, all your girls aren't single anymore and some are, as you so eloquently put it, sprogged up and *my* mates are getting all couply, so that pretty much just leaves us".

He had a very depressing point, so I focussed on the other issue in hand. "You just flew right past the vegetable confrontation, didn't ya?"

Marcus looked me up and down in mock disgust. "You've eaten crap all week, you need a better diet. Besides, you just ate a carrot!"

I jumped back on to the kitchen counter and stated my case, "A carrot's not a vegetable, it's a coloured dippy snack".

He looked like he was going to say something and then changed his mind; resistance was futile. "*Anyway*, I figure we'd be fine on our own. I mean, we live together, so we know we get on". He put a tea towel over the vegetables. "Well, most of the time". We both smiled.

I jumped down, got some wine and three glasses and took them into the lounge, then crept back in and on to the counter. I really liked it up there, the extra height made me feel like I was gaining ground in the conversation. I opened the cupboard door behind my head and got out an opened box of breadsticks and started chomping away. Marcus looked disapprovingly at me and gestured towards his dinner, while I shrugged and rubbed my stomach to indicate a state of deprived hunger; it was like charades with a difference. "So I saw one deal in particular that I think would be perfect for us".

Marcus put down his knife and now that he was unarmed, I felt infinitely better. He turned to face me. "Let me guess..." Marcus put a finger to his lips and a hand on his hip. "Two weeks all inclusive sleeping on a bar floor in Shagalluf?" *SO* gay.

I replied in the same sarcastic tone. "*No!* Two weeks in a five star hotel, half board, *actually*".

"Shagalluf *has* five star hotels, does it?"

"But of course. Also I checked... the bar serves cocktails in coconut shells". I could see Marcus was trying not to laugh but he was beginning to falter; I needed to seal the deal. "I think we should strike while the iron's hot".

"And the iron's hot then is it?" Maybe I underestimated him.

"Well, it feels a bit tepid at the moment but I'm hoping if I give it a few more minutes, it'll warm up". It was time to bring out the big guns; I was beaming my very best dimpled smile (OK, so cute smile, not the big guns I'd normally bring out, in a hostile male negotiation but breastage not really a winner with Marcus, the dimples, however...)

"Fine. Bring the stuff home and we'll look at it over the weekend". He fell for it everytime.

"Oooh, thank you, thank you, thank you". I jumped down from the counter and ran over to hug him.

Marcus was smiling at me, as I saw something poking out from under the tea towel that looked suspiciously like broccoli. I was gonna have to go and sit down.

Chapter 8

After dinner, I dragged out the laptop to nervously check if Sally had put the pictures up on Facebook from the other Saturday, she'd kept pretty shtum about it, since the unveiling of her evil plan last week. I checked my email account and there was nothing from Sally but suddenly I felt my stomach tighten, when I saw I had an email from Carly.

Carly Phillips' family moved to our village in 1986, when she was 8 years old. On her first day of school, she found herself surrounded at lunchtime by some of the cruellest boys who thought they were the coolest. I sat with my friends watching them pick on the new girl with interest, trading our packed lunch items and taking it in turns to share an earpiece of Emma's Walkman listening to the week's charts that she'd taped. I would've jumped in sooner, I hated bullying but it's not good school politics to get involved when a new student is being initiated *and* also it was my turn on the Walkman and Huey Lewis and the News were playing. However, this day was different as Carly, with her dark brown hair and green eyes was an exceptionally pretty girl, so the boys were particularly mean and *way* too hands on. I put down my lemon curd and Nutella sandwiches and started to make my way over against the wishes of my friends, I shouted from the back of the circle of boys, "Why don't you leave her alone!" Then all of a sudden there was a huge commotion (which I *thought* came from my noble interference), the crowd came flying back and two boys hit the deck and a moment later a red-faced, angry young Carly strutted out from the centre, practically dusting off her hands. For a minute, there was complete silence, as the tumbleweed practically flew across the playground and all eyes were on Carly as she huffily walked away and I found that an enormous smile had taken over my face. It was the cries of both floored boys that finally broke the silence and the whole school laughed, even the Dinnerladies.

She'd only been there a day but Carly was the talk of the school, with most of the other girls deciding that they didn't want to be friends with the new, scary girl but I was drawn. I saw her after school waiting with her younger brother for her mum to pick her up; everyone was stood around whispering about her, including my own friends, so I ignored them again and went over to talk to her. I praised her for her lunchtime antics and offered her half of my Wagon Wheel, she seemed grateful for the chocolate and the compliment. We talked and giggled about boys and other lame stuff until her mum showed up. Her mother smiled and waved at the other mum's and looked perfectly pleasant until she saw me talking to her daughter. My little skirt was on the wonk, my knees were grazed, there were dirty marks on my white bunched socks, my shirt collars were up and my tie was skew-whiff. To Carly's mother, I must have looked like a St Trinian's reject. Her face turned from sweet to sour in about two seconds flat, it was a stare that could scare a rhino at twenty paces and she grabbed Carly's hand, gave me a warning glance and dragged off her children towards the school gates. Carly turned back and smiled and I knew I had a friend for life. Well, that's how it should have been.

I wasn't the only one who was impressed by Carly. From the moment she knocked him to the floor and humiliated him in front of the entire school, Pete Richardson was smitten. For years he flirted, fawned and pined over Carly, constantly pretending he wasn't attracted to her but it was obvious to anyone that saw them together; he was hooked. Pete was comical and always playing the fool. He wasn't traditionally good looking and was a stocky fella but his sense of fun made him very attractive. Along with his good looking mates, he wasn't short of girls around him but unlike his friends, he was definitely a one-woman at a time kind of guy. He'd had plenty of relationships but no-one ever really compared to Carly, which was why it was pretty astonishing that he hadn't plucked up the courage to ask her out until his 21st birthday drinks. He had waited for the moment for thirteen years and as a consequence was crippled with fear, so when the moment came...? Well, due to an unforeseen inarticulate delivery, Carly was more likely to think he was a cross-dresser, than hopelessly devoted.

"Hey, how are you? Errr, you having a good time? Nice shoes". What did he say that for? He hoped she didn't notice.

"Thanks..." Carly looked down at her shoes a little quizzical, to see if she'd actually put on her slippers or maybe two different shoes by mistake, "...and yes, I *am* having a good time. How's it feel to be 21?" Carly playfully hit his arm which must have affected his brain and speech.

"Good, yeah, it feels good, erm, in myself, you know, I feel... good. That's a nice dress". What the hell was going on? Did he have clothing tourette's? Maybe if he was lucky, the floor would open up and swallow him.

Carly was totally bemused and looked behind her to see if the other boys were there playing a prank and then looked back at Pete and answered gingerly, "Thank you". There was silence for a second, Pete was looking down at his drink as if he was searching for the answer to life's mysteries, so Carly chimed back in, "So, what did you get for your birthday?" It was simple and safe; she was determined to salvage the conversation. She was tapping her feet and her glass along to the music, trying to impart some calm on to Pete, only the song that was playing was The Prodigy's 'Firestarter', which wasn't exactly Café del Mar on the zen front.

Pete however, looked relieved; he could answer this question without screwing it up. "Mum and Dad got me a new errr…" He suddenly looked terrified. What was the name? He couldn't remember! Oh no, he couldn't remember! "…it was a… errr…" He was looking around for help and didn't find any. He looked back at Carly; she was downing her drink out of desperation. Finally, an out! "Can I get you another drink?"

Carly looked down at her empty glass and then towards the bar where she noticed Luke, Jenna and I talking and her eyes lit up. "Great! Yeah, I'll come with you". Perhaps a little bit *too* enthusiastically.

Pete, confused, followed her smiley gaze over towards the bar and realised she had cunningly engineered an escape plan, he was totally dejected; his one chance and he totally blew it.

Over at the bar, Luke was only just telling Jenna and I how Pete had confided in him that he planned to ask out Carly, just as we saw them walking towards us, so we quickly silenced Luke.

Carly grabbed my hand and said "Come on mate, we need the loo", and practically dragged me across the dancefloor towards the queue for the toilet. "I just had the *weirdest* conversation with Pete".

She relayed the whole awkward experience to me, as the queue moved painfully slowly.

"Maybe he's pissed?" I tried to give him an excuse, I didn't want to get involved or ruin his surprise, but then again, he'd pretty much ballsed the whole thing up, without any help from me.

"He's not! He's only had a few. I don't know what's the matter with him, unless I was cramping his style and interrupted him in the middle of pulling someone. Maybe it's drugs!"

I thought that maybe deep down, after all these years, she secretly knew he liked her but at that moment it was crystal clear that she was *completely* oblivious. It was time. "I don't think you interrupted hon. I think there's a strong errrm, possibility, maybe... that he, in his own special way, might have been trying to tell you, that he... likes you". I blame that Collins fella; there were far too many words in the English Dictionary.

"*Likes* me? What do you mean, *likes* me? Of course he *likes* me, we're friends". Carly was not processing, or maybe the last half an hour of her friends going all 'Rain Man' on her, not being able to form a complete non-stuttering sentences, she wanted it spelled out clearly.

I decided, unsubtly, to go for the latter. "OK... He *likes* you Carl, he always has. He's *sweet* on ya, he's got a *thing* for ya, he's the Romeo to your Juliet, he's the yang to your yin, he's the Maverick to your Charlie".

Carly was looking in to space, I waved my hand in front of her face, to see if she was responding, or if I'd have to call in the paramedics. She was frozen and then as if she'd only just heard what I said, still staring in to space, she frowned and answered, "Wasn't Charlie his flying partner?"

With her gaze still unbroken, I was fascinated she had managed to respond, it was like sleep-talking. I tried to follow her gaze and work out what she was staring at but it would appear she'd just fixated on a mirrored post. I looked back at her comatose form but just couldn't let it go. "Err, no hon that was Goose".

"Huh". She nodded and then as if she suddenly heard the rest of what I'd said, "He likes me". A smile crept on to her face and her eyes, literally lit up. "He *likes* me".

We talked some more about it and I told her what Luke had told me, I didn't like to betray a confidence but it was Luke that had half-eaten it, I was merely passing on the left-over's. We returned to the bar and Carly was bubbly, sweet and blatantly giving Pete a million chances to try again and ask her out but the poor bloke was so mortified at his last attempt, that he couldn't bring himself to repeat the experience. Finally, at the end of the evening, we were all off dancing and Carly, who was sick of waiting, intercepted him on the way back from the gents. Apparently he looked so frightened, Carly thought he might phone his mum to come and get him. She suggested that it would be good if he could swing by on Wednesday, say 8:00pm, as she liked to break up the week and it would be nice to grab a bit of dinner. She put him out of his clothing tourette's misery and told him that it would also be really nice to have a chance to talk properly as due to the music, she didn't really hear what he'd said earlier and then maybe he could tell her all about what he'd got for his birthday. Bless Pete, over

Best of Friends?

the years; he'd distorted the story, so that Carly was the one that was all over him, dying to ask him out. She always smiled and let him get away with it.

I sat there for ages staring at Carly's email address and the title 'Nicky and Marcus - 30th Birthday Party'. So I knew it was about the party but they'd already RSVP'd, so I didn't know why she'd written to me. I really wanted to read it but then again, I really didn't. I missed Carly, *everyday* but maybe too much time had passed. Our falling out had been my fault (well mine and alcohol's) and Carly had said that unless I could see what was going on right under my own nose, there was no point in trying to sort this out. I didn't really know what she'd meant, I think she was trying to insinuate that I had a drinking problem which was ridiculous; sure I liked a good drink but I was no alcoholic. Anyway, they left for Brighton and I hadn't heard from them since but now, after all this time, she'd made contact.

Marcus noticed that I was just staring at my computer. "What's up chick?"

"Erm... It's Carly; she's sent me an email".

Marcus eyed me suspiciously. "And you're against modern methods of communication?" He knew why I was freaked; he was just playing with me. "Or are you worried that news of your stunner from the other Saturday has reached her?"

I narrowed my eyes but couldn't hold back a small chuckle. "Do you plan on showing *any* remorse for that comment?"

"Well, I have a bugger of a job finding shoes to fit my cloven hooves, if that makes you feel any better?" He nodded in the direction of my laptop. "So what does it say?"

"I don't know. I haven't opened it". Marcus didn't need to say a word; he just sat there with his eyebrow raised as I continued, "It's just… I'm not sure I want to read it, I'm kinda scared of what it might say".

I'd really laid myself open for some sarcasm and I wasn't disappointed. "Yes, words are a terribly frightening thing. I cower in the presence of them. I shudder when I know they're near. I get goose bumps when…"

I cut in quickly before he did himself an injury and his face accidentally fell on my foot. "I know how stupid that sounds, so I don't need a lecture, OK". Marcus put away his mocking for a second and once I felt he'd holstered his weapon, I proceeded, "I wanna know what it says, of course I wanna know but I just... don't think I can. I don't know if I can handle it, if it's written in a shitty tone, you know? Like, what if it says 'Hey I'm only coming to your party for Marcus, oh and by the way, I hope you get sucked in to a fiery vortex of hell', sort of thing?" Aaand I was off.

He winced and scratched his head. "Nice pity party you got going there, you need paper plates or you got it covered?"

"OK, so maybe that's a little dramatic". Marcus just raised an eyebrow. "I'm serious though Marcus, what if this is it? What if she's laying down the ground rules about us keeping a distance at the party? What if she doesn't wanna know me anymore?"

Marcus' face gave away his imminent sermon. "For one, I don't think she's quite as creative as you with the phrasing and two, do you *really* think that she'd write to you, three years after 'the big fight', *just* before your birthday to… what now? Mess with you? You think that's Carly?" He was clearly upset that I'd questioned her character and he was right. He'd brought logic into it and I hated it when he did that.

I let out a huge sigh and mini mock cry and flopped back against the sofa. I turned my head to face him with my best wounded puppy eyes. "Well, you *know* what I mean".

He gestured from me to the computer, "I suppose you want *me* to read it for you?"

I looked over with trepidation. "Would you?"

He smiled, knowing he'd fallen for it and held out his hands. "Give it here".

He began to read the email. Only he was reading it to himself. "Oi!"

He looked up startled. "What?!"

"You can't read it first! You have to read it aloud".

"You want me to re-enact it too?" I just sat and stared until he said, "OK, OK. It says 'Dear Nic'. What do you make of the tone so far?" He pulled a faux-frightened face.

I let out a big sigh and threw my head back on to the sofa. "You exhaust me".

He read the rest of the email aloud in a totally sarcastic, cheesy, upbeat, girlie voice. I expected nothing less.

< *Dear Nic,*

I was really glad to receive the invite for yours and Marcus' 30th Birthday party. I replied to Marcus last week *and told him we'll be a bit late. We're coming down the day before and staying at Pete's folks, so we'll spend Friday afternoon with them but then we have to spend Saturday afternoon with my folks and you know what my mum's like, I figure it's safer to say that we may be a little bit late! I hope that's OK?*

Also, I was thinking, if you were free on Friday night before the party, it might be nice if you and I could meet up for a drink?

Don't worry, if you can't make it, just an idea. Looking forward to seeing you and Marcus in 2 weeks time.

Take care

Carly xx >

Marcus enjoyed that *way* too much. He looked at me with mock questioning, "Good tone?"

I sat quietly for a second and then sickly smiled, "Yours or hers?"

"Ooh, get you!" He sounded like a pantomime dame, which I could never resist and let out a loud chuckle.

A few moments passed, then I said sincerely, "Thank you".

He handed back my computer, smiled at me and then annoyingly ruffled my hair as he left the room, shouting back,

"You're welcome".

Chapter 9

It was the next day at work and I desperately tried to keep to myself again, away from office gossip as Amanda was watching me like a hawk. I was happy to be in my own little world today, my mind was buzzing. Firstly, there was Carly's email, I would need to figure out what that meant at some point and reply sooner, rather than later. There was our party coming up in two weeks and I just couldn't shake that bad feeling at the pit of my stomach, I think the vegetables that Marcus made me eat last night weren't helping. I had Marcus' actual birthday tomorrow and was a little panicked about whether or not he'd like his present (a big model version of the Millennium Falcon that had been hiding in my room for weeks which I know sounds lame but he always wanted one as a kid), I was worried he'd forget all our conversations and wouldn't get it. I was also thinking about the coming weekends, I had a couple of heavy nights out in the run up to the party; I was out with Marcus and his friends for a birthday drink this Friday, then next week, I was hitting the town with Sadie and her friends. That seemed to be par for the course these days, nights out with other people's friends, because most of my mates had coupled up and a few had kids, so if I wanted to spend any time with *my* mates, it either meant pre-arranged dinner party gatherings or a night in after the kids go to bed with a hot cup of cocoa, I was not a fan of either.

I wasn't *quite* ready to hang up my dancing shoes and sidle in to the flannel pyjamas, just yet. Don't get me wrong, there are times when I feel that pang, like I've missed out on something amazing, you know like; when you see your friend's kids for the first time after they've been born or when they first say your name but then I'm often quickly reminded of why I also like my single, child-free life; I'm not covered in vomit, I don't have to check with my partner if it's OK to go out anywhere, I have time to do my hair, I can go shopping when I like and no-one moans about my purchases, oh and I don't pick up my child to smell it's arse, when I think it may have done a number two; why do mum's do that? I was however, becoming increasingly tired of the whole dating game, it was always the same, you doll yourself up, throw out some pheromones and then sieve through your catch. It was a jungle out there and aside from all the snakes and Cheetahs, throw some alcohol into the mix and you can think you're in bed with a Lion but wake up with a Rhino...

But then what did I know about relationships? I'd been running from commitment ever since I was old enough to spell it. I was a serial dater. I'd had a few men in my life that hung around for months at a time but never really anything lasting or stable. The only one that really became a relationship of substance was Rob. Rob and I met at Ruth's in the spring of 2002, there were hangovers, a queue for a brew and morning hair; he got my side order of toast and I got his black pudding. OK, so it wasn't the stuff of Jane Austen and Emily Brontë but I did feel the thunderbolt in my stomach when his hand touched mine as he handed over my

Best of Friends?

side plate (it *could* have been the 2:00am burger from the night before making its way round) but it was fair to say I was kinda struck by him. We agreed to meet the following week in Ruth's and from there we agreed to bump into each other at different establishments around town. Soon, he was a regular at mine and even joined us on Sunday night's on the sofa, where we'd cuddle up and take the piss out of Sadie for her Antiques Roadshow addiction. It lasted for about a year, he was my first real grown up, long-term boyfriend.

The story of how it all came to an end was staggeringly simple. I was out in town, had a few drinks and bumped in to Luke. Luke was jealous, looked upset, ordered more alcohol, we went home together; end of. Rob and I had taken a while to begin but just one night to end. He came round the next afternoon with a take-away from Ruth's, in case I felt rough from my night out with the girls; it was a sweet gesture and just made me feel worse. I couldn't look at him; I *had* to tell him the truth. It was the most horrible thing I've ever done, he was such a nice guy and I'd trampled all over him. It put me off relationships and I now had the perfect excuse as to why I wouldn't take the plunge and make the big step. I became like a defendant representing myself in court, I could cite a past case as the perfect reason as to *why* I should not do the life sentence. In the weeks following, I pretended like it wasn't a big deal and that I hadn't really cared for Rob in the first place, it was the only way I could actually stomach the guilt but the truth was, I was horrified. I hadn't set out to ruin or sabotage it, like I had done with other potentials, I guess this time I just did it subconsciously, my brain was automatically doing it on my behalf now.

Marcus used to moan about Rob and the amount of time he spent at our place. He grumbled that Rob left his shoes lying about in the hallway, that he'd used all the hot water or that he'd eaten up the last of the breakfast cereal. Silly things. The irony was that no-one was more upset than Marcus, when Rob and I split up. Marcus wouldn't accept the footnotes and wanted to hear the whole, sorry tale and it was the first time *ever* that he wouldn't back me up. He would normally mock, tell me what an arse I was, yada, yada, yada and then relent, jump to my aide, pick me up, help my foot back in to the stirrup and give me a leg up back on to that horse... but this time was different; he was most definitely *not* on my side. Judging by the reproach I received, it was the nature of our split that incensed him; I had *cheated* on Rob and I had *cheated* on him with Luke. He ranted about how Luke only showed up when I was vulnerable, about how I lose any rhyme or reason when he's around, how my personality changed and apparently I become selfish and cruel when I'm with him. Don't get me wrong, I had felt like shit about what happened with Rob and I was *not* proud of what I'd done but Marcus' reaction had crushed me. Things weren't right between us for some time after that and it got so bad that at one point, I even considered taking up Line Dancing, just to prove how much I hated myself. It was our first real big fight and neither Marcus nor I wanted to remember it.

I guess it was the start of Marcus' *real* dislike of Luke because it seemed from that moment on; he avoided him at all costs. He never really got to grips with the arrangement that Luke and I had (OK, so I admit after the Rob thing, I was struggling with it myself) but Marcus used to love hanging out with all the lads, yet suddenly if Luke was going to be there, he didn't want to know. Yes, of course I felt responsible but Marcus was a *big* boy, I really thought he'd get over it.

Pete never gave up on Marcus though. He'd worked out on his own that Marcus had issues with Luke, so about three months after Rob and I split, he arranged a night out that he knew Luke wouldn't be able to attend and Marcus happily agreed. They all went out on a proper town pub crawl and from what Pete told me, until Vom's, it was a great night. Club Vom's was always the last stop and Greg, Simon, Craig and a couple more of their friends were chatting to some girls near the dancefloor and Marcus was at the bar, passing the drinks back to Pete when suddenly they heard a voice carrying over the cheesy music... it was Luke.

Marcus froze, facing the bar but could see him in the mirror and Pete headed him off and didn't hide his surprise. "Errr, Luke. What are you doing here?"

"Ahhh mate, I was bored shitless at that wedding. My cousin looked like a giant fat duck in her dress". Luke was back and insisted on being centre of attention, so didn't notice that Pete was less than impressed.

"Her and her fugly mates were dancing round like Weebles, I obviously weren't gonna get any, so I fucked off early". He was well on his way, slurring a little with the odd stumble and treating the lads to a large dose of loud and obnoxious.

"Well done, son!" Craig was congratulating Luke on his escape.

Luke slapped Pete on the back and said, "Pete, my boy, get us a drink in then, you tight arse!"

Pete walked away biting his tongue and went straight over to Marcus, who hadn't moved a muscle. "I'm really sorry, mate. I didn't know he was gonna show up, he was at that wedding in Hertfordshire. The stupid bastard's driven back, even though he's already had a skinful". Pete felt terrible and kept apologising about Luke's unexpected arrival, so Marcus tried to alleviate the tension by joking that Luke couldn't even leave town for a day. It was an ongoing joke that Luke never travelled outside of a 10 mile radius that he needed to have jabs and a passport to finally leave the village.

They both looked over to see Luke at the other bar with Simon, Craig and Greg doing shots. "Go and join 'em, mate. I'm fine, I'm just gonna go". Marcus tried to reassure Pete. "I've had a blinder though, honest. I just wanna leave on a high".

"OK mate, I hear ya. Give us a call though, yeah. We'll go out again soon".

Marcus and Pete were exchanging a friendly hug goodbye, when they were interrupted. "Hey! How's my little gay boys". Luke was behind them and put his arms around them both.

Pete answered, "Leave it out, Luke".

"What?!" Luke was having trouble standing. "Just 'avin a bit of fun. Marcus can take a joke, can't you mate?" Luke was just hugging Marcus now and slapped him on the chest. "He's a big girl now, he don't need 'is boyfriend to look out for him".

Marcus stood still and looked straight forward, not making eye contact, while Pete tried desperately to get Luke off of him. "Come on Luke".

Luke threw Pete's hand off. "Where's that drink?"

Pete thought Luke was a prick the best of times but it was obvious those last shots Luke had done had really tipped him over the edge. "I think you've had enough, mate".

"Fuck off! What are you now, my mum?" People had started to stare.

Pete tried to grab hold of him but he kept shrugging him off. "Luke, you seriously need to calm down".

"What's your damage? Just 'avin fun, hanging with my homo here". Luke was laughing at his own joke.

"That's *enough*, Luke!" Pete finally managed to grab hold and pull Luke away.

"Whoa, seriously dude". Luke was straightening himself up. "I was just trying to find out from your man here where Nicky was tonight". He was trying to stay upright without swaying. "Saturday night's alright for fighting mate but I wanted to get a little action in!" He was laughing so hard at his own joke, that he didn't see it coming.

Luke was out cold on the floor and Pete was pulling Marcus away before the bouncers saw him but it was too late, they were on their way over. Poor Marcus was subsequently banned from Vom's for a year and he wouldn't talk to anyone about what had happened that night, I had gotten all my facts from an embarrassed Pete. The lads tried their hardest to get Marcus out again but if Luke was going to be within even half a mile of him, Marcus declined.

After hearing about Luke's choice phrasing regarding Marcus' sexuality that night, I didn't blame Marcus one bit for hitting him but I had never known him to get into a fight before, it was just *so* out of character. Whatever his reasons, one thing was for sure, he *really* didn't like Luke.

Chapter 10

I set my alarm extra early today, got up, made a brew, poured some orange juice, heated a couple of croissants put some butter and jam on the side of the plate (it was as close to making a cooked breakfast that I got.), I put it all on a tray and knocked on his door. It was Marcus' birthday. "MORNING! I thought you might like a bit of brekkie on your big day". I put down the tray and ran outside to get his cards and presents and then jumped on the bed with him. "Come on, budge up". Marcus was clambering to sit himself up, he was used to it, I did the same thing every year. "Sleep well?" I was bouncing on his bed.

"Like a baby". Marcus was yawning and rubbing his eyes.

"What, you woke up screaming a few times and wet the bed?" I was smiling and eating a bit of his croissant.

He sat and frowned at me for a second. "Yep and you're sitting in the wet patch".

"Euuwww". I actually got up momentarily to check and Marcus shook his head.

"So, what's it feel like to be 30? You can tell me, I can handle it". I was like a boisterous puppy dog this morning. It was a rare occurrence, I grant you, but I *could* do perky in the mornings when I had a purpose... and a large amount of caffeine.

Marcus let out a giant yawn again and stretched. "Well, I can feel my skin sagging as we speak, my brain has slowed to half speed and it's as if God's flipped a switch and all my internal organs are on a slow shutdown". The puppy just got neutered.

I'd had tried for weeks to convince Marcus to take the day off work but he was having none of it. He said he had a mountain of work but Marcus *always* had the Kilimanjaro of workloads to climb though, so dragging him away from the office was no easy task. He worked as a Tax Manager at a local firm in town and earned really good money. I had no idea what he did but I knew he was hard working, put in all the hours and was always acquiring new qualifications, so he deserved his success. Unlike me, he had never once, in twelve years, been late to work and he wasn't about to start today.

He patted me on the back. "Come on, move your arse, I need to get up".

"Just *five* more minutes". I was sticking out my bottom lip, trying to look cute and pouty but instead it looked like I'd been stung by a bee and was having an allergic reaction. "You haven't opened *my* pressie yet".

Confused, he looked back through the pile I'd given him. "There's *not* one from you".

"Ahhh haaa!" I jumped up, trying to indicate the element of surprise but actually scaring myself in the process. I ran outside and brought in my present and put it on the end of the bed, waiting nervously, while he carefully unwrapped. It was intensely annoying; he hated to tear paper, I think he got that from his dad Neil, it took him *forever* to open presents. Personally, when handed a gift, it doesn't matter if someone's taken the time to carefully package and spruce with bows and tags, I tended to obliterate. I got impatient. "Errr, gonna be late for work there Sparky, remember?"

"OK, OK, nearly there". He finally unveiled the present. Was that a smile? Yes! We have smile. He liked it but did he *get* it?

He looked over at me as if I'd handed him the world on a stick. "I've always wanted one of these!" Phew! He got it. He ran over and gave me a massive hug. "Thanks hon, you rock".

Marcus got himself showered and ready for work in record time and with a hop, skip and small jump (well, it was still very early), he went off to work. He kissed me goodbye and told me he'd see me tonight for dinner; we sounded like a married couple. I then got myself showered and changed and looked at my watch... it couldn't be? I thought my watch must've stopped so I checked with the wall clock in the kitchen, jeez it *was*, it was only 8.00am. If I left in a minute, I could catch the bus at ten past and I would be in work by 8.30am at the latest, half an hour early! I grabbed my stuff and left the house with a hop and a jump (I left out the skip due to a childhood trauma at double-dutch) and I was on my merry way. Fate then spoke, the Gods intervened and it was apparent I was not *meant* to be early to work, as there were roadworks near the High Street, the bus was caught in traffic and I walked in at *exactly* 9.00am. I decided that from that point on, it would not be sensible to tempt fate again.

Best of Friends?

Thank God Marcus was picking me up tonight to drive me home. I had never known an afternoon to drag so badly. I'd been marvelling in the morning at how full of energy I felt and hadn't realised how much late nights and hangovers really slowed me down and I was *beginning* to think it was the way forward until the clock struck 3.00pm and my early start suddenly hit me with a fiery vengeance. I drank three coffees in under thirty minutes, causing a nervous twitch but my body was still screaming 'power nap!' The only thing that kept me going was the promise of a lovely dinner, as Samuel and Neil were taking us out for a meal in a fancy restaurant tonight *and* that I wouldn't have to ride the stinky bus home, giving me extra time to get ready, so we wouldn't be late...

We arrived at the restaurant ten minutes late and Samuel and Neil were already waiting at the bar. The waiter took our coats and then walked us all over to our table. I was looking round in confusion, really eyeing up the place. I tutted, huffed and puffed a couple of times, without realising it until Samuel looked curiously at me and asked, "Is something wrong Nicky?"

"What?" Suddenly I clicked back. "Oh no, nothing at all, it's lovely". I was back to studiously looking around the room. As I approached our reserved corner, I was checking out my seat and the table thoroughly as I sat down.

"Sturdy enough for you?" Samuel was looking at me with some amusement now.

"Errr... yes". I had both hands grasping the table as if I was shaking it. "Don't make 'em like they used to, huh?"

Samuel looked a little concerned and looked towards Marcus, probably wondering why he'd agreed to take the mental patient out for the evening.

Marcus gallantly answered for me. "She's trying to think of a good nickname for the place, Dad". Oh, he knew me so well.

"Nickname?"

Marcus gave Samuel a brief glimpse of our world. "Yes, we affectionately name all the places we enjoy. It's like a seal of approval".

"Well, I am pleased… I think". Samuel looked thoughtful for a moment, then he turned his attentions back to me, obviously determined to play along. "And have you had any luck, Nicky?"

"Not yet. I think I'm going to have to rely on an incident during the evening".

"An incident?"

"Yeah. A sauce spill or a plate break, maybe". I was practically beaming at the thought of being gifted such an easy disaster to aide me in my naming process.

Samuel nodded pensively and then asked, "Does it have to be negative?" He was *good*.

"No, not at all. We never limit ourselves when giving a nickname. It could equally be a nice wine or a good bathroom that swings it". I was happily relaying the rules and trying to ignore Neil's gawp on the other side of the table.

"I'm glad to hear it". Samuel was smiling as he looked down at the menu. Neil on the other hand, looked as if the whole thing had flown so fast over his head that it left scorch marks on his scalp.

The waiter had a fancy French-cum-Spanish accent which I was sure was fake, just to make the restaurant seem posher. "Amuse-bouche?"

I just couldn't help myself. "Yes, it is rather".

"I'm sorry Mad*ame*?" A tone of confusion in his over the top Italian-cum-Welsh accent. Marcus let out an involuntary chuckle and immediately tried to compose himself. The waiter looked from him back to me as we sat like naughty school kids, trying not to laugh. Samuel interjected, "Err... yes, that would be lovely".

The waiter raised his eyebrow took our wine order in his ridiculous Russian-cum-Greek accent and walked off.

Marcus was giggling, Samuel was smiling and shaking his head and Neil was clearly *not* amused. I figured he must have been conspiring with the waiter. We all took a moment to peruse the menus and then Señor Fancy Pants was back with some small food, a bottle and his Mexican-cum-Dutch accent. "Would you like to taste the wine, sir?"

Samuel smelled, swished, swirled and sipped and then Fancy Pants half filled our glasses; I was going to need more than that to survive the accent, let alone Neil's constant uncomplimentary looks in my direction. We quietly ordered our food.

Over the years, I'd spent a lot of time with Samuel and Neil; they were a really nice couple. I especially got along with Samuel, probably because he was just an older, bearded version of Marcus but tonight felt a little strange, it almost felt like a double date and Neil was not in the best of moods. I was actually struggling to think of conversation but it was soon apparent, that I wasn't the only one.

Marcus started the ball rolling. "It's a nice menu".

Samuel, Neil and I all answered at the same time, "Yeah, nice".

I thought I'd help. "They've got a lot of nice things". It wasn't my *best* work.

"Yes they *have*". Samuel was very firm with his answer, trying to back me up.

Marcus followed. "It *is* nice". He then gestured towards some meals that had just been brought out. "*Looks* nice, too".

"It *does*". Samuel was again firm with his response.

"Yes". Neil seemed a little pre-occupied and so wasn't playing the game as convincingly as the rest of us.

Quiet fell on the room for a minute.

"*So*". Samuel was smiling in my direction. "Have you thought of a name yet?"

"I'm not pregnant; it's just an unflattering top". Well, if that didn't break the ice…

"Oh God, no, I *meant* for the restaurant, a name for the restaurant". Samuel looked horrified. Marcus was laughing.

"I know. I'm just kidding, I'm sorry". I tried to pull a sincere contrite look.

Marcus stepped in. "She does that a lot".

Samuel nodded as if he'd just remembered. "I know, I walked *right* into that one". I laughed and luckily Samuel joined me but Neil however, looked extremely uncomfortable which cut the laughter off in its prime.

A few more moments passed in quiet again before the silence was broken. "*So*". Bless him, it was Samuel again. "Have you two decided where to go on your holidays this year?"

Neil looked as if someone had just woke him up and Marcus answered, "We haven't quite found a compromise yet, so nothing's set in stone".

"So, it's just the two of you?" Neil looked between Marcus and I, not managing to hide the look of disapproval.

Marcus again, took point on our defensive line. "Yeah, well we live together and we've been going on holiday together for about thirteen years. It's just *this* time most of our friends have got other agendas".

Samuel was trying to help with a light mock. "Ahh, you're getting to *that* age now, people getting married and starting families".

I chimed back in. "Don't remind me! We've got *three* wedding invites for next year".

Neil's eyes narrowed. "What together?"

Marcus was looking strangely at his father. "Well, we do have most of the same friends, dad. It seems silly for them to send two separate invites to the same house".

Neil looked back down at his drink and Marcus looked quizzically from Neil to Samuel and shrugged his shoulders. Samuel shook his head as if to indicate that Marcus shouldn't worry and then Señor Fancy Pants was back with his Ukrainian-cum-Irish accent and our food. "More wine Mad*ame*?"

I flashed Fancy Pants my best dimpled smile. "Ohhh, yes. Keep it coming". Unfortunately for me, he was immune to my dimples and dribbled a tiny amount in to my glass.

The silence went on for what seemed like an eternity, when suddenly Neil sat jolt upright and winced. He threw a dirty look at Samuel and then decided to add in some polite conversation. "I love those lamp shades". He then bent down and rubbed his shin.

Marcus answered first, "Hmm, nice".

"They *are* nice". Samuel pitched in with the same firm tone from earlier. It would appear we were back on *that* Merry-go-round. I looked over at the lamps standing in the corner, they were very ornate with dark pink shades, shy of having Barbie's printed on the sides, they belonged in a girl's bedroom. Unfortunately, I'd started to speak before I processed, "Yeah. They're a bit ga… err… g-good". Shit. Hopefully, they didn't notice.

Marcus was staring at me like a bunny caught in the headlights; I guess *he* noticed. I was used to speaking freely in front of Marcus, probably because he normally started it but in front of Samuel and Neil? Err, no. I was officially mortified.

Marcus tried to help me. "Yes, they are good. They're nice".

Samuel firmly retorted. "They *are* nice"

And so did a more sinister sounding Neil, "Yes... they are".

Marcus did all the work on his birthday, he was the one that managed to fill the rest of the evening, engaging everyone with talk about work and holidays and then he spent some time talking about his drinks planned for tomorrow night and the crowd that was going to be there. The boy did good but on the cab ride home he didn't seem very happy. "I'm really sorry Nic; I don't know what was wrong with my dad tonight".

He didn't need to differentiate between dads. "Hey, don't worry about it. I'm sure it's nothing to do with either of us; he's probably just had a really crappy day at work. I have them all the time and *frequently* take it out on my friends". I was flashing a big knowing smile at him and he laughed.

"Yes you do", he smiled and patted my leg. He then turned away and looked pensively out of the window "And as you say, I'm sure it's nothing to do with us".

Chapter 11

I struggled to get into work again today but I was determined to be on time. Only five minutes late, not bad. I was straight in, coat off, computer on. I had an Email from Alice, she'd sent it to both my work and home email addresses, it was obviously important. After reading one line in, I realised very quickly that Alice's important and mine were on a whole other level. She said that Greg had been up all night worrying about the theme of 'Black and White'. What did it mean? Who's wearing what? Is it like formal wear? Should the presents be black and white? Of course the questions had nothing to do with Greg and everything to do with Alice's need to conform. I couldn't help but laugh. She really couldn't do anything without checking with everyone else first.

I did feel very sorry for Alice; she'd had a tough childhood. Alice Mason was a happy, shiny blonde, carefree, petite, little daddy's girl who was more than capable of making her own decisions; then her dad got sick. He'd had advanced liver cancer and died within the year, Alice was just *nine* years old. It was the first time any of us had experienced any kind of loss and I still remember it, as if it were yesterday. The plucky young Alice became introverted, we knocked on her door every night but she wouldn't come out and play. We still saw her at school but most lunchtimes, if we'd let her, she would just sit and read on her own. In the background, our folks rallied round Alice's mum, looking after her as only other mum's know how, with a home-made crumble and a bottle of Chardonnay. I didn't understand at the time how that could *possibly* help and it would be much later in life that I discovered the healing powers of the vino, good food and a great mate. Finally, when she started to come out of her own haze of grief, Mrs Mason realised just how much Alice had cut herself off and forced her to come back out but she wasn't the same girl. She'd lost her fight and her drive and I often wondered how different Alice would be if she *hadn't* lost her dad so young.

Greg Matthews was a smart, polite and homely kid but also easily led. He and Luke became best friends and Luke was only too happy to demonstrate the benefits of skipping school, getting trashed and womanising from a very young age. With his dark blonde hair and cobalt eyes, Greg was handsome in a boy next door kind of way and he had learned from the master on how to play on it. Fortunately for Greg, Luke's penchant for trouble, had him expelled from our school in the third year, allowing Greg the space to be his own man and steadily achieve. He began to keep Luke at arm's length outside of school and became more of a joiner, helping out at local events and even playing football for the local team but when he was 21, Greg's life changed dramatically again when his mum died in a car accident. One minute she was driving to the supermarket for the weekly big shop, and the next... Greg went off the rails and he and Luke became thick as thieves again but that's also when he turned to Alice for comfort. It was just a friends thing at first, two people that totally understood what it was like to lose a parent but then his visits increased to three or four times a week and finally one night, he asked her out to dinner.

Alice was suddenly terrified, she phoned Emma, Carly, me and then Jenna. Emma instantly sprung into action wanted to book the restaurant for her, told her how she should act, what she should wear and what she should say. Exhausted, she needed some perspective, so she phoned Carly, who was happy to tell her how moving from friendship into a relationship was a natural progression not to be scared of. Then she wanted some cheering up, so she phoned me and I told her that during mating, the honey bee's testicles explode and their penis snaps off. Then finally, she felt she needed advice on keeping her cool should the evening move back to his place and this was her biggest mistake as Jenna told her to get a few drinks down her neck, to take the edge off…

As threatened, Emma booked the restaurant on Alice's behalf, which was a bit fancy and not really Alice's sort of thing but Emma was *insistent* that it was ideally romantic. Alice had a few drinks over dinner to calm her nerves, which weren't improved by the fact that every twenty minutes, Emma was texting her to see how she was getting on. They were getting on great, why wouldn't they? They were good friends; they had nearly twenty years of material that they could discuss, so they weren't short of conversation. After dinner, Greg helped Alice on with her coat and as they walked out in to the late night, Greg checked his watch. Sure enough, it was too late to get into the pub before closing and seven years ago, the only other place that would have been open past 11:00pm was Vom's. Not really the sort of place you took a first date, even if you had known them for years. Greg casually asked Alice if she would like to come back to his for a drink as his dad was out of town on business again and wouldn't be back for a few days. Alice's stomach flipped, she obviously hadn't had enough to drink and so *warily* agreed.

"Vodka?"

"Lovely". Alice was sat on the edge of the sofa as if she was sitting on a pew in church.

"Make yourself at home. Do you want lemonade with that? I don't have any ice, I'm afraid".

Alice shifted back on the sofa about two inches but maintained the same position with her knees firmly together and her hands on her thighs, looking like she was promoting the Health and Safety Guide for Correct Posture at a Computer Workstation. "Lemonade's great". She didn't really like lemonade but was answering involuntarily now. Greg poured the drinks, handed Alice a glass and sat down next to her on her right. Alice then moved another two inches but this time to the left. She downed her vodka and Greg hadn't even taken a sip of his. "Oh, errr, I didn't realise you were *that* thirsty. Here, let me get you another". Greg got back up and wandered over to the drinks cabinet and dutifully poured. This time he put the drink three feet in front of her on the coffee table, it had come down to a simple choice but he must have figured it was a winner both ways; 1) if she wanted the drink, she would have to shift out of the holier-than-thou stance she'd fashioned, and 2) if she didn't want to move, she *couldn't* down the drink. You had to admit, it was a noble effort.

He sat back down next to her on the sofa and then after a few minutes, moved closer. The lounge had quite a few open containers strewn around and Alice nervously babbled, "What's with all the old stuff in the boxes?"

Greg looked upset as he answered, "Oh, that's my mum's stuff. Me and dad have been cataloguing everything. She collected a lot of antiques and we wanted some to go to different people, her sisters and friends. It's too much to keep them all in the house".

"I'm *sooo* sorry, I didn't think".

"That's OK. These boxes down here are stuff she would've wanted to give away, anyway. The stuff that reminds us of her, the really *valuable* stuff is all upstairs". Greg put his hand on Alice's knee and she lunged forwards and upwards, trying to lose the hand and grabbed for the other vodka which she managed in one swift move. She stood for a minute and drank it down.

"Is everything OK?"

"Mmm, hmm". Alice nodded, she couldn't answer, the lemonade was gassy and she needed to burp.

Luckily, Greg excused himself and went to the bathroom and she let out said belch, which was closely followed by a hiccup. She raided the drinks cabinet and quickly sneaked another large vodka, straight out of the bottle. Alice noticed a picture of Greg's mother staring out at her and really hoped she couldn't see her right now. When Greg came back, he was surprised to see the drinks cabinet door down and Alice perched back on the edge of the sofa but swaying slightly. By now, she was pretty well hammered.

Greg moved nearer and realised Alice was staring at the wall. "Alice?" Her gaze was broken and she looked up but as she did, let out another hiccup. Greg leant down by the side of the sofa and tried to look Alice in the face. "I think we need to get you to bed".

Best of Friends?

Alice froze. She totally mistook his meaning and the onset of panic must have started the chain reaction as she looked at Greg and then started to heave. Greg rushed her to the kitchen, where she promptly threw up in the kitchen sink. He held her hair and stroked her back and then when he was sure she'd finished and after copious amounts of water, he took her upstairs and put her in his room, gave her a t-shirt and shorts to sleep in and put a bucket next to the bed. He pointed out the bathroom, said his goodnights and headed off to sleep in his dad's bedroom.

In the morning, Alice awoke very uncomfortably, her neck was crook and it felt like she was lying on a mattress that had popped every spring. It took a little while for the fog to clear before she realised it was far, far worse.

During the night, she had gotten up to go to the bathroom, still pissed when she came out, she must have gotten turned around and she had gone into the guestroom, climbed on to the bed and not even noticed that she had spent the night sprawled across Greg's mum's priceless, favourite, fragile antiques. How she'd gotten on to the bed without breaking anything was impressive, how she'd slept the night on top of the antiques without noticing *or* breaking anything was nothing short of a miracle, now how she was supposed to get off of the bed without breaking anything, was a whole other ball game. Then she heard the toilet flush; Greg was up.

Alice thought she was going to be sick again as she heard Greg walking across the landing; it felt like every footstep was causing an aneurysm. Eventually, she heard him go downstairs and she could relax for a second while she tried to work out how the hell she was going to get out of this. Alice had done pretty well in school, staying on for A-Levels and then off to University with

Emma for a few years but she hadn't specialised in Physics. She would need to work out the distribution of weight on the artefacts, so she could remove an element at a time without breaking or subsequently causing added pressure on another item. Well, *that* or she could just try and launch herself off the bed...

Alice, with large amounts of alcohol still in her bloodstream and an obviously impaired judgement, opted for the latter. Needless to say, things didn't turn out *quite* as she hoped and the giant thud caused Greg to shout up the stairs, "Alice? Everything OK?!"

Alice panicked, rubbing her knee and grabbing her foot. She'd managed to launch out of bed and straight into the dresser and was still hopping around, when she noticed a few things had fallen to the floor. She shouted back mid-hop, "Errr, yeah! Fine. I just errr... I'm OK!" Alice cursed her own lack of imagination.

"Do you take sugar in your coffee?"

Shit, he was making coffee. "Errr, two please!" Alice didn't take sugar in her coffee but she thought it might buy her a few more seconds. Alice was rushing to get everything back on the bed, even though it really hurt when she bent down, when she noticed one of the items was cracked. Should she put it back and hope they don't notice, or should she take it away and try to get it fixed? Greg was now making his way up the stairs; he stopped as he thought he heard a noise coming from the guest bedroom; shook his head and knocked on his own bedroom door. "Alice, I have your coffee. I hope you're decent, I'm coming in". Greg set the coffee down on top of his dressing table, went over towards the curtains, opened them up and drew his blackout blind. He apologised for letting the light in but then realised Alice wasn't there. Confused, he went back out on to the landing and looked pensively towards the guest room, he slowly walked towards the room and turned the door handle, when suddenly he heard the shower go. Of course, she was in the bathroom! He knocked on the door. "Alice, I've left your coffee in my room. There's plenty of towels in there you can use. Also I've put the top you were wearing last night in the washing machine, so I'll put some t-shirts out on my bed for you to choose from, OK?"

Alice was standing in the middle of the bathroom, clutching the broken antique vase. "OK, thanks!" She was officially in hell.

I guess every cloud *does* have a silver lining though because after that, Alice didn't feel *quite* so embarrassed around Greg. I guess once someone's held your hair so you can be sick, your levels of bashfulness begin to diminish. We were all pleased, they were well suited; not just because they shared a common bond but also because of what they both wanted out of life. Greg (always egged on by his 'best mate') was not a monogamous man but he was also desperate to stay in a relationship, so what he needed was a girl who would turn the other way when his window shopping turned to buying and Alice, not willing to go out and grab life by the proverbials, needed someone who would bring everything home on a plate. It was a match made in... Well, one of them!

Sally popped some post down on my desk and then informed me that she had some free time when she gets home, so might put those pictures on the internet tonight. She threw her head back and cackled her evil plan laugh that echoed round the office as she left. Well, it felt like she did but to be fair, I could have imagined it.

Chapter 12

Thank god it was the weekend, again. I've often thought if I could travel back in time, I'd like to meet the sadistic bastard that came up with the idea of the working week being five days and the weekend only two but it's probably just as well I can't, I'm not sure I could be responsible for my actions.

I rushed in from work and checked my emails. Sally, after all her taunts, had finally been true to her word and put 'those' pictures on to Facebook and I'm *really* not loving her right now. The pictures are a surprisingly accurate reflection of the alcoholic journey that we'd all taken that night and thankfully, they do back up my story that up until Luke's arrival, I had been *relatively* sober; I could at least show Marcus that. Then of course, it reveals (extremely close up, I might add) that my night had gone rapidly downhill. I decided it was best to un-tag myself from a few photo's as after all, I had a couple of friends on Facebook who were relatives and I think my Auntie Jackie could quite happily live the rest of her life *not* seeing those images of me or then feel the need to discuss them with my mother, the next time she phones. I had *finally* learnt my lesson regarding photographic evidence of friends drunken exploits but I didn't feel that at nearly 30 years of age, it also warranted a telling off from my mum!

Sally wasn't the only person who'd tagged me in some embarrassing pictures; Emma it seemed, had also downloaded some gems of me with her children. There was a lovely shot of her eldest daughter Abigail jumping on my head and another special shot of her youngest Jessica kicking me in the stomach; what a lovely day that was. About four months ago, Emma and 'That' Justin decided to get Jessica christened but Jessica, I might add, is 2 years old; an age where splashing water from that big holy bowl into the face of the old dude in a dress would be hilariously funny. The ceremony itself was comedy gold, probably because Emma looked so mortified, that her kids were *so* out of control. Afterwards, we all went back to Emma and 'That' Justin's for drinks and food. It was the first time we'd been invited round to their new house, even though they'd moved a *year* beforehand and Marcus summed it up when he whispered in my ear, "Jesus, it's like museum in here, don't touch the glass!"

Everything was way too smart and neat and then I realised, "Where are the kids?"

"Oh, they're in the back, in the playroom. We don't let them come in here". Emma handed me my glass of bubbly.

Huh, they had a playroom, so that they didn't disturb Emma's perfect sofa or Emma's perfect carpet... interesting.

After a couple of hours of mingling and socialising, watching Emma do her best Delia Smith impression and some serious jaw ache from all the fake smiling, I was bored and wanted to leave but Marcus was engrossed in a conversation with 'That' Justin's parents (he was no doubt getting all the scandal, good boy) and my curiosity finally got the better of me, so I went back to find the kid's hidden room. With my cunning powers of deduction, I was able to locate the playroom; it was the one where all the high pitch screams were coming from and the occasional thud on the door that shook the pictures in the hallway. I was tentative, from the sheer magnitude of the thud on the other side; I wasn't sure what I was going to find when I opened the door. I also thought I heard a growl, maybe I was wrong, maybe this was where they kept Cujo? When I finally mustered the courage to push the handle, I couldn't *quite* believe my eyes. I took a moment to drink it in; it was like someone had handed the Tasmanian Devil a bunch of crayons, pushed him in the room, wound him up and let him go. As I stood there marvelling at the Devil's creation, Emma came up behind me, scaring the life out of me. "Be careful not to let them out", as she scooted off with a tray of mini sausage rolls.

I turned and looked at Emma in disbelief and then looked back at the kids, Emma was terrified of her own children and judging by this room, I wasn't surprised. For a brief moment, I wondered if anyone had checked their heads for numbers and then instantly felt terrible, berating myself for my negative thoughts towards these *lively* minors. What was I thinking? These were just kids, how bad could they be? They probably just wanted some attention, someone to play with, so I stopped being so judgemental and gave them a chance. I put down my fizz, took off my jacket and hung it on the door handle (so that rescuers could follow my trail) and stepped into the Lion's den to join in their fun and games. *Well*, I got an arse kicking that day, that I'd really rather forget but instead, Emma had finally worked out how to put the pictures up for all to see, to bring back those happy memories.

Emma was an academic achiever with phenomenal organisational skills and took the reins in every situation; she *had* to be in control. It was ironic that what Emma couldn't control was her own emotions, which had clearly rubbed off on her kids. Unlike Alice, Emma *did* have goals and ambitions but they all centred around one thing; all Emma ever wanted since childhood, was to get married. I know, it's hard to believe that in today's climate, where intelligent women can think for themselves and have the freedom of choice, that Emma's was to don the white dress, have the picket fence and raise the rugrats. Suffragette's, who'd chained themselves to railings, had simply wasted valuable drinking time when it came to Emma. This is why she got so upset if she didn't get a call back after a first date; she looked at every man she met as 'the one'. For this reason, she hadn't had a lot of luck with men (saying she came across as a little needy, is like saying Johnny Vegas likes the odd pie) and poor unsuspecting males must have been frightened for their lives, leaving scorch marks outside her dorm room but you couldn't fault her determination, she *never* gave up. She was desperately searching for the qualities she wanted in her perfect man. I had *no* idea what those qualities were but Marcus and I compiled an imaginary list once, they were; will stick around for second date, tucks shirt in, has bunny for boiling, will do as told.

I can only assume that her life must have felt like one long relationship, as she went straight from one man to the next, never stopping for a breather. She was just one of those women, who really didn't know how to be single and what's worse is she hated being around other singletons; like myself, for example. She felt *extremely* uncomfortable when I was sans boyfriend, like it was an embarrassing illness; I was 'terminally single' and she might catch it! Because of this, I knew that if I got a call asking me round, it was either a) to show off her new boyfriend or b) set me up with her new boyfriends *brother/cousin/friend (*delete where applicable). I wouldn't mind if they were at least *half* normal but she'd set me up with some shockers over the years.

At 23, Emma had a relationship with Oliver or 'Olli' as he was now known. Someone I had dated from school which suddenly became a problem, as I found out one night when she invited me out. "Every time I'm with him, I imagine him with you".

She'd caught me totally off guard, I hadn't even taken a sip of drink, yet. "What?"

"Olli. I really like him but every time I'm *with* him, I imagine him with you".

I responded in the only way I knew how. "Are you saying you're having dreams about me?"

"What? No! I'm just saying… I know where he's been and it freaks me out".

She looked disgusted and I waved to alert her to my extremely insulted presence. "Err, hi! Still sittin' here!"

She ignored me and carried on. "It's just when I kiss him, it's like I'm kissing you".

I laughed out loud, put on a silly voice, pursed my lips and sidled up. "You wanna kiss me?" Lead balloon anyone? I'd got the brick wall, the spotlight *and* the microphone but I was dodging the flying cabbages.

"I'm serious. They say that when you sleep with someone, you sleep with everyone they've ever slept with".

She'd obviously been reading way too much Cosmo, so I nodded in mock approval. "At the same time? Jeez, *busy* night".

As the tumbleweed passed and I realised my stand-up comedy days were over, I decided enough was enough and played it straight. "OK look, if it makes you feel better, I didn't sleep with him, not even close".

She looked up with hope in her eyes. "You *didn't?*" The trust didn't last for long. "But you two went out for ages? You're trying to tell me that you *didn't* go there?"

I laughed in disbelief and tried to sound forceful. "No, I did *not* 'go there'. We went out for two months when he was 15 and I was 14, for Christ's sake".

"Was it *that* long ago?" She was actually counting on her fingers, trying to do the math.

I thought we were finally at the beginning of a breakthrough. "Yes, it was! I was *far* too busy playing dot-to-dot with his acne".

"Oh". She cheered up and smiled. "That's cool then". Then just as quickly, the frown was back. "But you *kissed* him, right?"

Oh my God! I did the biggest sigh and dramatically slapped my hand onto my head for effect. "Jesus Em, I was 14! I imagine it wasn't my best work". I was getting a headache, I needed a stronger drink.

"Yeah, you're right". She was nodding very seriously to herself. "You were probably crap". I was looking at her in sheer amazement by this point but she didn't notice and was gazing deep in to space; she was off in galaxy far, far away. "He wouldn't be thinking about you, I mean your hair was shocking when you were 14".

She was recalling my young, pre hair-straighteners image, one that I'd hoped was behind me. "Thanks!"

She dialled up more horrors as the thoughts came into her brain and shot straight out of her mouth, without edit. "*And* you were flat as a pancake then".

OK, that's it! The chest was off limits. "I was *not!*"

My shout must have suddenly snapped her out of it and she turned and laughed. "You *so* were. Some of the boys called you 'two backs'". I was definitely getting the uncut version and I was not enjoying the trot down memory lane that I was being subjected to. I rubbed my temples and asked her to pick another subject but she was on a roll. "And didn't you have braces?" I tried to defend myself but it was madness to engage with the enemy, it just encouraged her. I managed to compose myself and I changed tact. "Look hon, I'm fairly sure that *'Olli'* doesn't even remember my name. Can we please leave it there?"

"Wait!" She suddenly looked up beaming excitedly, she'd evidently recalled something important and a weight had been lifted. "He *does* remember you... he called you Metal Nicky!"

I bit the inside of my mouth and let out a big sigh. "That's great, Em".

After my grilling, Emma only ended up dating Olli for three weeks, citing irreconcilable differences. After further investigation we found out he was a Vegetarian, which ruled out half of Emma's favourite restaurants and apparently this was high on her list. Fortunately for me, I'd managed to steer her away from dating anyone else I'd gone out with, I just couldn't risk her bringing up my 'Bros' years or the time I forgot my PT kit at Elementary school and was forced to play mixed football in my vest and days of the week underpants. She was obviously a font of knowledge on my past humiliations and I had to make sure she didn't overflow.

It was a few years later, at a mere 25 years old that the search was finally over; Emma met 'That' Justin. Within a year she had moved in, gotten married and had a kid on the way; once she'd secured her man, she didn't hang about. 'That' Justin was dependable, committed, dressed like his dad and was boring as hell; all things that sent shivers down my spine but seemed to tick the boxes off Emma's precious list.

Marcus broke my daydream and brought me back to the present day with a time update; he knew how easily I got distracted. "One hour, Nic!" Shit, I hadn't realised the time. I needed to get my arse in gear and get ready for Marcus' drinks tonight and you know how I hate to be late.

Chapter 13

Isn't hindsight a wonderful thing? As I sit here with a brew, looking back on last night and feeling sorry for myself, I can *easily* pinpoint where things went wrong but at the time, they didn't seem like such a big deal. See, we'd arrived at Dribbler's fifteen minutes late (yes, it was my fault) which prompted a round of applause from Marcus' mates. I loved going out with them, you could have a darn good drink, boogie and a giggle, without getting hit on by idiots all night. There were eight couples there including Mitchell and Daniel and both the couples we'd holidayed with last year. The bickerers were remarkably still together but I could see them arguing over a pack of Pork Scratchings, so I guess some things never change. I got fed up waiting to be served at the bar, as there were loads of people that came in after me but thanks to the only bartender being a woman, the good looking men were top of the heap. I realised how blokes must feel when it's a bar*man* and all the female of the species has to do is accidentally flash some flesh and their waiting time is instantly culled. I'd also foolishly sighed and tutted aloud which had been clocked by the dog-on-

Best of Friends?

heat barmaid, so I'd added to my waiting time. This is why, when I finally *did* get served, I decided to get in a double round; teeing off the evening with mistake number one.

The first drink had slid down my neck *way* too quickly and an eagle-eyed Marcus noticed and frowned. All I could think to do was shrug. Well, explanations and reparations seemed futile, there was nothing I could do about it as the drink was already warming my stomach, so I just quietly moved on to the next one. Mid second drink, my phone shouted 'Good Morning Vietnam!' from my bag, causing every eye in the whole pub to wander my way. I shouted, "Sorry!" As I sheepishly backed off, checking my phone to see who it was and *quickly* switch it to silent. I evidently showed my surprise as Marcus mouthed, "What? Who is it?"

That's when I made mistake number two. "Oh, nothing, no-one. Just Jenna". I don't know *why* I lied to Marcus... it was Luke.

I moved away from the crowd, standing on my own to read it. All it said was, "*Chupta? x*". That was Luke's version of 'what are you up to?' The English language, or certainly the bastardised text version, could be a wondrous thing.

I texted back, "*Just out 4 a drink with Marcus n friends. U? x*". I'm not sure why I added the 'You?' Often, I found it better *not* knowing what Luke was up to.

I was surprised, to get a message straight back (fortunately, this time, it just vibrated). "*Out drinkin. Wanna meet up? x*".

I wasn't *entirely* sure what he meant by that but knowing Luke, I had a pretty good idea. I knew I had the power, I could stop this right here; all I had to do was close the phone, put it away and rejoin the group. I closed the phone and put it in my bag but before I took my hand away, I thought it would be pretty rude not to reply; I should at least extend him the courtesy of a 'thanks, but no thanks' text back. I mused for a while over what to send back when Marcus caught me mid-ponder. "Everything all right there, luv?"

"Hmm?" I looked up from my phone. "Oh, yeah… Jenna was just asking what we were up to. I was just trying to figure out a way of not letting on where we are, in case she turns up and hits on all your friends". I smiled nervously as the lies just snowballed.

Marcus assumed a deadpan face and monotone voice. "Babe, they're gay".

I laughed anxiously. "Like that's stopped her before!"

Marcus thought for a second and nodded. "Good point, well made".

Marcus' friend Jacob collared him, so I walked further away and turned back to my phone. I hated lying to Marcus, so I had to nip this in the bud. I really didn't know *what* to reply, so I went for short and sweet. "*Sorry, can't. With the boys. Maybe sum other time x*". It was brave, it was bold, it was the new me; I *could* say no! I was just about to put my phone away when I looked up and saw the truffle hunter that Tamsin from work had pulled a few months back at Julie's drinks and it was my chance to redeem myself for the God awful pictures I'd flaunted of them. I sent her a quick text and warned her that not under *any* circumstances, should she frequent 'Dribbler's' tonight.

Now, I thought good deeds were rewarded? Obviously not, because had I *not* done my good deed for the day, had I *not*

Best of Friends?

forewarned Tamsin, I would have put my phone away and *not* received his reply; my good deed had facilitated mistake number three... The phone buzzed in my hand and I *had* to read it, I wondered how he had reacted to my new found bravado? After all, Luke was not accustomed to the word *'no'*. I opened the text with apprehension. *"Really? coz it looks like ur on ur own! Nice dress, btw x"*

He was here. I looked up and around and couldn't see him anywhere, then I looked through the bar and suddenly there he was on the other side, looking as fit as ever. God damn it!

I looked over towards Marcus and the boys and they were happily engrossed in some old anecdotes and then I looked back towards Luke who was leering at me and I could feel my resolve disintegrating. I smiled back, a little embarrassed and looked down at my drink, shifting uncomfortably on my feet. Was I actually going to go round there? I could feel his gaze boring in to me and I desperately tried not to make eye contact but it was no use; I let out a big sigh at my lack of courage and made my way over for mistake number four.

I assured myself that I was only going to stay for five minutes and he smiled at me as if he'd won; the worst part was, in a way, he had. I was angry at myself but it passed far more quickly than it should have and certainly didn't stop me from outrageously flirting with him, both laughing as we tried to outdo one another with comedy pick up lines. He was staring again but this time he was up close and personal and it totally unnerved me. I asked him in a roundabout way if he was out on his own, trying (not very subtly) to find out if he had plans to meet friends, especially friends that were girls and that maybe ate cheese and onion crisps. I asked him about his work which embarrassingly turned in to what sounded like an interview (all I needed was some glasses and a clipboard) but I did however, manage to find out that he'd left the Life Insurance Company that he worked for and was now an Estate Agent – which was not *really* a surprise; Luke had had more jobs than I'd had unhealthy dinners. It was at *that* point I thought my interview technique was on to a winner, when I realised he was coming across as very articulate, not something I had *ever* thought about him before and I started to feel bad that I had not credited him with enough intelligence in the past. Well, that was until I asked him about his new job, "And how do you find that?"

He looked confused for a second. "Easy, it's just up the High Street". I laughed and he didn't. I stood corrected.

Luke's attentions had made me lose track of time and before I knew it, I'd been talking to him for half an hour. I suddenly remembered why I was there and leaned forward slightly to look through the bar to check on Marcus. He seemed totally oblivious to my lack of presence and was laughing with his friends, so I figured I still had some time with Luke; just another five minutes... Hello, mistake number five. I couldn't help it, it was just easier being round the other side of the bar; for one, due to Luke's genetic make-up, he managed to get the immediate attention of the barmaid and two, I'd managed to get my own back on 'said' barmaid, as shy of urinating in every corner to mark her territory, she'd obviously tagged Luke for herself and was throwing me some *serious* evils, which cheered me up no end.

Luke's eyes were back on me. "*So*. Haven't seen *you* for a while. Although saying that, I saw someone that looked really like ya with some short, hairy dude in Vom's the other week".

I was officially mortified. I did the only thing one can in these sorts of situations. "Wasn't me, I haven't been to Vom's for months. I must have a double out there. Don't worry, I intend to hunt her down and kill her before she ruins my impeccable reputation". OK, so impeccable was a stretch but it didn't warrant the extended laugh that Luke gave it. Fortunately, he conceded that Hairy Kebab Man was hardly my type and that he must've been mistaken. Phew! I made a mental note to burn my clothes from that night, so that I could never be recognised again while we worked out how long it had *actually* been. I say *we* worked out; I pretended I didn't know the exact date and time, down to the second, of our last rendezvous and he genuinely didn't have a clue, so I threw it out there that it must have been about four months, whilst coyly playing with my straw. I felt my cheeks flush red when he remarked that it had been a pretty good night and I figured maybe I *had* drunk that first drink too quickly or maybe it was just the close proximity to Luke but as my brain flooded with visuals and my stomach began to flip, I knew at that moment I was hooked again.

Luke suddenly picked up his drink and gestured I do the same. "Come on, drink up. We're going to Job's".

I was about to follow suit, when I remembered, "I can't Luke, I'm here with Marcus". I knew I really wanted to be with Luke but I couldn't leave my best friend and it wasn't like I could invite Luke to join Marcus' group.

Luke looked through the bar towards Marcus and his friends. "He seems alright, he's with all his fancy boys, he probably won't even notice you're gone". I raised my eyebrows at Luke and he quickly responded, "You *know* what I mean! Look at him, he's having a laugh, he's fine. Come on, we'll have one in Job's and then on to Crusty's for a couple and I promise to have you tucked up in bed by 12:00am. Whaddya reckon?" Luke flashed his best smile; he could be *quite* persuasive... and so came mistake number six.

Chapter 14

In the interests of saving further blushes, I'm going to leave out mistakes seven through nine and move straight on to mistake number ten. When I woke this morning, Luke was gone; this wasn't the mistake or indeed a shock, I didn't expect him to hang around, due to Marcus. I didn't mind, it helped detract from any awkwardness either of you might feel or any unresolved issues of intimacy that friends might have when they cross those kinds of boundaries (OK, so I read that in a magazine). The last few years we had mainly stayed at his place, so that he and Marcus could be kept at safe distance but after all the things he'd said last night, I thought he might have dared Marcus' reproof, which brought forth a small panic. I was overwhelmed by a feeling of dread; what if he *was* still in the house, trying to talk to Marcus? I quickly got up, pulled on my dressing gown and giant, fluffy, comedy slippers and tip-toed towards the living room.

Marcus was sitting on the sofa watching TV with his back to the door. I was gingerly scouring the room with my eyes, ridiculously looking in places that a grown man couldn't *possibly* hide. "Hey, how goes it bud?" What was that? Bud? I never called him bud and I was *way* too chirpy for a Saturday morning. Way to give yourself up, Nic.

Marcus didn't turn round, continuing to watch telly. "Oh, hi".

I stepped in through the doorway looking in the corners I couldn't see before and trying to see out towards the kitchen. "Err... Where's Sade?"

"Still in bed". Marcus didn't move.

"What're you watching?" I wasn't really interested; I was just trying to keep him distracted, while I looked behind the door.

"Just that film I plussed last night".

Lucky for me, Marcus still hadn't turned round; he was obviously in to the movie, so I tried to edge sneakily towards the kitchen. "Err, yeah? The one with that bird from Buffy in? Any good?" I could see the top half of the kitchen and it seemed to be all clear but I was now in Marcus' peripheral view and looked round to see he was staring at me. I stopped in my tracks and smiled. "Hi".

"Hi". Marcus had a pretty sadistic look on his face, either he was *on* to me or he didn't approve of my slippers.

There was silence for a few moments before Marcus finally cut the air. "Where did *you* get to last night?"

Did he know? Or was he just fishing? "I bumped in to an old friend".

"An *old* friend?" Marcus nodded with interest and looked back towards the TV. "What 'old friend' was that?"

I panicked; I knew I couldn't tell Marcus it was Luke. Problem was, it was a bit late in the game for me to remember that Marcus and I had the same friends. "Remember Danny Jefferson?" I had booked my plane ticket to hell.

"*Donny* Jefferson?" Marcus slowly turned to face me with a quizzical look, correcting my mistake.

I pretended not to have made one. "Yeah, you know, Don. He had really curly hair, used to wet himself a lot". And I'd upgraded my ticket to Business Class.

"Don Jefferson, eh? Wow. I heard he'd moved to Australia". Marcus was smiling and waiting for me to prove him wrong.

"Err, yes, that's right, he had. He was back... visiting his mum". I was choosing the movies I was going to watch on the in-flight entertainment.

"Really? I'd heard he *went* with his mum".

"Did I say his mum?" I let out a little laugh at my apparent mistake. "I meant his mum's sister, his Auntie... Dora". I'd now been bumped up into First Class. I just couldn't seem to stop, I *wanted* to but I couldn't, the lies just kept tumbling out.

Marcus looked weird like he was going to laugh or was it cry? I really wasn't sure which. A sickly sweet smile had taken over his face. "You'd have thought that Dora would have gone with them, seeing as she *is* the Explorer". Ahh, that's what it was, he'd obviously been cueing up for a joke. Hadn't he?

At that point I had no idea, if I'd gotten away with it or not. Last night, when he asked me who I was texting, it was the first time I had ever out and out lied to him and by this morning, I was on a roll. Well, I say it was the *first* time; there was the time when we were 6 years old and I told him I'd completed the Rubik's Cube on my own, which was kind of true, except instead of turning the facets to correspond, I peeled off all the stickers and stuck them back on so they matched. Then we were 10, I accidentally broke his toy Ghostbusters car and blamed Pete, then when we were... Actually do you know what? It doesn't matter now, the point *is*, this is the first time I had lied to him as an adult and I *wasn't* proud of it.

"Kettles not long boiled, if you want a brew?" Marcus gestured towards the kitchen. I smiled and nodded, went in and flicked the switch back on. Maybe it was OK, maybe I was just being paranoid before, he didn't seem to mind at all. While waiting for it to re-boil, I turned towards the fridge to get the milk out and that's when I noticed the piece of paper on the side. I wandered over and picked it up. 'Cheers for last night, I'll call you later. Luke x'. Oh shit.

As if anticipating, how long it would take me to find the note, Marcus shouted through, "The strangest thing happened this morning…"

Oh fuck, oh fuck, oh fuck. My heart hit my stomach and I clenched my eyes closed. If I clicked my heels together, would I be able to get out of Kansas? I feared not, especially not in these slippers. I looked towards the ceiling for forgiveness. I knew I shouldn't have lied to him, this was bad, this was very, *very* bad. I walked at snail's pace back towards the kitchen entrance, where

Marcus was looking, as I slowly showed my head through the door frame.

He was dying to tell his tale, so I kept my mouth shut and let him talk. "There I was, just minding my own business, in my very own kitchen when in struts *your* friend Luke in his pants". I was frozen, my eyes had widened and my mouth was open. I looked like a Nun who'd accidentally stumbled into a Strip Club. Marcus continued with a jaunty little laugh. "Naturally, I was a little taken aback". Marcus' voice then became strained. "More so when he proceeded to pour himself a pint of milk, using the very last drop of it. He *saw* me staring at him but he apparently took that to mean something else and that's when he made a little crack about being half naked in front of me and that he'd better not bend down to get anything out of the cupboards". Marcus was visibly (and understandably) *not* amused.

I held my hands up to cover my nose and mouth and gasped, "Oh God".

"Ya ha. Nice huh? *Real* nice". Marcus turned off the TV but was still facing it. "You know how I feel about him Nic, yet you brought him back here and then lied about it". I'd never seen him so upset.

"I am *SO* sorry. I just didn't think last night, I..."

Marcus looked at me and cut me off. "That's the problem Nic, you *never* do! I don't want that arsehole in my house ever again, *got it?!*"

My mouth was dry, I tried to swallow. "He won't be, I promise". Marcus got up and walked into the hallway, where he grabbed his coat and I followed him out and pleaded, "Marcus, please. Where are you going?"

"To get some milk". Marcus put on his coat and left.

I showered, changed and slapped on the war paint but Marcus *still* wasn't back. I had no idea how I was going to make this up to Marcus, especially if Luke was going to be in my life. I thought about Luke and went over to my dressing gown hanging up on the back of my bedroom door and got the note out of my pocket. 'Cheers for last night' What the hell did *that* mean? Like I'd done him a favour; helped him paint a house or move a sofa?! 'Cheers for last night', what an arse! Suddenly, I had a flashback to Luke's actual arse... For God's sake, woman! Perspective, I needed to get back some perspective and assess my reality. Right, well, Luke and I are both single, consenting adults and last night our 'relationship' took a new turn, last night he told me he'd fallen for me and that all these years he'd really cared about me. Despite his note this morning, last night *had* felt like I was on the cusp of something with Luke and now Marcus didn't want him anywhere near our home. Sure, I'd left Marcus' drinks last night without saying goodbye but he was busy with his mates, he didn't need *me* there and yeah, so I bought a bloke home? Big deal! I pay rent, it's *my* home too; I should be able to bring home anyone I like! If Luke and I were going to be together, Marcus would have to get used to it. There!

Fortunately fate had other ideas and Marcus didn't return home to the 'it's my life' speech before I had the bright idea to check my mobile to see if Luke had called. It would appear I was incredibly popular this morning as I had loads of texts and missed calls but upon further inspection, I realised all the texts were from

Best of Friends?

Marcus asking me where I was and if I was OK. I also had five missed calls, so I accessed my voicemail.

Message 1: *"Hello Nicky, its Marcus. I can't find you anywhere, is everything OK? Call me"*.

Message 2: *"Hello Nic, Marcus. I looked all over Dribbler's for you, the crowd's moving to Job's now, just in case you wondered where we were. Call me"*.

Message 3: *"Hello Nic, Marcus again. Look, I'm getting worried now, you're not in Job's either, I hope you're OK. Just call me yeah and let me know you're OK"*.

Message 4: *"Hey Nic. I've just tried our home number and you're not there either. It's Marcus again, by the way. I'm freaked out Nic, you just disappeared. Just let me know you're safe"*.

Message 5: *"Nic? Marcus. I really hope you're sitting somewhere having a good laugh at all these messages. We're in Crusty's now and we're leaving in a minute. I'm not gonna get freaked anymore, I'm just going to assume you met yourself a good looking bloke and are... having a good time. I'm sorry for all the messages, I just... I'll be there in a minute guys!... Sorry about that. It's not like you to leave without saying goodbye; I got a little worried, is all. I've gotta go, I managed to talk them into going to Vom's, you'd have been proud. Well, I really hope I see you tomorrow. Love ya. Bye"*.

So now you're all caught up and know why I officially feel like a steaming pile of crap. I'd put my phone on silent in Dribbler's and forgotten to take it off, I hadn't felt my bag vibrating, so I missed *every* one of Marcus' messages. He sounded a little drunk on the last call which is why I suspected I had the 'love ya' thrown in and it just served to make me feel *even* worse. He was right, what he'd said to me after the Rob incident, he was right; I *did* become selfish when I was with Luke. I had to make this right with Marcus.

Finally I heard a key in the door and ran out into the hallway. "Hey. You were gone a while?"

Marcus walked straight past me towards the kitchen and I followed like a little lap dog while he explained, "The convenience store was shut; apparently they got done over last night".

It was just some more perspective to remind me that my life's not *so* bad. We made small-talk about the nice owner being OK and then he told me he'd gone shopping in town instead. After a few moments silence while he put the shopping away and I loitered with intent, I asked him, "Fancy hitting the sales today? We could check out those new trainers you liked? Also, we could go and see that movie you wanted to see and then maybe get a bite to eat?" It sounded fine in my head but out loud, it was a desperate, empty gesture.

Marcus however, didn't hesitate. "Sure, sounds good".

"….." I had breathed in, ready with my counter-argument but he agreed, just like that. OK, that had *never* happened before, we were always sparking, always retorting. I *was* prone to a little over-reacting and maybe that's what this was but I felt anxious, it was like the calm before the storm although I didn't have much choice but to play along.

We did as promised; went shopping, did our own fashion shows, went to see the film of his choice, chatted about how pants the acting was, got shushed by the woman behind us and I brought us dinner at a nearby Italian restaurant, where we had a few drinks and laughed about 'dough balls'. We'd had the perfect afternoon and evening together, which when you consider the morning that preceded them, was an absolute miracle. We got back and flaked out on the sofa to find a note from Sadie, saying that she'd be out in town and not back until late. Marcus put on a DVD and I went and got us a couple of beers from the kitchen and for the *first* time since we left the house that afternoon, I checked my phone. Luke hadn't called.

Chapter 15

The sun was shining, the birds were singing and Marcus and I seemed weirdly good. He was at his folks for the day and so was Sadie for her monthly home-made roast dinner and *so* on this glorious Sunday, I was home alone, preparing to reply to Carly's message. I got out the laptop and rustled up a brew, got a plateful of biscuits and I read the email again, trying to see if there was there any hidden subtext or subliminal messaging. After a thorough examination, I could find *nothing* to suggest Satan worship or that she wanted a repeat performance of the 'big fight', the message was clear; this was *really* happening, after all this time, she *finally* wanted to see me.

I sat down in front of the computer, waiting to make my move across the keyboard. I really wasn't sure what I would say after the way things were left but she'd sent a very cordial email and I needed to respond in kind. I sat back and let out an enormous sigh, then filled the air pocket with a Custard Cream. It was simple really, I just needed to break it down; so I thought about how to begin.

Well, 'Dear Carly' was a good start. Wait, was 'Dear' a bit too formal? 'To Carly'? That just sounded too nonchalant. How about "*Hi Carly*". Informal, friendly, done. What now? I ate another couple of biscuits and got crumbs on the sofa; Marcus hated that. I tapped my feet and started singing to 'The Verve' on in the background, it was way too distracting. So I used the remote, turned off the iPod and stared at the computer. Right, come on. 'I'm really glad you got the invite?' No. 'I wanted to inv...' No. "*I'm pleased that the invite found you, I hope it found you well?*" Hmm, very polite. OK. Next... I was going to need more biscuits. I got up, got the biscuits and was pacing the lounge, eating Custard Creams, I got easily distracted by that as well, as I was carefully eating the top layer of biscuit and then the filling, without damaging the bottom layer, it was an art form. OK, OK, I've got it. I ran back to the couch and back to the computer. "*Marcus told me you'd be arriving a bit late on the night of the party and after hearing why in your email, I fully understand, because you're mum is a fucking nightmare...*" Hmm, best not put that last bit in. I needed another brew. Maybe I should take a break for a while? No, not a good idea, I'll never finish it. I didn't anticipate how *hard* this would be. Well, I knew it would be hard, I just didn't think it would be painful; I was starting to get a headache. Maybe I should put something in there about the fact that she thinks I'm an alcoholic, a small rehab joke, perhaps? Maybe not. Wait... yep, here it comes. "*I think it's a great idea to meet up the night before the party, it's been....*" 'Too long?' No, that sounds needy. "*A long time since we've seen one another and so would be great to catch up*". Perfect. Nothing insinuated other than two old friends finding out what each other has been up to. No hidden messages, no different tone could be attributed to it. Job done. Sign off, right, 'Chuck us an email...' No, too cavalier. "*Let me know a time and a place and I'll look forward to seeing you then*". That's the kiddy. 'From' she put

'Take care', maybe I should use that too? 'Laters?', 'Ta ta?', 'All the best?' OK. "*Take care, Nic xx*". Aaand send.

It had taken one hour, a couple of brews, a few Custard Creams and a number of Hobnobs but I felt so much better now that was out the way. The thought of sorting out this mess with Carly, totally relaxed me, things just hadn't been right since she left and we hadn't spoken. I had so much to tell her, so much stuff that besides Marcus, only she would understand. I used to think Carly and I would end up old spinsters, sitting out on a porch in some rocking chairs with loads of cats, talking about the good old days over a bottle of bourbon (oh yeah, because we'd suddenly become American and it was the deep South) but I was really glad she had Pete. Sometimes you just know when you see two people together that they were meant to be.

Ever since that night at Vom's, Carly and Pete had been inseparable. They moved in together the following summer into a cracking flat that saw some stonkingly good parties over the years and I'd spent many a night crashed out on their lounge rug, sofa, bathroom floor; I wasn't fussy. Those were the days that all of our crowd would practically fill Ruth's on Saturday and Sunday mornings. I wondered what Carly looked like now? Obviously three years is not enough to age someone beyond recognition but I wondered what her hair looked like, what her style was these days? Carly was a tomboy but she was naturally pretty, so could wear a plastic bag and *still* look good. Even though Luke and Pete were supposed to be friends, Luke was always still trying his luck (but then she *was* female and had a pulse) but she was never interested. Note to self; must get that remedy from her. I pathetically checked my phone again.

Best of Friends?

I felt unsettled. I suppose today *was* unusual; Marcus, Sadie and I normally headed to Ruth's in the morning and then lazed around all day. I didn't often have the place to myself, so I'd been looking forward to watching the DVD's of my choice and raiding the goody cupboard but the novelty soon wore off. Although I considered myself an independent woman, I *preferred* to be around others, feeding off their energy and laughing at their misfortunes... and I'm still single? Shocker. The Carly email jubilation had quickly passed, my amusement from watching funny videos Greg sent had rapidly dissipated and my Sunday movie enjoyment had soon declined. I had checked my phone a good ten times today out of sheer boredom and Luke had not called and Luke had not texted. He and I had been doing this dance for a lot of years and I'd never really expected him to call before, maybe it was because of everything he'd said last night, that I finally thought that there was something in it. Also being a consumer of the English language, I had taken Luke's note at its literal meaning, as in 'I'll *call* you' = I'll *phone* you, I'll communicate via the telephone and 'later' meaning that afternoon, that evening, the next day; silly me. Knowing Luke, 'later' probably meant when I'm sat in a nursing home with a blue rinse and tartan fanny blanket and he's just had his catheter changed.

It's taken a lot of years to figure this out; millions have said it before me and until now I've been loath to listen but I've discovered the basic problem between men and women is that we use completely different sections of the dictionary. I don't believe we speak *different* languages, far from it; just that in our vocabulary, there's obviously a pink corner and a blue corner and never the twain shall meet. You know, like a, "You don't go into my dance space and I don't go in to yours". (Sorry, Dirty Dancing was on the list of approved Sunday hangover films and I've just watched it). "Nobody puts Baby in the blue corner". Sorry...

Hayley Coulson

We're not *allowed* to stray into their territory, it's defended better than Thermopylae, which means that women often take the *other* road, the road of second guessing. Second guessing is mainly a female thing, as most men if they don't get something, sensibly walk away but women are always trying to work out the hidden meaning. They spend hours of their lives and far too much money on ice-cream, pouring over a simple sentence. A practice usually exacerbated by the fact that men think they're being kinder by being vague; they're not, they're just subjecting the opposite sex to hours of agony over what they *actually* intended. Oh, the drama. Wouldn't it just be more refreshing if we all just told the truth? OK, so it might sting a little initially, like ripping off a band aid but you would recover much quicker, if you weren't sitting there wondering what it all meant deep down. I hated deep thinking; I preferred to paddle in the shallow end.

However, upon reflection, if you take away all the uncertainty, what would us girls talk about? Also, I kinda like ice-cream and a damn good excuse to eat a pot full. I just really wish I knew where I stood right now. Luke had made me second guess and at this very moment; I hated him for it, as I checked my mobile again. I *really* needed to get a life.

The day slowly dragged and by the evening, I was well and truly bored. I had earlier been momentarily excited by the prospect of *not* having to sit through the Antiques Roadshow but as the time drew near, I found myself hovering over the remote, "Ooh, they're in Salisbury this week!" I decided the programme must be hexed with some magical hypnotic power because I found myself *so* ensconced in some old girls spoon collection that I hadn't noticed when day turned to night and so it was seriously creepy when I heard something at the door, looked up from the telly and realised I was sitting in the dark. I muted the TV and could only hear my own breathing until... there it was again! It really sounded like someone was trying to get into the house, so I picked up my mobile, looked around and grabbed the first thing I saw, it was a cushion. It took a moment for my eyes to adjust as I crept down the grey hallway, keeping my back to the wall as I edged towards the door. I had typed 999 on my phone and I was hovering over the call button. I could hear my heart beating in my chest, I thought it might break free of the ribcage when I saw a shadow outside of the glass on the door, I was about to hit call when the letterbox opened and I dropped the phone and raised the cushion up.

"What are you doing? You silly cow!" It was Marcus.

"Fucking hell, Marcus! You scared the life out of me!" I opened the door to let him in. "What are you doing sneaking about? I could've really hurt you, you know!" I was panting, like I was out of breath.

"I went out without my keys and the lights were off, I thought you were out". He looked at my cushion and then down to the phone on the floor. "What were you going to do? Challenge me to a pillow fight and then scare me away with your Magic Roundabout ringtone?"

I folded my arms and tutted a lot, just adding to Marcus' mirth. I verbally bashed him and then came out with some nonsense about how he could've broken my new phone but he just laughed his arse off. In between his bout of hysterics, he took my phone, kissed it and handed it back. "There, it's all better, now".

"I can't believe you're mocking me". I wiped the phone, to show my contempt but a smirk was breaking through.

He wiped the tears from his eyes. "Ahh mate, someone has to", as he made his way into living room.

I assumed a martial arts position, which was supposed to look like a tiger but I looked more like a badger. "So, you didn't feel the danger awaiting you on the other side of the door?"

Marcus chuckled at my attempts. "I laugh in the face of danger... then I wait till no-one's looking, cry and run like a little girl".

I was *really* glad he was home.

Chapter 16

It was Monday morning again. How? Why?! I always thought that Monday morning's were proof that there *was* a God and he didn't like me very much. We had our usual Monday morning catch up at work of what had gone down at the weekend. Tamsin thanked me over and over for the text about her mystery minger in Dribbler's, Sally told tales of a new club she'd tried out with some mates outside of town and Julie regaled us with stories of her sister's Hen Weekend up in Newcastle. God, I loved Hen Do's and I'd been on some crackers over the years, as I slowly watched people I knew taking the plunge but they were even better when it was your closest friends, which is why my two favourites were Emma's and Jenna's.

Emma had decided on the very reserved option of spa treatments at a fancy hotel for the weekend. She figured that if we were all in a swanky hotel, with mothers, cousins and aunts, no-one would make her wear the condom covered veil, the L-plates or carry around anything phallic shaped; but then of course if she wanted class, she *shouldn't* have invited Jenna.

Jenna brought a massive case with her and we all took the mick, thinking she had about thirty different outfits in there for just the two nights but no, Jenna's luggage turned out to be like a Gimp's treasure chest and contained every vulgar Hen Night cliché that physically existed. Carly and I stood in Jenna and Alice's room and looked through the stuff Jenna had with her.

Carly rummaged with amazement. "Jesus Jen, it's like a travelling whore house!"

I laughed and then pulled out a whip. "Hmm, mobile masochism". Carly, Alice and I were laughing in sheer disbelief. I lifted up some 'furry love cuffs' with the hotel pencil, like a forensic scientist at a crime scene who's not wearing their gloves. "Where'd you get stuff like this anyway?"

Alice had a vibrator in her hand and was looking at it with a stare of sheer terror as Jenna answered proudly, "Well, there's a few shops in town where you can pick up some bits and pieces and some of it is from my own *personal* collection".

In the background, I noticed Alice suddenly dropped the vibrator back in the case and was looking for somewhere to wipe her hands. I desperately tried not to laugh. Carly pulled out a crotchless thong and whispered to me, "Is *this* one of hers?" So I used my pencil to take it from Carly, just in case. "What's the point of this?"

Jenna was straight in there. "Well, it's for…"

I cut her off pretty quickly. "I know what it's *for*, luv. I'm just wondering what the point of wearing anything at all is? I mean, *look* at it?" I was holding it up with the pencil, for the girls to get a proper look.

Carly turned her head to the side and studied it. "Well, it could double as a cheese cutter?"

Alice was still vigorously rubbing her hands on her jeans. "Or dental floss?"

I winced and laughed at the same time. "Euuww, I'm not putting that near *my* mouth!"

Carly was cracking up as Jenna snatched the pants and put them back in her case. She wandered towards the loo and shouted from the bathroom, "I've got some chocolate willies in there as well!"

I raised my eyebrow and looked at Carly and Alice, then shouted back, "Well, it wouldn't be a party without a chocolate willy!" I shrugged, pulling a face and we all quietly giggled until Jenna came back out.

We met for dinner that night in the hotel restaurant, full of middle-aged moneyed women who rolled their eyes when we walked in. It was just as well we were seated separately at the back, as Jenna pulled out a small assortment of her party favours in front of Emma's prospective in-laws. Emma was horrified and none of us had the heart to tell her that was just a warm up.

The next day, we had the full works and got thoroughly pampered for the day, lazing around in our robes. Carly was reading the brochure as we lounged by the pool and said to me. "It says here you can have a Shiatsu".

"I think we'll all be having one, after those Mung Beans last night".

We all laughed without moving, not even turning our heads to look at her as she continued on, "It also says you'll come out looking like a new person".

I jumped in first. "Bagsy Angelina Jolie".

"Damn". Jenna sounded bitter. "I would have gone for her. Can't you be Reese Witherspoon, she's more your height".

I was frowning at the height jibe, while Alice cheerfully added, "Carly could be Maggie Gyllenhaal".

Carly smiled. "Thanks". Then tried to half sit up as she remembered, "Hang on, isn't she the S & M Secretary girl?"

Alice winced. "Errr... yeah, sorry".

Carly thumb gestured that perhaps that was more suited towards Jenna, who was lying with a towel over her head and we all silently chuckled.

Alice asked in a little voice. "What about me?"

I studied her for a second. "Well, I think you could be a Nicole Kidman".

"Really? You think I could look like a Nicole?"

"Sans the ginge, yeah, there's definite potential".

Emma threw a flip flop at me. "Oi!"

I diplomatically answered. "You're not a ginge darlin, you're a red-head, there's a big difference". Emma smiled, shook her head and lay back down.

Carly tactfully changed the subject back to Alice. "Definitely a Kidman and a Moulin Rouge Kidman at that... but without the singing... and the flying about..." there was a silence for a second before Carly added the most important, "And the slutty clothes".

I flopped back on to the lounger and giggled for a minute while Jenna, still with the towel on her head, re-joined the conversation. "She's too *quiet* for a Moulin Rouge, she's more of a Days of Thunder Kidman".

Alice's burlesque happiness was short-lived and she looked disappointed at her new bad-permed persona. I felt the need to defend Alice and end the madness. "I think the point is that it's *not* us and also, hello! No matter how much Shiatsu we have, after that steam room earlier and tonight's escape from Mung Bean Hotel, we're more likely to go home tomorrow looking like Keith Richards".

Alice looked at me like I'd just told her Santa wasn't real. "So you don't think I could look like Nicole?"

I frowned and thought about answering when Carly saved me by singing, making up her own words to Elvis' Heartbreak Hotel. "Well, since my burger left me, we found a new place to eat, it's over the hill and tastes of pig swill, its Mung Bean Hotel..." We all laughed until we were nearly thrown out.

Later that night, despite the joy at being able to eat burgers and drink beer, instead of tofu and aloe vera, we were yawning and falling asleep at the tables until Jenna came up with the bright idea of double vodka Redbull's all round... which is how we ended up with the anecdote of Emma's Aunt, a whip, three men and a small donkey. We left the hotel the next day feeling worse for wear and Emma felt cheated that her perfectly serene weekend had been defiled. Jenna congratulated herself on a job well done.

The following year at Jenna's own Hen Night however, was everything you expected it to be. There were drinks, there were men, there were drinks, there were more men, there were more drinks, there were strippers, there were a few more drinks, there was a nightclub, there were more men and I think… yes, a few more drinks. Jenna's Hen Night consisted of a hotel in London and a Party Bus that took us from pub, to pub, to pub, to club. Carly and I had psyched ourselves up for that night for a whole month. We'd been improving our drinking and practising our 'I've got a boyfriend' rejection lines (as I was seeing someone at the time as well). We'd also been working on our stamina, so we could last as long as the metabolic marvel that was Jenna.

Carly was my saviour that night, as I'd decided at the beginning of the evening that it would be a great idea to do a shot in every bar we went to, on top of our round of drinks. Carly, just shy of spraying on some Ralgex, handing me a Lucozade and rubbing my shoulders, reminded me that it was a marathon and not a sprint, so I abstained. Jenna however, did not. After seeing the results at our final venue, I was eternally grateful to Carly for the restraint. Jenna, drunk and disorderly, went round all her friends one by one asking them the same question and now it was my turn, as she slurred, "Can you believe I'm getting married?"

"Actually Jen, no". I was just being honest, I *couldn't* believe it.

"I know! Me and the old ball and strife, who'd 'ave thought it!" Carly went to correct her but then thought better of it; it wasn't wise to disagree with a drunken Jenna.

Jenna then asked Emma, who was clearly not impressed by Jenna's display which was made worse because she was soberly heavily pregnant at the time with her first child and she *really* didn't want to be there. We had practically forced her citing the 'Good Mate Codes of Practice'. "No, Jen. Especially as you just snogged that bloke, two bars back".

"What?!" Jenna looked insulted but promptly ruined it with, "Which one?" I looked over at Carly and laughed.

Jenna straightened her hair and smoothed down her dress and addressed her mini crowd of revellers. "It's my last night of freedom…"

Alice spoke up for the first time in about half an hour, reminding us she was still there. "But you're not getting married for another three weeks". We all gasped in unison.

Jenna was not amused. "It's my *last* night of freedom, out with my *girls*!" She was getting louder and we were getting more embarrassed.

Alice however, was on a roll. "You've got another Hen do next week that the mum's are coming to!" Carly hid her face in her hands, awaiting the onslaught. Good old Alice.

Jenna shouted, "It's my *last* night of freedom *without* the sodding parent police, *with* my girls, I can do whatever the hell I want to night out, *alright*?!" Jenna was swaying and daring Alice to reply but she quietly sipped her drink, looking slyly contented at her brief act of living dangerously. I wanted to pat her on the back and say, "That'll do pig, that'll do".

"I've made a few mistakes in my time, let me tell you". It was starting to sound like a Frank Sinatra song but we were soon reminded that this performance would carry none of the finesse of 'Old Blue Eyes'. She was holding up her finger and pointing it at us all but then she stumbled on her heels and the finger nearly went up Alice's nose. Carly helped her stand up straight again. "I've done some things that I'm not proud of…" She held up her hands and sullenly nodded, as if to correct the cries of 'never!' from the crowd but she was more likely to get a rousing chorus of 'no shit!' from us. "I'm not the beshhtest friend I can be". She lurched in my direction this time and put her arm around my shoulder. If I'd have done those shots, she would have taken me down with her, I was silently grateful to Carly again. I tried to move my head away, as my eyes nearly melted from the Sambuca fumes that emanated from Jenna but it felt like she was hanging on for dear life at that point, so I was stuck. "I could have seen the funnier side". She meant to pat me on my upper chest but instead she was patting my breast. My arms were full, holding her up, so all I could do was raise my eyebrow in protest and look down at her hand. Carly and Alice were laughing their asses off… but not for long. "I could have been more virginal". She was pointing at a *very* surprised Carly; it was my turn to laugh. Then she spun a bit too quickly on her heel towards Emma, luckily (or unluckily), I kept her up. "I could have been more in touch with my emotions". She nodded at Emma, "And I could have been more…" She held her hand up and put her finger to her lips and whispered, "Mousey like you". She was looking at Alice and none of us laughed. Alice responded with a glare. I didn't know she was capable of menacing looks, let alone have the courage to throw one at a drunken Jenna, so I steered Jenna away and *quick* before she noticed.

With Carly's help, I managed to sit Jenna down before she did herself and others with her finger pointing, an injury. Carly held on to the back of her dress like a dummy while Jenna continued with her oration. "I need to thank my mum, God rest her sole…"

(I should point out at this juncture to save confusion, that Jenna's mum wasn't dead but apparently her sole needed resting and we weren't going to argue). "She sat me down last week and told me the key to a good marriage". Carly and myself snuck a quick glance at one another, bit down on our bottom lips and grimaced in anticipation. "Sex, and lot's of it!" We weren't disappointed. Jenna cackled like a witch. "Can you Adam and Eve my mum telling *me* to have lots of sex?! That's like trying to teach Granny to suck balls!"

For a moment, Carly forgot herself. "Err, that's egg's there, Jen".

"What?" Jenna swung her head round so quick; I think we were all surprised it didn't fly off. Carly was berating herself and pretended she didn't say anything as Jenna continued her 'sermon on the couch'. "I've had my fair share of men... all shapes, sizes, colours and... sizes". Jenna wiggled her little finger, became fascinated by it and went into starey mode.

Carly thought she would seize the opportunity to change the subject and get us out of there. "OK! So who fancies a dance?"

However, Jenna wasn't finished. "Size is a funny thing. It's like one of those tom... tom... roller things at a fair, you stick your hand in but you never know what you'll get!" Jenna was laughing at her own joke and Carly and I used the excuse to openly laugh *at* her now, hiding the mirth was starting to hurt. Jenna went on, "And you know what they say, a little knob is a dangerous thing". Carly let go of Jenna's dress as she laughed and Jenna nearly fell off the couch.

Emma was horrified. "What? Who says that?"

I was wiping the tears and leant over and whispered in Emma's ear. "I think it's supposed to be knowledge". Emma looked strangely relieved and I suspected this spoke volumes about 'That' Justin.

Jenna was now moving in to Gwyneth Paltrow, Oscars speech, territory. "I *love* Dave, I really love him, he's the only one for me, now. He's..." Jenna stopped mid-sentence because she was distracted by a bloke at the bar. He was a Ten-to-Twoer if ever I saw one (you know, the unattractive member of the opposite sex, that you'd only ever consider talking to, right before the club shuts) but she didn't seem to care and we were given a lucky reprieve as Jenna sent us off to the dancefloor, while she approached her next victim.

Carly, Emma, Alice and I did as we were told and took Jenna's work friends with us, where Carly and I made the most of a bad club by ridiculously silly dancing to 'The Nolans'. We left Jenna to it, it was the only way really, once she'd decided on something, God help those that got in her way.

At work, Julie finished telling us about her Hen Weekend and fortunately for me, it was Julie and her hangover that had Amanda's attention today. Maybe this week wouldn't be so bad,

after all...

Chapter 17

I was wrong. Work had been insanely busy and Amanda was still gunning for me. I knew I was being monitored, so I forwarded all my non-work related emails to my home address. It didn't help that thanks to the upcoming party, I'd never received so many personal emails in my life. When I got home, I chucked on my trakkies, crashed out on the sofa, cranked up the laptop and started to go through my messages. There were loads of party emails from friends, more funnies from Greg, a chain mail 'if you don't send this on, you're dog will die' type from Emma and yet another panic message from Alice.

I hadn't seen Emma, Greg or Alice for ages and I missed going out in our crowd. Maybe I was unnecessarily worried about our party, maybe it would all go smoothly and now that we're older and wiser, we'd just relax and have fun, remembering why we were friends in the first place? Then again, we'd all kind of been thrown together at our tiny school in our tiny village; it was our parents that brought us together and parents have a lot to answer for. I mean, every child takes after their parents, right? 'The apple never falls far from the tree' (I'm sure Jenna would tell you that it was a banana and a hedge) but it was true though. I mean, knowing Alice and Greg's sad tales, their behaviour wasn't hard to figure out and perhaps it doesn't come as a shock that Sadie's lack of common sense, comes from her 'Darwin Award' dad who practically blew the roof off their house when he'd tried to weld a crack in the gas pipe... Jenna's mum had been known as the village bike, long before Jenna took on the mantle (or in this case, the saddle), so no real surprises there and Luke's parents were both fancy Doctor's who were *never* around... oh and both having affairs – hmm, there's got to be some Freudian crap relating to *that* one.

Me? Well, I guess it wasn't *too* hard to see where I came from either. Mum was the daughter of a Catholic Priest, brought up with *extremely* good morals and values and Dad was the son of a shipyard welder, brought up with a good sense of humour and the *extreme* capacity to drink. They were from opposite ends of the scale but they must have genuinely cared about one another because they made it work. My saintly grandfather passed away before I could meet him, which I think is just as well, he wasn't a fan of my dad's, so I can only imagine what he would have made of me. I probably would've been subjected to daily Hail Mary's and a good weekly scrub in a bath of holy water. My mum was still heavily involved in church activities and went regularly, no doubt to beg forgiveness for her family's indiscretions (and by family, I of course, mean me).

I wouldn't mind, but I wasn't *that* bad, I had good morals and good values, I just didn't always openly demonstrate my knowledge of them. I had proved time and time again that I *could* follow the rules but there was no denying a rebellious streak that would come out when I least expected it (and I do mean that

Best of Friends?

literally, after one Christmas party, when Jenna and I did a topless run down the High Street, Jeez that was cold, I nearly had an eye out). I constantly battled to suppress the renegade within and it wasn't easy, I can tell you. It starts with little things you know, like half inching a Woolworths pick-n-mix, then it moves on to the heavier stuff like not returning a film to the rental store and before you know it, you're in for a life of sex, drugs and debauchery. Well, I'm sure that's how my mum saw it anyway. I was never lacking in smarts, I've just always been a firm believer that life is to be experienced, which is why in my later years, I spent so much time at Ruth's recovering and why in my younger years, my mum spent so much time at my Head Teacher's office, trying to keep me in school.

If there was trouble, it generally found me like a homing pigeon and as much as my mother's religious background probably convinced the Principal that I wasn't *wholly* evil, it was Carly's good grades and her honest face that managed to talk me *out* of mischief and countless detentions. Carly was definitely the angel on one shoulder and there were no prizes for guessing who was the devil on the other. Jenna was always the ringleader but for some reason, constantly got away with murder; it was like a protective aura that was impenetrable. She'd stolen exam papers, left friends in a puff of smoke as she ran from countless attempts to catch her with a ciggy, stole money from the village hall fund, trashed a cheating ex-boyfriend's car and it was Jenna that caused a really nasty incident involving Simon and his testicles, when we were just 10 years old…

I should explain. In the year that we all had a crush on Marti Pellow and all the girls were Wet, Wet, Wet – Simon's only interest was fiddle, fiddle, fiddle. He had a penchant for the old pocket billiards and thought no-one noticed the juggling through holes in his trouser pockets. One lunchtime, Jenna ran over in the middle of a quick game of footy, kissed him and promptly ran away. He just stood there in shock, while all the other kids made "Ooooh" sounds in unison. We had no idea what she'd done until she ran back giggling to tell us. It was after the bell rang and we all walked back to class that we noticed Jenna's evil plan had began to work as Simon started to gurn and couldn't sit down properly in his chair. His head was twitching and he put his hand up, asking to be excused from class. Our teacher, ironically called Mr Cox, wouldn't let him leave, saying that he should have gone to the toilet in his lunch break and it was a good ten minutes before Mr Cox noticed Simon had gone bright red, with veins popping and tears streaming down his face and *finally* took him outside. When Jenna had kissed Simon, she'd held his hands, transferring the itching powder she'd mercilessly applied to her gloves, so that the next time that Simon, ahem, took matters into his own hands... well, I don't need to tell you the rest. Jenna totally got away with it of course but I think Simon was emotionally scarred for life.

Now see, if I'd done anything like that, I probably would have forgotten I had the powder on my hands and rubbed my eyes or chewed the glove, either way, I'd have injured myself more than my victim. Any pre-determined act from me was likely to end up in tears. Like the time, I wrote something derogatory about a teacher on a school toilet door but the red pen leaked all over me and I was *literally* caught red-handed and not forgetting the time I was looking after one of the school pets in the summer holidays and accidentally flattened the guinea pig in a freak, back garden bowling incident – *that* wasn't pre-determined but it's when I got caught trying to blow him back up with a bicycle pump...

Emma wasn't always so sensible either; she had proved her entertainment value with the incident at London Zoo. It involved a school trip, a pencil eraser, a monkey, Luke and a chocolate ice-cream. Luke had been picking on her, so she used the rubber to get the monkey's attention, the ice-cream was wiped on Luke and the monkey loved the ice-cream. I wish we'd had digital cameras back then, to really capture the moment.

Alice had also had her fair share of rascality. Up until the loss of her dad and her subsequent Marcel Marceau impressions, Alice could be *really* naughty when she wanted to. It was Alice who let down the tyres on Mrs Denby's new car, it was Alice that repeatedly spitballed Mrs Denby during our maths lesson and it was Alice who put a spider in the arachnophobic Mrs Denby's draw. Come to think of it, Alice really didn't like Mrs Denby.

Marcus was the quiet one. He was never a ringleader or really a willing follower but he *was* a martyr to the cause and constantly put the group's needs above his own and you can't fault that kind of dedication. I really don't think he wanted to join in when we played Knock Down Ginger in the pensioners quarter of the village (for those unfamiliar with the game, don't worry, it's not a sick car prank with the auburn tinted, it was a simple game of knocking on doors and running off). I'm pretty sure he didn't want to be involved in our camping weekend at Glastonbury festival either, when we all got trolleyed and coated in mud *and* I really don't believe he was up for the Ultimate Pub Crawl Challenge that we'd set up one Bank Holiday weekend, where we intended to go to every single pub on the High Street; all twelve. Needless to say, after getting carried away in the first one, we only actually managed a total of seven but Marcus came, Marcus drank and Marcus fell down with the rest of us.

Despite our differences, I guess you could say we all fitted together like a jigsaw puzzle, even if the picture on the front was a little disturbing. However, over the years, the dynamic of the group shifted so much, especially between us girls as we approached our mid 20's. Emma broke away from the group because we were obviously stifling her chances of finding Mr Right and began her steep decline into tedium. Alice was so content in her 'blind eye' relationship with Greg that Emma's 'less-drama-on-a-night-out', version of life seemed more appealing and I started exercising more control over my *own* behaviour in an attempt at a trouble-free existence, which left Jenna to take on my share. Jenna's drinking had reached Winehouse levels, she'd go drinking until the cows came home (and if she could have found a club that would *take* cows...) and to top it off, she'd taken to joining Luke in a regular game of 'Whose Line is it Anyway?' with the nose candy. Her antics had diminished in their ability to be funny anymore and we seemed to spend most of our time talking about or cleaning up after Jenna and as a result, Carly and Jenna really began to fall out. That's why we were glad when Jenna met David, although he was about as much fun as a smear test, we were thankful that she seemed to be curbing her impulses and was on her way back to the straight and narrow (well, maybe a little wavy and wider than most but it was a good attempt). As for Luke, whenever Jenna got around *him* she briefly reverted back, like at Carly and Pete's leaving do. *Nothing* was the same after that night, Carly and I, Jenna and Carly, Pete and Luke and Luke and I, it was a mess. Luke changed after the 'big fight', I don't know if he blamed *me* for what happened, I had no idea but he definitely he treated me differently after that. It had obviously affected his ability to use a telephone because he still hadn't called.

"Dinner's ready!" Sadie was making dinner tonight, which was always pretty scary, I wasn't good at the culinary but Sadie burned soup. I suspected we might be in line for Ravioli on toast or something equally as glamorous. Sadie came bounding in with three bowls of macaroni and cheese and plate full of slices. Pasta with bread; sometimes I hated being so right. "Have you two sorted out your holiday yet?" It was the contentious question of the week.

Marcus answered first because I had a giant mouthful of food. "No, apparently the only place to go in the world is Magalluf".

Sadie was dunking her bread. "Shagalluf? I couldn't agree more!"

I did a thumbs up in Sadie's direction; I still couldn't talk. I really did need to cut down on my volume-to-fork ratio; Marcus was getting *far* too much air time. "We missed the perfect deal that Nicky found us last week, so now she's looking for more deals in... yes, you've guessed it, Magalluf!"

I gestured but I still had my slice in my hand. Marcus raised his brow. "Are you trying to frighten me, waving your bread around?"

I finally swallowed the last piece. "Well, it's downright terrifying to a Celiac". I put my bread down and turned to Sadie. "*Actually* Sade, we missed the deal because Mrs Fussy Pants over here couldn't make up his mind".

"That's *Ms* Fussy Pants to you and I *made* up my mind! I was perfectly happy to go with that one you brought all the stuff home for".

"But if we *see* a deal, we have to jump on it, we took too much time and missed the boat, we need..."

We were on our usual roll and it would no doubt go on, and on, and on. Sadie was used to us now, so just gave up listening and turned up the telly.

Chapter 18

I felt like a child who crossed off days on a calendar with a big red X, as I slowly counted down to our party. It was Thursday and I was glad we'd broken the back of the week, Wednesday was touch and go for a while but we'd come through the other side and now Friday was within our grasp. All I could do was thank God, as it was turning out to be a really crappy week, with a little bit of shitty thrown in for good measure.

Respect seemed to be the theme of the week and it ain't been pretty. First up, Luke hasn't rung. I've regularly checked my phone and even got Sadie to text me, to see if my mobile was working. Where is my *self*-respect you ask? Good question! I've started to really dislike myself for being such a feckless gullible idiot and I'm really starting to dislike *him* for being such a smarmy, self-centred... Ahh, see this is my curse, this is where I start to feel bad, I'll call him all the arseholes under the sun and then suddenly panic that the reason he hasn't called is because he's been trapped down a mine or a well. I've actually taken to following barking dogs, just in case they 'Lassie' me to his location. The word pathetic doesn't even *begin* to cover it and I'm *still* single? I know, it's a shocker!

I was also punishing myself, for my lack of respect for my friends. Marcus had previously commented that I changed when with said well-dweller and now that I was beginning to cotton on, I couldn't deny his astute assessment. I was never *quite* myself in front of Luke, always striving to be what *he* wanted because I was not convinced that the real me was good enough and as a consequence, I had been convinced to run out on my best friend's birthday drinks; what kind of a 'friend' did that make me? I had desperately tried to make it up to Marcus. Making dinner twice, sitting through a whole night of Bruce Lee films, taking him for lunch, making a thousand cups of tea and did I *mention* the Kung Fu movies?! Plus, I'd also done all the house chores but it wasn't *nearly* enough. He *said* he was OK but I knew he wasn't.

By Wednesday things went from bad to worse, when Amanda announced she was conducting our mid-year reviews. Not a great week for an appraisal, especially considering the fact that lately, Amanda was not my biggest fan. As well as the late mornings, this month had seen an increased number of hangovers from hell.

She was loving the superiority. "Sit down Nicola". Nicola? Now I really *was* in trouble. "Of all the mid-year reviews, I've found yours the hardest to do. I find you an enigma. When you get your head down, you can be incredibly hard working and there's no one better at really *selling* than you". Then came the low blow. "I see *myself* in you". Oh Lord, kill me now. "But your attitude at times can only be described as disrespectful. Your open display of disinterest on occasion is not only disrespecting the business but disrespecting me".

I was given a moment's reprieve as there was a knock at the door, it was Julie. "Hi Amanda, sorry to disturb you but I've got Father Bolton on the line for you. It's about their annual trip to Rome, he says it's urgent".

Amanda huffed and puffed. "It's always urgent with that man; tell him I'll call him back in about half an hour". Julie quickly left the room and shut the door, while Amanda shook her head and made a note to call him. "You're a Catholic aren't you? I don't know *how* you put up with all their nonsense. So anyway, where *was* I?" "I believe you were discussing my lack of *respect* for you".

"Oh yes". She continued, unaware of the irony. "It would appear your *only* consistency is your ability to show up late". Amanda was in her element and full of her own self importance, proceeding with her nose so far in the air it was grazing the artex on the ceiling. "So, I've been going through this mid-year review and I want to read you something and I want you to tell me if it's fair". Good job I didn't have any rope at the time, otherwise I'd have secretly fashioned a noose under the table. Question was, would I have made one for me or for her? "Nicola is a bright young woman with tremendous communication skills. She is intelligent and lively and has the capacity to go far within the company. However..." Here we go. "She often lacks drive and with her constant tardiness, shows a lack of ambition that I find displeasing". I was biting down on my tongue so hard that I thought I might chew the end off. "*So*, what do you think of that?"

Let's see. I suppose 'shove it up your arse' is out of the question? I smiled sweetly and answered, "I think that you've captured the communication aspect to my job well".

She narrowed her eyes and then scribbled something down. "And how do you feel about my *other* comments?"

Errr... 'You *so* need to get laid?' I decided to be more tactful. "I think that pertaining to recent weeks; your comments on my tardiness are sadly just. I'm afraid I've had some trouble at home the last month but I hope to get things sorted very soon. I can assure you that it won't be an issue in the future". I had no idea where it came from but it was good, damn good; total bullshit of course but what the heck, I'd already bought my house in hell, now I was just picking out the furnishings.

Amanda shifted uncomfortably. "Oh God, I'm sorry Nicky, I didn't know. What kind of troubles?"

Oh shit. Ermm... "I'd rather not say, if you don't mind? It's very personal". I sullenly nodded, took a deep breath and woefully looked up to the ceiling; it was a Golden Globe performance. "I'm sorry I brought my personal issues to work, Amanda. It won't happen again".

With that, Amanda reached across the desk and held my hand. "I'm *so* sorry; I wish you'd told me. I haven't sent this to Head Office yet, I'll see if I can re-word it and we can work *together* towards a better future".

I tried to get out as soon as possible before I a) vomited from all her saccharin bollocks and b) laughed my arse off. "Thank you, that errm... means a lot".

I was utterly amazed, it was the first time I'd managed to talk myself *out* of trouble as opposed to *in* it. Marcus would be so proud. Although I knew that with *my* track record, my Karma was going to make me pay for this in some shape or form, I enjoyed the euphoria of success while it lasted.

Life had taught me some important lessons this week and although I'd paid attention, it was soon apparent that 'respect' wasn't done with me, as the latest example was delivered, quite literally, this evening by Emma. 'That' Justin had to work late, her parents were out of town and Alice wasn't answering the phone, so Emma turned up on our doorstep with her delightful children asking us to look after them for an hour, while she went to Pilates. Yes, she really *was* trying to dump her kids on us so she could go stretch and fart in a room full of hormonal women. She was clearly hoping Marcus would do it, as Sadie was out and it was blatantly obvious to anyone who'd met me, that I didn't have a maternal bone in my body. Emma was gone before I could say 'not on your Nellie' and as soon as the door shut, Marcus magically pulled an excuse out of the air and cunningly palmed the kids off on me; claiming a prior engagement, he *knew* I was too busy kissing his arse this week to say no.

Time passed in silence, as the kids stood in the hallway with their coats on, holding matching dolls, wearing matching clothes and just staring at me. I was the adult, I *needed* to claim my ground. I swallowed and steadied myself, bravely bent forward and held out my arms, cheerfully asking, "Hey! How you doing?" Nothing. I injected a bit more pep into my next question and slapped my hands on the front of my thighs. "You wanna watch a DVD?" Nada. I was swinging my arms and clapping my hands now. "You must be hungry, *right?*" Zilch. My smile had distorted as I was dying a death, this was a tough crowd and if I threw in any more arm moves, I'd look like a cheerleader. "Errr, why don't you both take your coats off? Here, let me help you". They both took one step back. Abigail eyed me suspiciously for a moment and I thought I could feel her eyes burning into my head. I put my hand up and checked my skin was still intact. We all just stood there in silence, listening to the clock resonate through the hall, until *eventually* Abigail let me take her coat and once she gave in, Jessica followed. I hung up the jackets and walked towards the lounge, I turned to beckon them in and... Christ! They were right behind me, I could almost hear the music from the Omen as I tried to regain my composure; kids were like dogs, they could *smell* fear. "Why don't you two hop on to the couch there and I'll put a film on".

Nearly an hour passed before Marcus returned. "Hey, I thought I'd come back and see how you ..." Marcus stopped in his tracks as he came in to the lounge and saw me on all fours, pretending to be a 'horsey', while Abigail sat on my back pulling my hair as the reins and Jessica stood there, repeatedly hitting me round the head with her doll. Trust me, this was preferable to when the funny film was on and I turned round to see why the kids weren't laughing and they weren't looking at the TV, just staring at me. I felt a shiver go down my spine. I thought they'd remembered the Christening and wanted to finish me off this time, so when Abigail suddenly jumped on me, I thought an apocalypse was imminent. However, when she followed it moments later with an Arm Wringer, a Backbreaker and a Full Nelson Slam, I realised that perhaps 'That' Justin had allowed them to watch *way* too much Professional Wrestling. So, I gave up and joined in, it *did* look like fun.

"I'll just go and put the dinner on then". Marcus was backing out of the room, looking frightened and he was right to, I was thinking of practising a Mountain Bomb on him.

Another forty minutes later, Emma *still* hadn't returned and Marcus started to fret. He said something inaudible as I was lying on the floor holding off Jessica who was trying to asphyxiate me with the cushion. He then put on the most absurd voice, like he had no nose, so the kids wouldn't understand. "Do you think that… you know, s*he* is coming back?"

I put on the same silly voice, in the hope he'd realise how ridiculous it sounded. "Of course *she* is". From the look on his face, it worked. I was now holding my knees up and hiding behind them, trying to protect my face from the oranges being pelted at me.

Marcus tried to keep his distance whilst picking up the fruit and returning them to the bowl. He thankfully went back to normal speech but whispered, "She said she'd be an hour, it's nearly two". He walked back out to the kitchen but then came back in almost immediately. "She didn't look a little *strange* to you when she turned up?" He was holding some celery.

"Errr, put it away hon, you're scaring the kids". I was trying to get the little people off me, so I could sit up.

He comically hid the celery behind his back. "She's *never* done this before; I just think it's weird".

I was back to my orange defence, Marcus had just re-armed them. "She's been a bit weird for years, mate. Ouch!" I'd taken a direct hit to the ear.

Marcus was collecting oranges again but this time kept hold of the bowl. "I think something's going on Nic, I'm worried about her".

I was sat on the floor rubbing my ear, which I suspected now looked like a rugby players. "I think you're jumping to conclusions there, hon"

"No jumping, not even a hop, it was more like I was tip-toeing and the conclusions were right there".

I was sat with my back to the couch, my legs ajar, absolutely exhausted. I turned my head to face Marcus and smiled. "OK, I hear ya but I think it's a little too *early* to send out a search party, dude". I'd foolishly let my guard down and didn't notice until it was too late; a charging Abigail flew into my groin area with an extended knee, catching me square on the pelvic bone. I managed to let out a high pitched squeal before toppling over, which seemed to amuse the kids no end and I could see Marcus grimacing as he crept back into the kitchen.

After the pelvic injury, I also retreated to the kitchen, leaving them to bash ten bells out of each other with the cushions and fighting the temptation to fill them with bricks. Marcus laughably wanted to cook extra of *our* food to give them, so I took over and made them toasties and we all sat down together to eat. It felt weird; like Mama and Papa Bear but with psychopathic cubs.

Three hours after she dropped them off, Emma *finally* returned to pick up her children. I wanted to shout "Adrian!" when she walked through the door, as I suspected I looked like Rocky but I knew she wouldn't get it. Seeing her was a whole mix of emotions; I was relieved, I was curious *and* I wanted to kill her, slowly and painfully. She looked *really* sheepish and avoided any eye contact as she put on their coats. "I can't thank you enough. One chore turned into another and the time just ran away from me".

Marcus smiled at her. "It's not a problem; they were no trouble at all". I looked over at him open-mouthed, wincing as I shifted on to my other leg because my groin injury was still smarting (and it's not the sort of thing you can rub better in public). Marcus added,

"You may want to ring your mum and Alice and let them know you're OK. I made a few calls".

Emma took a deep breath, looked at us both with sheer gratitude and said some very heartfelt thank you's. Wherever she'd been or whatever she'd done, she obviously *really* needed it. Marcus and I just smiled back; she took the kids' hands, turned and left. They were gone.

Marcus walked back in the lounge with the thousand yard stare. "I feel so… violated"

"I don't remember you being wrestled or tangoed?!" He pulled a mock grimace again and very briefly threw a questioning glance towards my nether regions. I shook my head and held up my hand. "Don't even *go* there. I feel the need to get drunk and totally trash the place".

Marcus looked around the room. "The kids have already trashed it".

I held my hands over my ears, begging him not to mention the 'K' word again and he more helpfully suggested we go and drink enough so that we'll never remember the night again. I happily agreed.

Chapter 19

Saturday. If ever there were a cause to celebrate; it's that one, beautiful word. We'd made it to the weekend and tonight we're off out clubbing and tonight I had a plan. It wasn't a complicated plan, it was poetically simple really, I planned to end up inordinately inebriated (two words I suspected I wouldn't be able to say later). Now normally I wouldn't have been so brazen with my planning, as everyone *knows* it's a mind over matter thing. If you *plan* to stay up until the wee hours, you end up knackered by 10:00pm and forcing your drinks down, which is why I saluted the 'I'm just having a quiet one' nights. The night's where you end up very merry, very happy, dancing like your gangster rapping and singing songs at the top of your lungs that during the cold, harsh, light of day, you would pretend you'd never heard of. However, a plan was needed as up until Thursday night, it had been a weekus horribilis and I needed to *seriously* de-stress.

I say up until Thursday, because after our close encounter of the kid kind, Marcus and I did something very out of the ordinary and broke one of our *own* rules and walked to a village pub. This was normally a *big* no, no because local pubs are likely to be frequented by... well, local people (namely, your parents or their friends). We chanced the pub nearest to us and were pleasantly surprised, not only did we *not* find a legal guardian in sight but it was traditional, oldy worldy and my personal favourite, cheap. We sat up at the bar, had a few beers, chatted to the landlord and giggled until closing time. We walked home vowing to go back to "Smokey Joe's" (so nick-named for its log burning fire) for a Sunday roast. Maybe it was the night air on the walk home or the buzz of laughing so much but the next day, nothing could faze me and the day passed without incident.

I was late meeting Sadie's girls in town, as I gave Marcus a lift to Mitchell and Daniel's. I was gutted he couldn't make tonight but he'd promised to sample Mitchell's newly acquired cooking skills at their swanky dinner party. Mitchell had also invited his new single friend he'd met at cooking camp, so Marcus was also being set up on a blind date. This wasn't the first time Mitchell had played Cilla, so Marcus knew what to expect and as much as he loved Mitchell and Daniel, he really wasn't looking forward to tonight and knew alcohol was the only option.

The girls were already at their second venue and going for it big time, by the time I arrived. It was obvious I had a *lot* of catching up to do but I was parking my drinks. The mind over matter kicked in early and I was *desperately* trying to shake it off. Thankfully, I was kept amused by their antics and their one-legged walks as we headed on to the next venue but it was an absolute joy and relief to get a really sweet text from Marcus wishing me a top night but underneath it said 'GOJF!!' Now the 'Get Out of Jail Free' text was a time honoured tradition between good friends, that if one of us was on a bad date or stuck somewhere we didn't want to be, we'd just text 'GOJF' to the other. The 'GOJF' was usually followed by a number exclamation marks that correlated to the *severity* of the situation, for example; [!] = bored, [!!] = ugly, [!!!] = scary. The receiver of said text would then ring with an emergency; ie. the dogs sick [!], the car or house has been broken in to [!!] or [!!!] respectively, and in extreme cases [!!!!], you could always rustle up a dead grandmother (but this was reserved for horror movie status only). Marcus had sent a two [!!], so I needed to phone with a car vandal/accident story.

I went outside, away from the noise in Crusty's and dialled his number, Marcus answered immediately, he must have been clutching his phone and was talking extra loud, so everyone at the dinner party could hear him. "Nicky! Hi. How are you? The car's been what?"

I was on the other end laughing. "You are such a big fibber. I take it he's a bit of a troll?"

"Looks like it's been hit by the back end of a bus, eh?" Marcus played this double-entendre game so well.

I needed to keep talking on the other end of the phone to give Marcus a suitable, realistic conversational gap, so I wittered on for a second about my sobriety and then got distracted by the music in Marcus' background. "Christ, is that the 'Mama Mia' soundtrack?" I was embarrassed that I even recognised it but poor Marcus was the one that had to sit through it.

He was still keeping up the pretence that I was giving him a car diagnosis, so I just received a very strained, "Ya ha", in answer to my question.

"So is the whole evening a total bust?"

Marcus went for the knock-out. "Hmm, a *complete* write-off?"

I could hear Mitchell closing in. "The car's a write-off? Let me talk to her". Shit.

Marcus must have covered the phone's speaker, as there was some inaudible mumbling and then Mitchell was on the line. "Nicky, what's this about Marcus' car?"

My partner was in trouble and I'd been tag-teamed. These are the moment's friends train for. "Hi Mitchell. I hope you're having a lovely party and I'm sorry to disturb you but apparently someone's hit Marcus' car whilst drunk driving and the Police need Marcus to come back and decide if he wants to press charges". I had no idea if that was factually correct, it didn't *have* to be, as long as I was convincing in my delivery.

Mitchell hit me with a left, right, left combination. "You haven't seen the car? You weren't there? Why did the Police phone *you*?" God, he was good.

I was a little winded but managed to get myself off the ropes. "No I wasn't there and haven't seen it, I'm listed as the second driver on the vehicle, they contacted me when they couldn't reach Marcus, he must have missed their call during dinner". Mitchell asked Marcus if he'd missed a call and he replied that he'd switched his phone off whilst eating, as it would have been rude. An impressive uppercut.

Mitchell was back on to me. "Can't *you* go and sort it out? We haven't had the cheese and biscuits yet".

He'd taken a beating but just *wouldn't* stay down and as 'Take a Chance on Me' rang out in the background, I realised I needed

Best of Friends?

to land the killer punch. "I can't Mitchell, the car's registered in Marcus' name, only *he* can press charges". Ding, ding, end of the round. There was silence at the other end (well, apart from the fact that 'Waterloo' had just started up) and I was already jumping up and down, holding up the belt and celebrating my victory with an imaginary Rocky theme in my head.

Marcus came back on the phone. "Thank you for letting me know, Nic. I'm most exceedingly obliged". I could practically *feel* him smiling down the phone. We would have to hide the car for a few days; while it was being 'fixed' but we had won this bout.

I headed back inside and the girls were on the shots again; I abstained, my good deed had given me a *natural* high. It was rapidly approaching Vom's o'clock and although I'd never been there sober before, I was *actually* looking forward to appreciating the moment. After all, you can't beat the experience of a nightclub; as you wait your turn in the queue, subtly sizing up the other revellers, you can hear the music seeping out the door and the anticipation tingles as you just can't *wait* to get inside. The gauntlet has been laid, you've still gotta get through the queue, pay the woman, smile at the doorman, queue again to drop off your coat, queue once more to get a drink before you can even attempt a go at the dancefloor but you're overwhelmed as the bass hits you, the second you walk through the door. You can feel it vibrate through your head, swiftly moving to your shoulders as they start to feel the flow and your blood now pumps in unison with the heavy bass. Your arms begin to loosen and the beat is now in your chest, feeling like it's gonna break through your ribcage as the sound envelopes you. You feel the melody around your waist like a strong pair of arms and as its hands move to your hips and the rhythm pulsates down your legs and in to your feet, you find that you *can't* stop moving...

Except, that's not what happened tonight. Despite the fact that Vom's is the cheesiest club known to man and wouldn't know a decent tune if it slapped it round the face with a large trout; a fight kicked off in the queue and one of Sadie's friend's lost her wallet, the doormen were grumpy after the fight and asked her for ID, knowing she couldn't produce it; game over. Well, for *her* anyway, her mates gave her money for a cab home and ran in to the club, leaving her standing outside. I guess I was appreciating *my* friend's right about now; we would never leave the field of battle if we were a man down. When I walked inside, I *was* overwhelmed but not by the bass... by the smell. Christ, was it always like this? I guess this was the drawback to the anti-smoking laws in public places now. I was a reformed smoker and hated the smell but even *I* thought a nice pack of Marlboro Lights would have covered up this foul stench of bad feet, a treat. As I tried to shield my ears from the crackly speakers, I realised my usual pre-Vom's diet of copious amounts of Vodka, must normally numb all my senses. I tried desperately to soak in the ambience but there wasn't any, just some cheap coloured lighting, crap smoke effects and really nasty carpets.

The girls were surrounded in seconds as they took to the dancefloor and I was trying to fend off a plastered, shouty bloke that kept spitting. I only managed to understand about three words; drink, dance and booze (or thinking about it, where he was staring, the last one could have been something else). Without my trusty vodka, I was unable to translate but suspected, I normally would have understood every word; one could only hope I wouldn't have encouraged any *further* interaction. Sadie seemed to be chatting to a nice bloke but I couldn't help but notice he had exceedingly long arms. I was *all* too aware of my environment and my sudden snobbery was no doubt a contributory factor but it wasn't the only thing impeding my ability to get my groove on, I was seriously lacking rhythm tonight, I looked like a frog in a blender and I think it was because... yes, I was still *sober*. It was a sad realisation at my age, that I couldn't actually dance unaided by alcohol. It was my own fault, I had put the mockers on it, I had purposely set out to party and now my mind over matter theory was in full swing. I excused myself from the group and found the bar on the other side of the dancefloor which was always a lot quieter. Miraculously, there were a few stools free, so I plonked myself down and ordered a drink.

I was sat on my own at the bar for about ten minutes, turning round every now and again to laugh at Sadie and friends on the dancefloor. I was contemplating my next move. I couldn't leave just yet; if I could *just* last half an hour, *that* was acceptable. I was miles away in my own little world, wondering if Marcus was still up and so didn't notice the tall girl standing next to me. "I do that when I'm bored". I looked up and realised she was talking to me. "The glass swirling and straw stirring, it's a *dead* giveaway". She was smiling.

"Oh, yeah, sorry". I laughed and embarrassed, promptly put down my glass. I did what I always do now and glanced briefly to see she had a band on her wedding finger, so I was a little relieved to find this wasn't one of those moments, like our Amsterdam trip seven years ago, when I was innocently chatting away to a local at the bar, unaware that her shoes aired on the side of comfy and it wasn't until an awkward moment later in the ladies loos, that I never *ever* want to talk about again, that I realised she was being more than friendly.

The tall girl ordered her drink; you couldn't help but notice she was very pretty and had one of those familiar faces. I felt the need to explain my solo act at the bar and gestured towards Sadie.

"My mate's indisposed with a new 'friend' and I'm hiding from that pissed bloke over there".

She took in the scene and nodded her acceptance, then looked pensive as she watched Sadie and her new acquaintance dancing together. "Wow! He's got *really* long arms".

She was *totally* on my wavelength and I perked up as she shared *her* story. "I got talked into coming out at the last minute by my mate. She's over there, with the guy with the really large ears". She was pointing towards more gyrating revellers. I pulled a faux-grimace and she nodded. "His twat of a mate kept trying to hit on me. I was thinking about leaving but we've not long got here, you've got to give it at *least* thirty minutes haven't you? Do you mind if I hide out here, while I finish my drink?" She pointed at the empty stool next to me.

I let out a little chuckle. "No, not at all". I held out my hand. "I'm Nicky".

She shook it. "Lyndsey. Nice to meet you".

We turned our stools to face the dancefloor and watch our friends and their chosen partners for the evening and Lyndsey laughed as her friend tried to dance to 'Girls Aloud' and nearly fell over. "So Long Arms doesn't have a friend with scarily Long Legs that you fancied then?"

I chuckled. "Unfortunately not, although I did spot a guy with freakishly large hands that I thought had potential".

She was laughing and trying to swallow her drink. "I think I'll have one more drink and then leave her to it".

"I hear you. I was thinking the same thing myself". I decided to confess my evening woe. "I was *really* up for a big night out but then it just wasn't happening".

"Always the way when you plan it. Although saying that, mine was all a bit last minute and I'm *still* not up for it. My boyfriend, sorry, my *fiancé* had to work late, so my mate made me come out and celebrate". Lyndsey explained. "I got engaged last night. It was *totally* unexpected; my boyfriend hasn't even got the ring yet! So he gave me his pinky ring until he buys a proper one". She was shaking her head when she showed me the plain silver band on her left hand.

"Wow, congratulations though, that's great". I couldn't help but feel a twinge of jealously. This girl was really like me, she thought the same and even looked a little similar, she was obviously *way* prettier than me but her sense of humour, everything... she could *be* me and for the briefest of moments, I wanted what she had and wondered, why *isn't* it me? "At least this way you get a say about what the ring looks like, right?"

Lyndsey raised her hands partially in the air in a 'Eureka' moment, I was obviously the first person she'd told who'd gotten it. "Exactly! That's *just* what I thought. *So* many blokes get it wrong".

We sat chatting and laughing for ages until Lyndsey looked at her watch. "Well, I guess it's OK to go now. It looks like *she's* having fun", gesturing back towards her drunken pal kissing Noddy's best mate. "And so does *your* friend", pointing towards Sadie and Long Arms getting *very* up close and personal.

I shook my head in disbelief. "Christ, it's like a school disco!"

She laughed out loud. "Thanks for letting me hide out here and thanks for the laugh, I *needed* that".

I was smiling back. "Pleasure. I wish you well for your engagement. I hope you get the ring you want".

"Me too! Thanks again, and take care". She looked genuinely sincere in her well wishing, so I returned the compliment. I think I've made a new friend.

Chapter 20

Now if only I'd left right then and there. When Lyndsey left, I checked my watch; I'd made it! It was perfectly respectable to go then but I didn't, I decided to finish my drink. I could have left it, I didn't want it anyway and I could have gone home with warm, fluffy and happy feelings but no. Instead, that extra five minutes set a course in motion that changed everything. As I took the final sip and got up to leave, I realised there was someone standing behind me. "You look good". I froze, I knew that voice anywhere... it was Luke.

He moved beside me and I anxiously tried to hide my face, desperately wanting to play it cool. "Thanks". I briefly glanced at him and threw in a nonchalant. "So do you".

Luke smiled and nodded as if to acknowledge my perceptiveness; arrogant arse. "*So*, you here on your own?"

I didn't want to look at him. "No, I'm with friends". Luke looked around us, his face questioning their existence, so I pointed to

Sadie and Long Arms, who were now engaged in what looked like a cannibalistic ritual. Embarrassed, I *quickly* turned back round.

"Can I buy you a drink?" He was leering again and leaning *far* too close to me at the bar but he was off his game, obviously feeling the chill of my cold shoulder, he was using all his usual tricks but there was no *way* I falling for them this time.

"Sure, knock yourself out". I had no intention of drinking it; I would leave it on the side untouched, it would make a nice statement. I felt proud of myself, I was doing well and I was oozing calm. Well, OK, maybe not oozing, more like dribbling it but *I* was in control.

Luke knew he was in Arctic territory and was likely to get frost bite, if he didn't think of something quickly. "I got some pretty good commission today". I was still facing the bar; it was easier to be mean this way. He carried on with his best smiles, "So, you know, I'm spreading the wealth with my favourite people".

"I didn't think there was any money to be made in the housing market at the moment?" I sighed, feigning boredom and trying to show disinterest but I should have just kept quiet as he ignored my tone and saw my response as an invitation to sit himself down.

"Oh no, there isn't, I'm not working there anymore; I've got a *new* job".

"Really? Shocker". I injected as much sarcasm as I could muster. I needed *him* to leave as my legs were shaking and I couldn't physically move.

"I wanted to call; I've been a bit busy this week, what with the new job".

I looked at him unimpressed. I didn't need to say anything, which was just as well, as I may have maintained calm on the outside but my stomach was doing a merry little dance.

"Don't be like that, babe. You and me, we're... connected, you know. There'll always be something special between us". Arrghh, no way! Did he *really* say that?! What a cheese-monger. Surely I didn't fall for that crap from him?

Thankfully, due to his last statement, I felt the nerves start to lessen and I turned slowly on my stool to look him square in the face and tell him coolly and calmly, *exactly* what I thought of him, only he was looking at me like I was a cold beer on a hot day. "You didn't... I was waiting for..." I desperately tried to get my composure back and lose the stutter. I cursed those five minutes until I *finally* managed to get a sentence out. "You said you were going to call". For all my former bravado, it was a weak response. My voice had cracked and he *knew* he was in.

He raised his hand up to my cheek. "You know how I feel about you". What utter shite. I wanted to slap his hand away and leave but I needed help, I felt dead from the neck down, my arms wouldn't move and it was like I was glued to the stool, I wondered if maybe there was an ejector button under my seat? If I could just Daniel Day Lewis up my left foot to check. "You've always been special to me". He continued on and was getting closer and closer. "No matter what Lyndsey told you". He was about two inches from my face now...

Wait a minute. "*Lyndsey?!*" I felt a tingling in my fingers and the sensation start to come back across my body.

Now it was *his* voice that was cracking. "I saw you two talking just before..." My expression was baffled and his changed to panic. "I thought that's why you were upset?" My expression changed to alarm and his moved on to fear. "I saw she showed you the ring… It wasn't *my* idea to get engaged, it was all *her*".

Oh my God! I knew I recognised her; Lyndsey was the Cheese and Onion Ho! Except, she wasn't a ho, she was really nice and he was a…. "You WANKER! You total, two-faced, lying, cheating, *wanker!*" It was one of those moments, where despite the fact that vinyl left Vom's with the reversible jumpers and Babycham, you expected to hear the record scratch and the music come to an abrupt halt but even without the dramatic sound effect, I'm pretty sure the entire club stopped what they were doing to look round.

The world took a second to catch up with us, as I found the strength in my legs to stand and Luke stumbled backwards off his stool, trying to defend himself. "Look, come on, you know me, I'm not…."

"Yeah, I *know* you and I know that you're the biggest *arsehole* that ever walked the earth. Yet I kept coming back for more, because unlike your cheesy fucking lines, I actually *did* believe that after all these years, there was something there…" I only stopped momentarily to draw breath. "But it turns out that all our history counts for shit! You *constantly* manipulate and worm your way round people, you… ARGGHH!" I held up my hands and just yelled in sheer frustration and by now, we'd gained quite an audience. Luke looked around in shame, shrugging his shoulders at our voyeurs, as if to say 'I've never seen this crazy bint before in my life!' I was looking to the ceiling and clenching my fists, desperately fighting the urge to clock him one. "I can't *believe* that I fell for your bullshit again!" Luke was trying to think of a response but didn't manage one before more horror flooded my brain and I realised, "Ahh man". My head was in my hands now. "You were still seeing her the other week, when you came back to mine. All that stuff you said, you were just ..." I was shaking my head and pulling my hair back off my face, tears now filled my eyes but I was biting down on my bottom lip, desperate not to cry. I lowered my voice. "I'm *such* an idiot; I can't believe I fell for it".

Small groups had amassed, all pretending to have their own conversations, while they listened in to my infinitely more interesting flip-out. It was mainly girls and to my relief, they were all shaking their heads and throwing Luke dirty looks. It was time to go, before I totally broke down, if I could walk out of here without crying like a baby, I could still maintain at least *some* dignity. Luke, visibly mortified at my public display, tried one last gesture of taking my arm but I threw off his hand and shouted, "Fuck you, Luke, FUCK YOU!"

So much for the dignity.

Chapter 21

After my outburst at Luke, I had gotten my coat and ran outside. There were no cabs and a queue of people waiting. It was 1:00am and too late to try and call anyone, I did wonder for a moment if Marcus was up but that *so* wasn't fair, I had abused our friendship lately and I didn't want to ruin the only thing I had left that I *really* cared about. I wondered about what Marcus would say when I told him what happened. I don't think he'd be *too* chuffed about the fact I considered myself at the start of a 'relationship' with the arsehole but I think he'd be pretty happy about me calling him a merchant banker in front of the *entire* town's drinking population.

I was marvelling at how things had gone so terribly wrong. I felt publicly humiliated, I was lucky if I could *ever* show my face in Vom's again (mind you, while I was in there breathing in the fetid aroma, I wondered if I ever *wanted* to go back there, I don't think I did; certainly not sober, anyway). Also, if I thought about it, there had been plenty of nights in Vom's that *far* outweighed the humiliation factor of this one; Hairy Kebab Man practically bounces to mind. Although this time, I *had* drawn quite a large amount of attention to myself; this one would be talked about for *quite* some time. Until the next scandal arose, of course.

Right now, I just wanted to be home but I couldn't wait in line for a cab, I didn't want to run the risk of another unpleasant encounter with Luke *or* give him the chance to try and make it up. That's when I saw Lyndsey at the front of the taxi line, waving and smiling at me, so I hid my nausea and did the same back. She gestured for me to jump the queue. I shook my head, smiled and mouthed, "No thanks". I motioned that I was going to walk home, waved again and turned away quickly. I could feel the tears welling up, so I moved at speed down the road. A small part of me had wanted Luke to come out of the club looking for me and causing a scene, so Lyndsey would see him, so she would know he was there and *know* he was a liar. I had no interest in hurting her as she seemed like someone I could definitely be friends with but I wanted her to know what she'd gotten herself into. That's why I didn't look round, I was scared if I did, I'd go running back and tell her everything. I could only hope that the audience that had gathered to watch our little performance contained one particular person; her friend. I realise it was a big ask for our little drama to drag the inebriated young lady away from the allure that was 'Big Ears' (or indeed for her to remember her own name at that point) but I just hoped she'd seen Luke there and found out what was going on.

Even though walking the six miles home *had* been done many times before, without my beer coat or vodka scooter, it would definitely not be an option tonight but I figured if I kept walking, I had a better chance of flagging down a cab on its way *back* to the club. I had been walking now for about ten minutes and the fresh air was actually quite soothing but everything was going over and over in my mind. I couldn't believe Luke; I couldn't believe he'd done this to me. He'd done some pretty crappy things over the years to countless other girls but I'd known him most of my life and we were *supposed* to be friends. We'd read Billy Blue Hat books together, learned to roller-skate together, discovered cigarettes and alcohol together and we'd been bumping uglies together for the last ten years.

I had always fancied the pants off of Luke and wasn't afraid to show it but he was a flirt and a tease and you never *quite* knew where you stood. Luke had a pretty crappy home life and never got the attention he craved, so he often hung out at my house playing pranks, like hiding my mum's Rosary Beads or putting lipstick on her statue of the Virgin Mary but we were only ever 'just good friends', until the night of my 20th birthday. Luke was paying me an inordinate amount of attention and *everyone* noticed. Carly pulled me to one side and told me to keep my distance, that it would only end in tears but then due to his persistence in his attentions towards *her*, Carly had never really liked Luke, so I ignored this sound advice and dove right in. He said he didn't want a relationship because it would spoil our friendship. The old cliché but he told me that *after* our first bout of carnal gymnastics, saying that it would be really cool if we just got together when we're both single. I was mortified at the suggestion but then he went to great lengths to explain the idea, playing *wholly* on my commitment-phobia. See that's the thing, friends know one another, he *knew* my weaknesses, he knew if he threw in words like 'monogamy' and 'committed' that I would want to run, screaming for the hills. After a while, I thought it sounded like an excellent plan, 'friends with benefits'. All the fun but with *none* of the hassle, it was perfect and I was convinced that I loved the idea.

At first things were great, exactly as we'd planned; no pressure, no issues, no dramas. Every couple of months, it was a regular thing that we were both perfectly happy with. Then after 'the big fight' three years ago, things went rapidly downhill. I had blamed Carly, I had blamed Pete and I had blamed myself but I never *once* thought to blame Luke. I was so frightened of losing him and his friendship that I constantly made up excuses for him. I knew things had gotten bad when I turned to Jenna for advice and no doubt seeing that I'd become so dependent, is when he *really* began to treat me like crap.

That's when I noticed (well actually that's not true, *Marcus* noticed), that whenever I got into a relationship that had *any* form of future potential, he would come prowling and sniffing around again like the alpha male, marking his territory and thus scaring away any budding suitors. Clever, when you think about it, if I were forever single, then I was forever available when *he* wanted it. Serves my naivety right for not crediting him with the appropriate amount of intelligence, he certainly had *me* fooled. Marcus had tried to warn me a thousand times but I'd never listened, I pretended to; you know sat there, nodded and made all the right noises but I never really took it in. He saw Luke for what he was and now *I* looked like a fool.

While I'd been patiently awaiting a phone call this week, wondering what had happened to him, Luke *had* been busy, he had proposed to a girl. He'd actually cared enough to ask someone to marry him and he'd asked a girl that was just like me; not *me*, but a girl exactly *like* me. Wow, that stung. Maybe he hadn't *meant* to propose, maybe he was just telling her what she wanted to hear, like he did with me all the time and she, like me, had taken him literally. Either way, it was clear I had never been good enough for Luke but someone *just like me* had.

I was crying so hard now that my chest hurt and I struggled to get a breath. In *all* my years, I'd never had a meltdown like this and I think that's because sobbing was not an activity that was familiar to me and once I started, I found it *impossible* to stop. I was glad that there were no cabs for a minute. I was glad of the walk (well, accept these frigging shoes were killing me, they were meant for dancing, not doing the steeplechase home) but the walk had turned out to be far more important than I could *ever* have deduced. Maybe it was the combination of the cool night air, my unplanned sobriety, the exercise and the release of tears but at that moment, my head cleared and I happened upon a strange realisation. I had just *assumed* that I'd gone all Norman Bates in the club and then fallen into my current state of Niagara because my heart had been utterly decimated... but it hadn't. The truth hit me like a Mackerel in a Swedish Fish Dance, if I'd had those sorts of feelings for Luke, they were *long* gone. Luke had become like an addiction to me now, a habit that I just couldn't break and the thought of not getting my 'fix' was tearing at my stomach. Maybe *that's* why I've been acting so erratically this week, I was ready for Luke Rehab. I had finally seen the light, only I didn't feel empowered, I felt lost; I was distraught that I had *wasted* all those years. I was still crying, I think they were tears of relief now and after ten years; it had been a long time coming.

Finally a cab rounded the corner and I flagged him down; it was Pork and Cheese Freddie. Normally, I would have whooped with joy at having scored the collectable cab driver but I was too far gone in my sobs. I just managed to mumble my address before I wept, really and truly *wept* again. Freddie looked at me in the rear view mirror and asked me if I was OK in his broken English. I nodded and carried on sobbing and sniffing, so Freddie tried to cheer me up the only way he knew how, he skipped a few songs on his CD, obviously trying to find the perfect one and nodded at me in the mirror as the gentle first few lines of 'Don't Stop Me Now' began to serenade out of his speakers. When the song kicked in full pelt, Freddie was using his steering wheel as a drum and head banging along and I managed a small chuckle in between tears but then realised just how appropriate the title of the song was, because you really *couldn't* stop me now. I couldn't stop myself from crying when he asked me if I'd had a good night and I couldn't stop when I paid him (nearly soaking the cash and causing him to look at me like I'd escaped from Broadmoor) but I knew things were bad when I couldn't even stop to appreciate the comedy gold when I saw he was wearing a yellow jacket and white vest top... I must remember to tell Greg.

I stood outside the front door and tried to compose myself before I went inside the house, so I wouldn't wake Marcus, I didn't want him to see me like this. I managed to stop the sobbing but the tears were still free falling and really stinging my raw cheeks. I took a few deep breaths, quietly unlocked the door and tried to sneak in. This is normally the part of the evening, where during inebriation, one's house has had the volume turned up on it, so that when you quietly try to sneak in, you miss the lock with your key, slip, hit the letterbox, drop your loud keys, get the door open, accidentally lean on it, it swings open and slams the hall wall. You drop your keys again, you bend down to pick them up, your ass knocks the door, slamming it shut and then you bounce off the walls down the hallway, like a pinball... but tonight, I was sober and quiet. I went in to the bathroom and looked in the mirror and almost didn't recognise the face that looked back at me; my mascara was streaked down my face and my eyes and cheeks were puffy and red. For a short space of time, I felt void of emotion, had I finished crying? I didn't know. The tears had momentarily stopped and I was on auto pilot now, I managed to wash and then brush my teeth in complete silence, my brain was still for a minute, allowing me to get ready for bed. I got changed and I climbed in under the covers but it was then that my brain switched back on and the tears began to flow once more. I sobbed and sobbed, not knowing how long for and I didn't hear him come in; he just walked round to the other side of the bed and climbed in. Marcus didn't ask me what was wrong, I guess he didn't need to, he was just there; he held me and I cried into his chest.

It was 2:30am and I must have fallen asleep on Marcus. The room looked blue, as there was a tiny amount of light coming in through a gap in the curtains. I propped myself up and rubbed my puffy, over-cried eyes. Marcus was fast asleep and breathing gently. He looked beautiful when he slept and he was slightly unshaven tonight, which actually made him look quite rugged. I'd never spent a lot of time *really* studying his face, so I hadn't noticed the little scar he had under his left eyebrow before, even though I *knew* it was there *and* how he had gotten it. We were 5 years old and he'd hit his head during a game of Swingball with me, it was kind of cute and I couldn't help but smile remembering it. He had thick, bushy eyebrows, I used to tease him about them all the time growing up but now, they really framed his face. He moved and I panicked; I tried to put my head back and pretend to be asleep but I flinched when I realised I'd soaked his t-shirt with tears and he opened his eyes before I could complete the slumber illusion, so I propped myself back up again. He breathed in deeply, he was looking up at me with his eyes half open and sleepily asked, "You OK?"

"Yeah, I'm OK". I *did* feel better now that I was all cried out and I had Marcus. "Thank you". I held his gaze for a second and he smiled at me. I looked down at his chest and raised a little chuckle. "I'm really sorry about that". He pulled his drenched t-shirt away from his body and looked down at it and laughed. He sat upright, I moved back and then he took it off. I was speechless for a second; it threw me a little off course. I took a guilty moment to look at him; I hadn't realised before quite how toned he was, I knew he looked after himself but he really was impressive. My admiration turned to shame when I realised I'd been caught, he *saw* me looking at him! I suddenly felt nervous, which was ridiculous and I waited for him to make fun of me but he didn't, instead he put his arms out, gesturing that I should go back to where I was. I laid back down and pulled the sheet up over my cold legs. My head was on his bare chest now and God, he smelled good. He was stroking my hair so gently. He was just wearing shorts and I could feel the hair on his legs and suddenly my stomach flipped. I could hear his heart beating faster in his chest and his breathing had gotten heavier. I moved my hand across his chest and I felt his stomach contract and heard him breathe in sharply. I slowly moved my head up and I was facing him, he was looking at me so intensely... then he kissed me.

Chapter 22

The next morning, I awoke twisted together with Marcus. I hadn't slept that well in… hell; I'd never slept that well, not *sober* anyway. I was perfectly, serenely content. Normally when you share a bed with a new partner, you tend not to sleep, you're always too worried that you might snore or unattractively dribble, sending your man running faster than a greyhound out of the tracks but this was Marcus, *my* Marcus and I'd never felt so comfortable. His arm was around me and I clasped my hand around his. I felt him stir behind me, so I slowly turned to face him but just as I turned, I heard a key in the front door. It was Sadie!

    I jumped up and tried to grab my shorts and vest top from the floor, suddenly feeling very embarrassed about my form in the harsh light of day and I tried to cover up. "Shit. *Quick!*" Marcus obviously hadn't woken up properly yet, he looked confused and wasn't moving. It took ages before he followed my lead and he didn't seem that fussed about rapid movement either and took his time collecting his shorts to put them on. I stopped for the briefest of moments to watch him without his knowledge. God, he did look good. I encouraged quietly, "Quick, *quick*!" as I tip-toed toward my bedroom door, trying to look through the gap. Sadie had come in and gone straight to her bedroom. Marcus was behind me now and I whispered, "Thank God! She's in her room. You can make it back or at least to the bathroom without her seeing you".

"Great". His tone was *not* one of pure joy this morning. I tried to ignore it and not read anything in to it as he really wasn't a morning person.

"Go now, *quick!*" He really needed to speed up if he didn't want to get caught, so I was practically pushing him out the door, when I suddenly thought. "Wait!" He turned to look at me, his hair without product, just fell across his face, it was so... focus, woman, focus! I pulled him back in and ran to the bed, then quickly crept back and handed him his t-shirt. I had to check the t-shirt as he looked at it as though it belonged to someone else. Sadie could re-appear any minute, so we didn't have time for pleasantries. Probably just as well; he didn't seem in the mood for them. I shoved him out the door again and gave him my best smile but I think he missed it. I watched through the gap in the door, as he made it back to his room.

I went into the bathroom; I couldn't quite believe everything that had happened last night. The row with Luke felt like a distant dream and as the water washed over my body, I thought about nothing but Marcus; it was a *very* long shower. I spent ages on my hair and make-up because I couldn't stop smiling or recollecting. Marcus was running his hand down my leg and...

"You wanna brew?" It was Sadie.

"Errr, yeah great. Thanks". Luckily Sadie was on the other side of the door and couldn't see that I'd gone bright red, I felt like I'd been caught in the act.

My thoughts went back to Marcus. OK, so things had been a little awkward this morning when Sadie came back but you know what they say, uncomfortable mornings are better than boring nights… and my night had been *anything* but boring.

I couldn't concentrate on anything and took forever to get ready. I thought I looked OK; I was good to go but then maybe just another coat of lippy. OK, I was *really* ready. I had agonised over what to wear, so decided to go with a t-shirt and jeans, I wanted to give the illusion that I was cool, calm and collected, the 'what *this* old thing?' approach to dressing. I left my room and headed for the lounge, my stomach was doing somersaults that would gain top gymnastic marks at the Olympics. I stopped and took a long, deep breath before I made my entrance. He wasn't there. I walked out to the kitchen and Sadie was just stirring the tea, I tried to act as normal as possible, as I had no idea if Sadie had seen my little altercation with Luke, I had no idea if she'd seen Marcus and I had no idea what had happened to her hair, as it was standing on end like Russell Brand's. I tried to conceal my disappointment at the Marcus-less kitchen. "Hey. How was the rest of last night?"

Sadie looked *really* rough, yawned, "Morning. I needed a brew to give me the strength to stand up in the shower. Then I plan on going back to bed".

"That good, huh?" I kept looking around the kitchen and towards the doorway, expecting him to suddenly appear. I was looking over her shoulder towards the garden, when I asked, "How was your stud?"

Sadie went bright red. "Oh, him. Me, Trisha and a group of us went back to his house, he got a bit fruity and then I threw up on his new bedspread".

"Ha ha. Ahh, genius!"

"You *know* me; I don't *do* one-night-stands. I think my subconscious must've stepped in and saved me". Sadie's face confirmed that she actually *did* believe her reflux was the work of fate and not the ten vodka's and countless shots she'd downed earlier. "Do you think people will know? I mean, a few people saw me leaving in a group. Oh God, they might think we had an orgy!" She was looking at me for answers but all I could do was stare back until she was ready to answer her own question. "No, no, what am I saying, you're right, that's just silly. People know me, *right?* They know I wouldn't just go off with a bloke I'd just met…. even though I did. I mean, I wouldn't you know, *go off* with him, like go off. People would know that, right?"

I was torn; I didn't know whether to ignore the insane rambling and go outside to check if Marcus was hiding in the shed or stay and tease the hell out of her. "Of course. Slut". I went for the latter.

"DON'T!" She looked like she was about to have an anxiety attack. "What if someone who knows my mum saw us, what if they woke her in the middle of the night to tell her what I'd been up to?!"

Normally, I would have stayed and played for hours, it was just *too* easy but this morning, I had a higher purpose. I decided to put her out of her misery and gave her a long speech about why sharing a cab didn't mean the bouncers contacted the local papers about the return of the gang bang and that her folks had no way of knowing but she *still* didn't look convinced. "OK, say they did get up at 3:00am for a stroll, past the local nightclub to… I dunno, walk the cat or milk the budgie, seeing you getting into a taxi with a group of people is hardly cause to ring social services or ground you". I grabbed a handful of Cheerio's out of the box and proceeded to eat them one by one.

"Yeah, cheers. You're right, I *know* you're right. I guess *you* do it all the time". Ouch! "It's just this morning, I didn't even know where I was to order a cab from, I had to walk down the street in last night's clothes, until I found a local newsagents that was open".

I was smiling, trying to get the image of poor Sadie wandering the streets with that hairdo. "Couldn't you have just asked Long Ar… err, your friend?"

"After the bedspread incident, he made me sleep in the lounge. I think Trish was in one of the other rooms with one of his friends, so I just grabbed my things and left. I feel so humiliated".

I was edging towards the kitchen door; he *must* be in his room, which will be my next stop when Sadie leaves for the shower. Sadie cut back into my daydream. "So, where did *you* get to anyway?" It was the million pound question. "I saw you and Luke talking one minute and the next you were gone and he was still there. What happened?"

She didn't know about the row. Could I go '50/50' or 'Ask the Audience'? Unfortunately not, I was on my own with this one. "I was knackered; I left Vom's early and came home. Sorry I didn't let you know". I opened up the fridge, pretending to look for something; I was desperately trying to hide my face.

"You bumped in to Luke and left without him? Wow. Did you two have a fight or something?" Sadie looked at me wide-eyed, as I closed the fridge door.

Firstly, I was amazed that Sadie must have been the *only* person in Vom's that didn't witness the spectacle of me and Luke and secondly, at her subsequent deduction that because I hadn't left with him, we must have had an argument. It would appear that everyone understood the Luke/Nicky dynamic better than *I* did. "I think it's fair to say that Luke and I are *not* the best of friends anymore".

Sadie winced, "Oh, I'm sorry".

"Don't be, I'm not".

Sadie fished out a biscuit, looked at it and breathed in deeply; this morning, it was her Everest. "Was Marcus in when you got home last night?"

Oh God, did she know? "Errr... maybe. I came in and went straight to bed. Why?"

"Oh right, I just wondered what he was so upset about".

Such a throw-away statement for her and pure torture for me. "*Upset?*"

"Yeah, I saw him in the lounge earlier, he asked me about what happened last night, I gave him the bullet points, you know... left out the part about me in matey-boys bedroom but told him about my walk of shame and he didn't mock me, not even *once!*" Sadie looked pensive as she broke off a piece of biscuit. "Actually, he looked kinda pale, like he wasn't well and then he just grabbed his coat, said he had to go out and left. Maybe Mitchell's cooking isn't all it's cracked up to be".

My heart sank. "Maybe, I errr... I don't know". I tried to act as natural as possible but I was failing miserably. Luckily Sadie was too busy deep breathing after the exertion of another yawn to notice any weirdness on my part. "I'll give him a call a bit later and see if he's OK".

"Cool. I'm getting in the shower. Call a Lifeguard if I'm not out in twenty". Sadie walked off taking her tea into the bathroom with her.

I laughed, trying to hide my bitter disappointment. "Will do, mate"

Chapter 23

Why had Marcus run out like that? Maybe it *was* the food? Maybe he *wasn't* well? Maybe... Oh God, was it *me*? Oh my God, it *was* me! He was sick with shame, why didn't I see it?! I went into the lounge, I had to sit down as light dawned and it suddenly all began to make horrible sense. When Sadie came home and I'd jumped up, he must have seen me again in all my glory and talk about a couple of stark reminders that I'm not his usual 'type'! I sat with my head in my hands, I was mortified as it all came flooding back. His face when he was putting on his shorts, he was obviously wondering 'what the hell have I done?' And when I handed him his t-shirt, that *look*; he probably thought 'this is when it all went wrong'. I should have read the signs, I should have known what was going on at the time, then maybe we could have talked, we could have worked it out. I sat up straight and took a deep breath; I needed to get a grip. OK, the reality is, if he'd told me to my face that he thought it was a huge mistake, I *would* have been upset. I thought about it for a moment... actually, I would have been *devastated*. My stomach was churning and I was beginning to feel sick myself, my chest suddenly felt like I'd taken a battering ram to it. How could I *not* have seen it? How could I *not* realise? Just how long *had* I felt this way about Marcus?

I needed to get out of the house. I dialled his number, it went straight to voicemail. Marcus and Carly were the two people I trusted with a problem, the people I relied on the most to help me through a crisis, so right at that moment; I was feeling pretty friendless. I walked quickly down the road, with no known destination and before I knew it, I was dialling her number, waiting ages for her to answer.

"Jen? It's Nicky. Jen, I need your help, advice, whatever. I need to talk".

I was sat nursing a brew in Ruth's for what felt like an eternity waiting for Jenna. I had tried Marcus on his mobile twice and he wasn't answering. I sat there looking out the window in a trance and it was it was Ruth that finally broke it. "On your own today, poppet?"

I looked up and smiled, "I'm just waiting for a friend".

"Don't you want any food to go with your tea?"

She had her pad and pen at the ready but I looked around and then at my watch, Jenna wasn't due for another thirty minutes. "I'll wait till she gets here, thanks Ruth".

"No problem darlin, you just give me or Ron a shout when you're ready". Ron was Ruth's husband of about forty odd years, they were about the same height and they actually even looked a little bit alike. He still pinched her bum when she went out to get something from the kitchen but with his arthritis now, I think he found it hard to let go. They were a lovely old couple and almost surrogate parents to all the kids of the village in the way they'd cared for us after *far* too many indulgent night's out. Ruth went back behind the counter and I went back to staring out the window. Being alone with my thoughts about Marcus felt dangerous this morning, I had made an interesting discovery last night when I realised I hadn't been heartbroken by Luke but I hadn't dared associate that with having feelings for anyone else; it had come on so gradually, that even *I* hadn't noticed.

I heard her before I saw her. "Can you believe it; they'd bloody sold out of the colour I wanted". Jenna had been in the middle of ordering cushion covers on the internet when I'd phoned.

She took off her coat and wiped the bench seat before she sat down. I handed her a menu and we spent a moment in silence perusing. "How long have you been here?"

I lied, "Not long".

Jenna looked around with her nose turned up. "Does that old broad still run it? What's her name, Ruby?"

"You mean Ruth. You know, as in the name, Ruth's?" I was staring at Jenna, who was totally oblivious to my sarcasm and inspecting cleanliness of the table.

Ruth came over and we both ordered. Bless Ruth for not laughing, when Jenna asked for the fat-free options, instead she replied that she might have some in next week and gave me a knowing wink. She left us to it and Jenna enquired, "So what was all that about, earlier? You sounded like you were in some kind of trouble".

She took some tissues out of her bag and proceeded to wipe the table space in front of her, while I shook my head. "I had a weird night is all. I just needed to vent".

I *never* went to Jenna with a problem but I didn't have anywhere else to turn. After Emma's little stunt with the kids the other night, she was obviously having some issues of her own and Alice? Well, she didn't really say a lot, which made her a great listener but I needed *feedback*, I needed someone to tell me what to do. It felt weird for me but I think Jenna was enjoying the role reversal. I wasn't sure I wanted to tell her about Marcus, so I figured I would just start with the argument with Luke.

I took a deep breath and put my hands on the table. "I saw Luke in Vom's last night". Jenna shrugged and I continued, "He inadvertently told me that he was engaged".

"What?! Engaged?"

"Yes".

"Luke?"

"Yes".

"Since *when?*"

"Since Friday". She suddenly looked relieved that she wasn't *totally* out of date with the gossip. So I told her about how he'd 'accidentally' told me whilst he was trying it on.

"Tiger's eh?"

I was understandably thrown by Jenna's random statement. "What about them?"

"Never change their spots".

I was staring at the table in front, wondering how much it would hurt if I just slammed my head down on to it. I thought the Jenna-isms were a drunken thing but it would appear they'd now taken on a life of their own.

Jenna sat open-mouthed, listening intently as I told her about the whole argument, about how Lyndsey was lovely and what a total shit *he* was, how I walked a mile in my new shoes (which then provoked a lecture from her about the *importance* of breaking in footwear which nearly prompted me to run home, get the new shoes and 'Single White Female' her with them) and then I told her about my very public display of potty mouth. I was amazed as she sat there listening and nodding; Jenna had never been so attentive.

Ruth brought over our food and we sat quietly eating before Jenna said, "Is that it?"

I didn't look up from my plate; I didn't want to give myself away. "What do you mean?"

Jenna was picking at her toast. "I dunno, it just feels like there's more you're not telling me. Is the girlfriend up the duff? Is that why he's marrying her?"

I sat there deciding whether or not I should tell her, I wanted advice and I wanted to share but at what cost? My hesitation was as good as an admission.

"So there *is* something else?" Jenna moved in closer, then lifted her elbows to check she hadn't leaned in anything and then propped herself forward again.

"No". It was weak but I couldn't, no matter how much I wanted to talk about this, I couldn't do it... Could I?

"No? Come on Nic, we're *supposed* to be friends".

"I *can't* Jen. It's not fair".

"Come on mate, you can tell *me*. You're obviously upset; I might be able to help". I'd never known Jenna to be so selfless, it was a refreshing side to her that I hadn't seen before and I really *did* need to talk about this, otherwise it would eat me up and drive me insane and after all, this was about sex and of that, Jenna was the oracle.

"You have to promise you won't say a word, Jen".

"Cross my heart". Jenna made a heart-crossing gesture... on her right-hand side.

I omitted two very important details regarding my feelings about both Luke *and* Marcus but I told her.

Jenna sat there like a teenage boy watching his first porn film. "Fuckin nora!"

I took a deep breath and clutched my mug. "I know".

"*Fuckin* nora!" Jenna threw down her toast crust on to her plate. "I actually thought you two might have done it years ago but not *now*! You're *30* in a couple of weeks! Blimey! I wasn't expecting *that* this morning". Jenna was shaking her head and reaching for her tea. "So how did you two leave it?"

"He's gone out somewhere. I think he's too embarrassed to be around me. He probably *hates* me".

"Hmm, good point". It definitely wasn't what I wanted to hear but she carried on regardless. "He probably thinks you tried to turn him into a hetro".

I laughed in disbelief, as I often did with Jenna. "You can't *turn* someone into *anything*".

"Well, look on the bright side; it's not the *worst* mistake you'll ever make".

I stared at her for a few seconds before I let out an involuntary chuckle. "That's comforting".

Jenna spent the next half hour grilling me about the gory details, while she used colourful euphemisms like 'Bedroom Rodeo' and 'Threading the needle'. She said it was better this way, that I'd got to have a 'taster' of the bread at home and if I was happy with my home-baked goods, then I wouldn't have to go looking round the bakery for something else. Her cookery doublespeak was almost putting me off my food, until she finished with a Jenna classic. "Well, you know what they say, a bird in your hand is worth two in your…"

"Yes! Thanks Jen". I managed to cut her off before the people on the next table choked on their muffins.

Chapter 24

After I left Ruth's I rang home and Marcus *still* wasn't there. I wandered around aimlessly, then headed over to the local park and sat on the swings. We'd spent a lot of time there as kids and I suppose I hoped he'd be there reminiscing as I was but this wasn't a black and white movie and he was nowhere to be seen. I sat there until it started to rain but luckily, my folks lived just around the corner, so I headed over under the pretext of a party reminder for next week. Who was I kidding? I wanted the company (and to score a bit of roast dinner).

I was sat on the edge of their sofa, drinking tea, it was our usual position. Only it wasn't until I arrived that I remembered I was wearing my 'Jesus is my Homeboy' t-shirt, so I couldn't remove my jacket, even though the heating was on and I was starting to cook. My mother did her usual and regaled me with local stories. "Mrs Jenkins died".

It was best to play along. "Really? I thought she died years ago".

Best of Friends?

She looked thoughtful. "No. She definitely died last week. Apparently, she hadn't been well for a long time, so I think it was a relief for the family..." I totally tuned out for a moment, I was staring in to space, I was thinking about Marcus, the way his hair fell on to his face was... "But then she was *always* a bit of a money grabber, so I wouldn't be surprised if she contested the will".

I took a sip of tea and rejoined the conversation. "Didn't she have pneumonia?"

"No, that was Mrs Davis". By that point, I wouldn't have been surprised if she wheeled out a flip chart and drew up a family tree that included ailments and career histories to accentuate her point. I tuned out for a bit again, unsurprisingly thinking about Marcus.

We sat down to dinner and Dad was pre-occupied watching football, only alerting us to his presence with a chuckle when mum announced we had spotted dick for dessert. *Now* I know where I get it from. My mum did all the talking, telling me every detail about my goody-two-shoes sister, Claire; she was at University and was a real smarty pants. She always volunteered for good causes and she and her boyfriend had been saving the whales and banning the bomb for years (yes, she was *so* far removed from me that it was a miracle we were even related). We weren't close and it was a shame, I could *really* use a sister right about now. To my parents, she was the perfect child, the child that rang home regularly and talked about what she was up to, the child that was always interested in the garden when she visited. The child that helped mum down at the Church and the child that *didn't* ring them at five in the morning asking to be picked up from an all-nighter and then promptly throw up in the back seat of their car.

My younger sister's contentment in her relationship was one of the greatest gift I'd *ever* been given. One child's felicity in love, inevitably takes the mantle of child-bearer away from the other sibling, so it was a huge blow to find out that their romance was on rocky ground as it meant that I may be looked upon once more to be the provider of grandchildren. My mum cut across my panic. "You haven't touched your peas".

"I don't like peas, Mum". In nearly thirty years, I hadn't touched my peas, I *hated* peas but growing up in the Thompson household, every Sunday without fail, my Mum served my roast dinner with peas.

"We all need a little green on our plate, it livens it up". Mum's favourite excuse for adding vegetables; personally, I couldn't see what was so fun about them.

We spent the rest of dinner with polite chit chat about mum's Church fundraising and dad's Gout and my work here was done. I reminded them about the party and almost made a clean exit when she looked me in the eyes for a moment, moved some hair off my face and settled her hand on my cheek. "What's the matter? Is everything OK?"

I wanted to tell her. I wanted to confess the whole, sorry story but how on earth could I explain this to her? She called Marcus the lovely gay boy. "Nothing mum, I'm fine". I tried to flash a reassuring smile back, we hugged affectionately and I left at speed. I was worried, as those immortal words 'What's the matter?' seem to be like a rain dance for the tear ducts at the best of times.

I'd had a brief reprieve at my parents, the chance to think about something else but alone again on the walk home; my head was swimming with the events of last night. I'd been responsible for some pretty infamous screw ups over the years but even for me, this was the one, the golden nugget, the *mother* of all messes. If this was one of the joys of turning 30, I didn't want it! Then it dawned on me, that's it! That's the way I had to look at this; for a few weeks, I was *still* in my 20's, this was just my 20's saying a monumental goodbye, a final farewell to my youth, a bon voyage to my tight skin, an auf wiedersehen to my motor functions. Now that I was approaching the big three, oh, I could be wiser, more focussed, more mature (I'd have to get myself enrolled on a twelve step programme for that last one) but I could make this work, this could be a *good* thing, I've turned a metaphorical corner, I'm looking ahead and… Damn it, I can see Mitchell and Daniel have just pulled up outside our house.

I was going to run into someone else's driveway and hide behind a wall but it was *too* late, they'd already seen me. I frantically looked around and luckily (or unluckily, dependent on how much you think I deserved Marcus' avoidance) the car wasn't there.

"Hi! How are you?" I tried to act like I was overjoyed to see them but this was Mitchell and Daniel, I should have known better. I may have been able to spin a good yarn over the phone but up close and personal, I was a crap actress. Proven at the tender age of 13 when I had a small part in a school production. All I had to do was come on, say one line, then go off again. I came on, my mouth went dry and my hands went clammy, the lights were too bright so I couldn't see a thing and before I could utter a single word; I tripped over my dress and wiped out the stage set.

Mitchell and Daniel eyed me suspiciously and Daniel answered, "We're good. We've just come to see Marcus and see how the car is". Daniel smiled; he was obviously trying to catch me out. At least I knew one thing, Marcus wasn't with them.

"I'm not sure *where* Marcus is Daniel but the car is probably in the garage being fixed. You're welcome to come in for a cuppa, though". Spoken in such common terms, I knew it would put Mitchell off with visions of 'workman's tea' out of a chipped mug.

"No, thank you. We were just passing by and thought we'd say hello". Mitchell was getting the car keys out of his pocket and pressing the button to unlock it in record time and Daniel was already half in. "We'd best be off. Pass on our regards to Marcus and don't worry about the party, all the decorations are in hand". They were in, the doors were shut and the engine on, they obviously weren't waiting for a response from me, so I just mouthed "Thank you", as I waved them off.

I unlocked the door and went inside, Sadie had obviously gone out for Sunday dinner and the place was dark. I tried Marcus on his mobile again and this time, I left a message warning him about Mitchell and Daniel and their detective work. I also left the obligatory (and now worn out), "*Please* call me".

I got myself a large glass of red and crashed down on to the sofa. I was exhausted and I wasn't surprised, it had been quite a month. I had slept with three different men in the last four weeks. If it were one of my friends, I would have whooped and cheered, slapped them on the back and said, "You go, girl!" Mainly because I wouldn't have really understood the reality. I would have been impressed by the gall and the guts to be *that* liberal with the most important thing I own. If I were Jenna five years ago, I wouldn't be worried right now, I wouldn't be fretting, I wouldn't even be *thinking*, I'd probably just be filling up with vitamins and Red Bull, ready for round four but I definitely wouldn't be feeling so licentious. Although, considering Jenna's recent confession, she hadn't really changed *that* much in the last five years, she was obviously still the queen of promiscuity, even with a gold band on her finger but then that was the point, I *wasn't* Jenna. I'd had my share of fun over the years but I was no queen, not even a princess, I had that small thing called a conscience. Damn my conscience! *Sure* it had saved me from shocking decisions on occasion but it had gotten in the way of some fabulously potential mischief over the years as well. I wondered why my conscience hadn't kicked in last night and then I realised it was because, for some reason, everything had just felt *so* right, even though I had gotten it so *very* wrong.

Chapter 25

It was mid-week and Marcus *still* hadn't come home. I've been going through the motions this week, totally on auto-pilot. You know that feeling when you arrive somewhere and you can't remember how you got there? You've done something *so* many times, your sub-conscious kicks in. Luckily, mine had gotten me up, showered, changed and in to work each day and did my job for me; must thank sub-conscious. I'd never known a time when I felt so detached from my own life. I knew that at some point, I would have to step up to the plate and take control again but I suspected for the interim that my sub-conscious was doing a *far* better job than I could.

At least now I'd stopped clock watching because Sunday night was awful, constantly waiting for the door to go and nearly wiping out the sofa when Sadie returned. She'd asked after him and I did what I seemed to be doing a lot lately, I lied. I told her that he wasn't feeling well, so was staying with his folks until the party, because he didn't want *us* to come down with it. I'd since found out that was *actually* where he was hiding, not returning

Best of Friends?

my calls. I wanted to go round there but I doubted he'd told his dad's the real reason for his homecoming and so wouldn't exactly appreciate my '*outing*' him. I'd also thought about waiting for him outside of his work but figured that might constitute stalking, so I had to be patient and wait for him to come to me.

I had to say, I was *surprised* at Marcus. It was obvious that he thought I was the anti-Christ; that I seduced him and tried to turn him to the dark side but he'd been there too and my *very* vivid memory of that night reminds me that he was an *extremely* willing participant. I had no idea if Marcus was in purgatory; if he was punishing himself or just blaming *me* but it definitely felt like I was the one being made to suffer. Ever since it happened, my mind had been so consumed with thoughts of recriminations and regrets; it was like there wasn't any room for anything else... like common sense. This could explain my rather extraordinary behaviour this week. It was on Tuesday that I had my most *bizarre* brainstorm to date, brought on by something my mother had said regarding the Church fundraising and a new curtain for the confessional box and that's when it hit me; Confession! My obviously deranged, mental state told me that it was *just* what was needed; someone I could spill my woes to, who would absolve me of *any* wrong doing and forgive me all my past indiscretions and the very thought of being 'forgiven' felt like a load off, so last night I made enquiries.

I was astounded to find that the local Church had its own website. It did give me my first laugh of the week, as I thought about all the fun a web designer could have with a Church website; like Nun icons and when you click on 'Confession' it shouts, "Sinner!" Unfortunately, their website was extremely dull and didn't even list their Confession times but there was a contact number on the top, so without much thought as to what I'd say, I decided to give it a ring.

"Hello? Is that St Francis of Assisi Church? Oh hi, yes. I just wondered, what are your opening times? Oh, I see, OK, that's great. See, I've got this friend who wants to come to Confession, is there any particular time for that? Christ! Tonight? Oh God, sorry, errm, I meant... I'm SO sorry. What's the dress code? Oh, right. Splendid. Thanks very much. Sorry".

I sat with my head rolling in my hands for quite a while after that, realising my IQ was dropping points like they were hot. Confession was that night from 6:00–6.30pm, so knowing my mum never went on a Tuesday (Ground Force was on Cable), I made my way over. The door creaked as I walked in and I expected everyone to turn round but they carried on staring forward, I was impressed at their resolve. Claire and I had spent most of our childhood here and to me; it was a big, cold, intimidating building with *really* uncomfortable seats that used to scare the pants off me, so I guess not much had changed. I headed over to the right and walked along the side of the pews and past a sweet little dwarf woman to what looked like a box. Suddenly a new-looking curtain opened right in front of me and a man in his mid 50's stepped out, it looked like he'd been crying. I looked inside and the little dwarf woman (or actually once she stood up from kneeling and praying, rather tall, frightening looking woman) quickly moved in front of me and sat down in the box, she leaned forward and yanked the curtain across. No wonder they needed a new one.

I headed to the pew where the tall dwarf had been kneeling and I went to do the same, except I'd got my new jeans on and the floor looked a bit dirty. There were mats but they looked like they'd seen better days, so I decided I would just sit and pretend to kneel if anyone came along. I heard the door go and immediately swung round, then berated myself for not exercising proper Church etiquette. It was overwhelmingly quiet, I tried to sneak a look round and everyone was in their own little world, some were frantically muttering to themselves, which looked a little disturbing. It didn't take long before I was bored, so I started tapping my feet and humming a tune which turned into a full rendition and earned me a sharp, angry stare from another pew-dweller.

The tall dwarf had been in there a good five minutes, God only knows what she had to confess (I had to laugh for a minute at the irony of that statement). She'd looked completely uninteresting but I suppose you *never* can tell, they say it's always the quiet ones. Maybe she was in there apologising for pretending to be a dwarf? No, she was probably begging forgiveness for burning last night's dinner or forgetting to leave a note for the milkman? Or maybe she'd had an affair? Ooh, that's more like it, or maybe she'd killed her husband? *Now* we're talking. Maybe she'd killed her husband, over an affair with the milkman and she put him in last night's burnt dinner? I was happily getting carried away when she came out looking a little flustered, so I settled on affair.

It was *my* turn. The Priest said some kind of blessing and then it went quiet; was I supposed to say something? I tried to look through the little holes and see what he was doing on the other side, then remembered I'd seen a film once where someone said, "Bless me Father, for I have sinned", so I said that.

Maybe I wasn't supposed to say that, maybe he thought I was taking the mick as it went deathly quiet again before the Priest replied, "When was your last confession?" Phew.

What was that? When was my *last* confession? Damn. "Ermm, well, it was... err..." I couldn't think of a good lie and it *was* the house of God (or at least a little shed in the garden of God) so I came clean. "I haven't been before, Father".

Suddenly answering simple questions became a challenge. He asked me my age and I wished I hadn't taken the option to lie off of the table but I guess it would have just defeated the object, so I told him the truth, which seemed to cause some surprise. "And in 'nearly 30 years', you don't feel that you've *needed* confession?" It was a loaded question. I'd needed it alright but I hadn't a clue where to start? I should have made a list before I went but would you make your list of sins alphabetically or chronologically? I thought about setting up a weekly appointment, so that I might get through most of the 90's by Christmas. I was berating myself for not being better prepared and not Googling this before I went and then musing that I wouldn't have been able to read any instructions in there anyway, it was *way* too dark and they needed a little lamp which would make it cosier... Thankfully, my thoughts were interrupted by the Priest, who'd taken my lack of response as a need for assistance. "Why don't you tell me why you came here today?"

Right, why was I there? I could answer that. Did I *want* to answer that? I knew he wouldn't approve but I couldn't hide it, I figured if this man truly *is* one of God's earthly vessels then he probably already knew what I'd been up to. "I had... 'relations' with a man that I shouldn't have".

There was a small silence before he said, "Are you married?"

Oh yeah, the whole sex before marriage thing. Just stick some horns on me and hand me a trident. "No Sir... errr, Father".

I nearly jumped out of my skin when the 'Magic Roundabout' theme tune echoed around the confessional box. I was desperately routing around in my bag. "I'm so sorry Father; I forgot to turn it off. I'll just... there". I managed to switch it off my mobile but not before checking who it was; ironically, it was my mother. I knew I'd never doubt God's existence again.

There was a long silence this time before the Priest carried on from where he left off. "Is the man you had these '*relations*' with, married?"

I let out an involuntary laugh and then tried to pretend it was a cough. Shit. "No Sir, errr, Father, Sir". I didn't want to offer any more information on his status as I suddenly realised I didn't know the Catholic Church's stance on homosexuality either and I didn't want this to turn into a lecture that incensed me and provoked a 'Tommy Lee' where I trashed the joint. It was at *that* point that I realised how little I knew about my own given religion, my upbringing, my family's beliefs; I had ignored this part of my life growing up and I'd cut out any remaining trace when I left home. I thought right at that moment how disappointed in me my mum would've been, maybe that's why she phoned, she just *knew*. I started to well up and it was a resultant sniffle that alerted the Priest to my teetering tears.

"By coming here, you have made the first steps towards righting your wrong. You need to ask God for his forgiveness. Repeat after me…" I did as I was told and then he said something else about a penance and absolving my sins and it went quiet again.

I sat there for a second wondering what was next when he said, "You can *go* now". Thank God (literally) but just as I was about to leave, he said, "And please tell your mother that the new curtain is a big hit with our parishioners".

Shit. He knew it was me, how on *earth* did he know it was me? I suppose when you're working on the big guy's staff, you know everything (well, that and my mum was always showing photos of me and my sister to anyone that would stop and look). I wondered how much Priest's can tell their fellow Church goers? I wondered if it was ethical or moral or going against the confessional codes if he told my mother? Like a Doctor/patient thing. "Err, this is just between us, right? And obviously... God". You could almost hear another ten points slide off my rated intelligence, at this pace I'll be a vegetable by autumn.

He let out a small laugh. "Yes, this is just between you, me and God"

Did I feel better for my absolution? A little, I guess. Although I couldn't *help* but feel I hadn't really earned it. I think that due to my omissions of circumstance and detail, perhaps the very nice Priest (who knew my mother, did I mention that?!) may have thought I was over-reacting to a little boy trouble, felt sorry for me, absolved me and then sent me packing, so that he could deal with some *real* issues. On the plus side, if he *did* get a bit loose-lipped about my visit after an over-exuberant Holy Communion or something, my mum would be none-the-wiser. It's important to appreciate the positives.

I spent the next few days constantly checking my mobile and landline to see if he'd called back and I'd left a couple of messages on his phone, let's say seven (because the actual figure of twenty is *just* too humiliating) and I'd not heard a peep, not one iota, not a sausage. Luke's lack of contact last week had annoyed the hell out of me but the silent treatment from Marcus was *killing* me. I figured maybe I needed more forgiveness? More purging, more cleansing. That's when brainstorm number two kicked in. I'd gotten a voucher for my birthday last year from Sadie that I'd never gotten around to using, it was for the local Therapy Rooms in town where she worked, so I before I knew it, I'd booked myself in on Thursday for a night of peace, tranquillity and repose, hoping to be relaxed and ready for the party.

Chapter 26

Sadie was a godsend and I think I would have gone loopy without her around this week (OK, so *more* loopy). She knew something was amiss but didn't ask questions, so it was Wednesday night before either one of us even mentioned the impending party.

I was in the kitchen getting dinner ready, when she came home from work moaning about having to do a pedicure on some woman's verruca'd trotters and I tried to rid my brain of the image, as I added the mini sweetcorn to the stir-fry. It was the only meal I could successfully cook, mainly because you just stirred... while it fried. "Did you invite any of your friends to the party?"

Sadie set the table (well, got the lap-trays out of the cupboard). "Yeah, I asked a few people but no-one can make it".

"Oh, that's a shame, everyone busy?"

Sadie rolled her eyes. "No, it's not that. Mel's had her hair cut, she hates it and won't go out".

I could only imagine what she'd had done to her hair to cause her own grounding. "Did she GI Jane it?"

Sadie gurned. "No, but it's a *really* harsh bob".

"Like Geldoff?" I was laughing at my own joke but it did a fly-by.

We sat down and both tried to eat our noodles without them slapping round our faces and Sadie continued, "Then there's Trish, she's just had her dog put down".

Perhaps I would have taken it more seriously if she hadn't a noodle hanging from her mouth but I chuckled again. "What someone told her it was fat and its mother never loved it?"

Sadie looked confused and said innocently, "No, it was sick". Shit, where was Marcus when you needed him? I felt my stomach flip at the very thought of him and I tried not to think of him again.

Sadie then told me that Long Arms had called her and I was very careful this time not to call him that to her face. His real name was Ash and apparently he wasn't overly upset about the barfing bedspread incident and had only told Sadie to sleep in the other room because he didn't want to take advantage of her while she was drunk. It was actually quite sweet and although not *exactly* Gone With The Wind, it was as close to a romantic gesture as you were going to get these days and I hadn't seen her *this* happy about a potential date in a long time.

"Wow. He must *really* like you". It was sincerely meant; if someone blew chunks on my new home furnishings, I don't think I'd have been so understanding.

"You think?"

"Absofruitly, my friend. So have you decided where you're going?" I was wondering where one with such long arms would frequent? A bowling alley maybe? A zoo? Tyre swings at the park?

"I haven't said yes. Do you think I should go? It's supposed to be tomorrow. He *was* quite sweet on the phone and was really nice about the whole vomit thing. He *was* good looking too, wasn't he?"

"He was very easy on the eye. I say give it a try hon and if it goes well, you can bring him to the party on Saturday".

She was wiping her face and hands with the kitchen roll. "See, I can *totally* pull a hot bloke. I told Marcus he was good looking and I don't think he believed me".

I looked up slowly from my noodles. Had Sadie been in contact with Marcus? Had they been meeting secretly at lunchtimes and he told her not to tell me? They did work almost opposite one another, maybe they'd run into each other on the High Street? I stopped guessing and asked, "Have you *seen* Marcus?"

"Yeah, the morning after I met Ash, before he got sick". I breathed a sigh of relief and then Sadie added, "I told him that besides you, I was with the best looking guy in Vom's". She got up and took her plate to the kitchen.

I was trying to finish off the last of my noodles, really needing a fork; the chopsticks had given me finger cramp. I was surprised at *just* how long it took for Sadie's comment to register. 'Besides me?' What did she mean, 'besides me?' "Sade?" I was in the kitchen like a shot. "What was that about Vom's, hon?" Even though I hadn't actually finished, Sadie grabbed my plate from me, scraped the remains into the bin and put it in the washing up bowl in one swift move.

Trying to get information out of Sadie was hard; she didn't always tell you the whole story. You'd often get footnotes and then find out something really integral to the story at a later date. "I told him that he was tall, dark and handsome and that he'd made a bee line for *me*". She was smiling to herself as she cleaned and rinsed her plate and put it on the side.

I didn't want to detract from her moment. "He did babe, he only had eyes for you". That was enough of that. "So what was that about Marcus and Vom's?"

She was slowly cleaning the next plate now in a circular motion; it was almost hypnotic. "He did, didn't he? He ignored all the other girls and came straight over to me".

Her rinsing was so mechanical and precise, I wanted to grab the plate and smash it but I was giving myself away and needed to exert some self control, so I grabbed the tea towel and began drying. "He did, *straight* over... Now what was that about Vom's and Marcus?"

She was beaming as she obliviously cleaned the Wok, it was torturous; even worse than the time she subjected me to an EastEnders omnibus. "Out of all those pretty people, he chose *me*".

"He did honey, just you". I needed to change tact. "Out of all those pretty people, like Luke for example, he's pretty, what did..."

She panicked and cut in. "Why would Ash go for Luke? Do you think he's *gay?*"

I inhaled very, very deeply. "No Sweets, Ash isn't gay and he wouldn't go for Luke, I was just merely noticing that Luke was a good looking man, like Ash and that you said something to Marcus about that. *What did* you say to Marcus about Luke?" I managed to get the entire sentence out in one breath.

She cleaned the cutlery while she thought about her conversation, "Errr, I think I said that '*I* was with the biggest fox there' and *then* I remembered and said, 'oh no, you were chatting to Luke but besides that, he was definitely the best looking'... or *something* like that".

"So he knows I was talking to Luke?"

"Yep. *Why?* Shouldn't I have said that?"

I picked up the cutlery to dry it, putting it away one by one. "No, no. It's fine, I was just... it's fine, hon". I flashed her a big smile. "Don't worry about Ash, he *obviously* likes you and he seems like a really nice guy. I have to go ring Jenna about tonight".

I was planning on cancelling with Jenna but suddenly I welcomed the distraction. The night was filled with the usual chit-chat; I commented on her shoes and she complimented my bag but then after a few sherbets she went into some very graphic detail about her illicit relationship. I sat looking at her while she talked, realising I'd seen her more in the last few weeks than I had in the last few years and that was a pretty sad state of affairs (poor choice of words considering the circumstances perhaps) but maybe that's why she'd done it, maybe she *had* turned over a new leaf but she'd felt so friendless and so alone that she'd reached out to the first person that paid her any attention; Barry, the delivery man.

Surprise, surprise, she hadn't spoken to her husband about their issues; she said she'd become too scared to. It wasn't that David was *physically* abusive, far from it, but he had certainly laid down the law (excuse the pun), about how he expected his wife to behave. She criticised their love life, as it used to be an ongoing joke that she was 'banged to rights' every night but apparently now she was more likely to be 'let off with a caution'. The old Jenna would have walked away from such a limp excuse (the pun's just keep on coming) but it was not surprising that the *new* Jenna avoided confrontation and found solace in the arms of another. After all, she still had the old Jenna's sex drive.

Jenna was about to order her third drink when she noticed I'd hardly touched my first. "Wow, you *really* are flogging yourself over this one, aren't you, Dobby".

I laughed, "I'm just not that thirsty tonight and I've got a busy weekend planned".

Jenna ordered another drink for herself and took a giant gulp. "Ahh yes, the *party*. Will you and Marcus be hosting it as friends or as a couple?" I told her all about Marcus' disappearing act and that I didn't know if he would even be attending his own party and she used the shock as an excuse to down another two large mouthfuls. She enquired after my busy weekend and I filled her in on Thursday's intended pampering, seeing Carly and then preparations for the party but her face turned sour. I'd only ever seen a change of look *that* drastic once before, when we'd all been out for a meal and Luke talked Greg into eating a jalapeño pepper and mid-conversation Greg went grey and started to sweat; I've *never* seen anyone run so fast. I looked at Jenna again; worried that she may suddenly start Sally Gunnell'ing it over the bar stools towards the toilets. Perhaps the wine hadn't agreed with her?

She downed the rest of her glass and proved that the wine and her were getting along just fine. "I didn't know you were in contact with her". She signalled the bartender and ordered up her fourth and I had a *déjà vu* back to my heated conversation with Marcus.

"I *hadn't* been but she sent me an email the other week, asking to meet before the party to catch up". My smile soon dissipated; it would appear I'd disturbed the hornets' nest, so I decided I'd better start drinking up.

"Catch up with *what?* She left *you* remember, when you needed her the most. I don't see how you can just let her back in your life like that". OK, so I hadn't just disturbed the hornets' nest, I'd clearly whacked it with a large stick. I *had* hoped she'd be glad I was trying to build bridges.

Honesty was the best policy. "I miss her Jen. I want the chance to say sorry for that night".

Jenna's volume increased dramatically, "I've told you, *how* many times? You don't need to apologise, you did *nothing* wrong. All you did was have a drink and a laugh; it's not your problem if she hasn't got a sense of humour". I sat quietly, not knowing what to say. "I mean, for Christ's sake! Who does she think she is that *you* have to apologise to *her*? You have to cancel tomorrow mate, you need to trust me... she is *not* your friend".

Can open; worms everywhere. Jenna obviously had an issue or two surrounding this and I didn't want to aggravate her any further, especially since she'd knocked a few back in a very short space of time and was now swaying on her stool. I suggested we walked down the High Street to Dribbler's, she happily agreed, thinking we were on a pub crawl but I just needed to get her outside, I figured the fresh air would do her some good.

Chapter 27

The longest week of my life was thankfully, *almost* over. Despite my fragile mental state, I made it in to work dead on 9:00am and I saw Amanda check her watch for effect as I sat down. She looked up, smiled and I clenched my teeth and semi-smiled back. Just *two* more days at work until the party, just *two* more days. I got my head down again and even managed to sort out loads of problems where customers had gone online to reorganise some of their own details but failed to tell us, so today, I was a hero. I basked briefly, as I was sure it wouldn't last but more importantly, it meant I brooked no opposition when I asked if I could leave early tonight, so I could run up the road just in time for my much needed treatments.

    I must have looked like a crazed woman when I arrived dishevelled, out of breath and wheezing like an asthmatic, in my ridiculous uniform. Luckily, Sadie was there, so she gave my name to her colleague who ticked me off the list and told me to take a seat. I'd brought some trakkies, a hoodie and some flip flops to change in to, as I was having a manicure, pedicure *and* an Indian Head Massage. I had no idea what the latter was but it was supposed to relaxingly relieve stress, so it sounded just the ticket. I had my hands and feet done first and then was whisked into a dimly lit, towel-filled room that stank of flowery things. There was some soft Amazonian music playing in the background as a young girl (whose name I didn't quite catch but it sounded like Chlamydia?) started rubbing oils in to my head. It was incredibly soothing and I nearly nodded off on a few occasions, only to be woken by sound of mating whales and fornicating frogs through the speakers. By the time she'd finished, I felt so light-headed; I thought I might float away.

Sadie was just finishing up and I needed some air, so I walked outside like a mechanical toy, while I waited for her to drive me back. My legs were stiff and far apart, my fingers and toes splayed and my hair oiled, ruffled up and part standing on end; I looked like Edward Scissorhands. It was of course, at that *very* moment, that the fate's aligned and decided to bestow upon me a piece of my punishment; *that's* when I saw him. I should have known, Sadie worked almost opposite and it was no real surprise he was working late, Marcus *always* worked late. He was running over the road and I wanted to wave but caught a glimpse of my reflection in the shop window and decided now *really* wasn't the time. He was running towards the alleyway between two shops to the car park when Sadie came out. We took the same alley and I just saw the dust kick up, as his car raced off.

Sadie excitedly talked about her date all the way home and I admit I was a little jealous. When we got in, she did a quick floor show in three possible outfit combinations; I chose option number two, so naturally, she went with number three. My French manicure had dried, so I helped straighten her hair, while she put on the rest of her make-up; she was good to go. I promised not to wait up, reminded her of the rules of the 'GOJF' text and waved her off. Our little girl was growing up.

I was alone in the house again and took a moment to look in the full length mirror and caught the complete, uncensored horror of my appearance. And I'm still single...? Yeah, you remember. If I were Marcus, I would've run from me too. I was back to wearing the hair shirt, the fibreglass pants *and* the barbed wire slippers. He was obviously running from *me*, so it begged the question, was he *ever* coming home? After all, this *was* his house, Sadie and I just rented off him. Marcus bought the house when we were 23, he bought it on his own but with the understanding that I would immediately move in with him; Marcus, like myself, hated to be alone. It was my idea to rent out the third room, he didn't need the money as he earned big, it was *me* that thought it would be fun to have more people around, almost like living at Uni. I'd sadly missed out on the University experience but I loved it when I went to visit Alice and Emma and wanted to recreate it. Well, that and I'd been watching *way* too much 'Friends'. Marcus didn't argue, I don't think he was too keen on the idea, but he didn't argue.

It was probably just as well there *was* someone else living in the house. Now that I know the old mattress jig was on the list of possibilities, Jenna could have been right, this *might* have happened sooner and our friendship could have gone down the can years ago. I wondered what my life would have been like if Marcus *hadn't* been in it and I honestly don't know what I would have done without him and I don't know what I'm going to do if he doesn't come back. I just wish I knew what was going through his mind; was it that he'd crossed a friendship or sexuality boundary? Or was it that he'd crossed those boundaries with me? There were also some external factors that had to be considered, like Luke. Marcus hated him; I hadn't realised *quite* how much until the other week when he found him in the kitchen and I now know (a little late in the game) that Marcus left after hearing I'd been talking to Luke but what did that *mean?* I know Marcus had banned Luke from the house but it was a bit much to expect that I'd never run into him in our tiny village or small neighbouring town. However, Marcus *didn't* know that I'd argued with Luke, maybe he thought that our 'chat' was more intimate. Oh God, I hoped not! It was like my own web of intrigue. For a very brief moment, I was nodding appreciatively, that *I* Nicola Thompson was at the centre of... I shook my head, this wasn't cool, this was happening now. Maybe in years to come, when I have the wondrous benefits of hindsight, I can nod appreciatively once more but right now, this was all pretty crap.

Enough was enough; I was starting to piss *myself* off with all the whining self pity, so I decided to look to the positives. I had an empty house and an empty house, meant that any wine I opened belonged solely to me, no-one would pinch my Minstrels *and* I had full power over the remote control. I was looking forward to tonight, throw in an evening of American trash TV and it was some of my favourite guilty pleasures all rolled in to one but clearly the fate's weren't done with me as there was a knock at the door. I jumped up out of my seat and ran down the hall, maybe he *had* seen me, maybe it had prompted him to come home but why did he knock? Maybe he'd forgotten his keys; maybe he was just being a gentleman, maybe?

"Hi Nic!" It was Emma.

"Oh, hi". I leaned against the hall wall not hiding my disappointment.

"Cheers, good to see you, too!" She looked me up and down. "Hungover?"

"Sorry mate. No, I'm fine. I was just… you know, finalising things for the party". It was the first thing that sprang to mind.

"Is this a *bad* time?"

Her smiles unnerved me, I couldn't help but wonder if she'd hidden her kids round the corner and was about to ask me to look after them again. She started talking and managed to explain in under sixty seconds that she *was* alone, 'That' Justin had the kids and she just wanted to get out of the house for half an hour, so thought she'd pop round. She gestured if it was OK for her to come in but I was still wary, if it was advice she was after, I was hardly in the mood but this is what friends did, this could be my penance, so I smiled and opened the door fully for her to enter. I poured her a glass of *my* wine and watched as she sat in *my* chair, while I took up residence on the sofa. I had to control the daggers from my eyes when I saw her reach for a Minstrel and I was on the edge of my seat ready to intercept any repetitive chocolate manoeuvres with a swift grab and twist of the arm, which would result in her somersaulting over and landing on her back (I learned that one from her kids last week). I had to quickly remind myself that this was my atonement and relaxed back into the sofa. We watched a little TV, we chatted for a while about what we'd planned for Saturday, she enquired about the food as apparently the children were on a special diet (probably eating other small children) and we reminisced about the joint parties Marcus and I had thrown in the past.

We *had* put on some impressive displays over the years that seemed to get more extravagant as we got older. Our sweet sixteen was a gun-toting, rootin tootin, Wild West theme, which was outdone by our sixties soundtrack, Dirty Dancing themed 18th party where we had the 'Time of Our Lives'. Our Circus oriented

Best of Friends?

21st saw people dressed as ringmasters, acrobats, fortune-tellers and bearded ladies, we'd hired jugglers and some fella on stilts (which turned nasty when he drank the spiked punch). Then our last big joint shindig was our 25th birthday, it was fancy dress *yet again* and this time the theme was Horror. Just as well really, as it all kicked off that night between Craig and Luke, so we pretended it was all part of the act (come to think of it, I've still no idea what that fight was about). However, it *was* a classic as Alice got upset because Carly lied about her costume, which naturally, Alice copied and bless her, she'd put quite a lot of effort into her 'Orc' from Lord of the Rings and was having trouble drowning her sorrows through the fake teeth but all the outfits that night were hilarious. Luke was supposed to be the Clown from Stephen King's 'IT' but he looked more 'Krusty' from the Simpson's, Emma came as Medusa complete with tinfoil snakes in her hair and 'That' Justin came as 'Chucky', the demented ginger doll but Marcus thought he was a dead ringer for Mick Hucknell. Mitchell and Daniel came as a *very* camp Freddy and Jason and then you had your generics, who lacked the creativity for fancy dress, as there were half a dozen Frankenstein's, a few Devils and I lost count of the number of Dracula's, although it did seem to be a source of bonding, over the mini quiche, as they discussed where they got their outfits. Marcus went as a very debonair Jack the Ripper and I went as Carrie, which in hindsight wasn't such a great idea, as I was coated in ketchup and it just made me feel hungry all night.

Emma and I laughed away the hours and she didn't ask for any advice, she didn't dwell on unhappy subjects, she didn't eat too many of my Minstrels and I didn't mind if she drank too much of my wine. It was a really nice evening, something Emma and I hadn't done in a *really* long time. It was well over two hours before she finally left and I didn't mind one bit.

Chapter 28

Carly and Pete arrived at lunchtime and spent the afternoon with Pete's parents, as promised and Carly texted me to confirm our meeting. I was really looking forward to seeing her but I was also feeling sick with anxiety, as Jenna's comments had shaken me. Tonight really *could* go either way and with the week I've had, I wasn't sure how much more I could take.

I left work dead on 5:00pm, desperate to start my weekend. Everyone wished me well and promised to see me the following night at the party. I'd even invited Amanda and her husband Brian to come along (I felt I had to) but I secretly hoped that their babysitter would let them down. Failing that, I had an elaborate plan B, where I would break-in to their house and sneak some laxatives in the dog water. As it stood, it looked like she was still coming... I'd best dust off the balaclava.

As I walked through the door of Dribbler's, I spotted her instantly. I wasn't late, I was *actually* on time for once but Pete was meeting the boys there, so Carly had joined him; she had back-up and I had to agree, it was a *smart* move. We'd timed things well too, we only had to fill the first fifteen minutes with light banter before our reservations at the restaurant. It was Pete who saw me first. "Nic!" He gave me a massive bear hug. "Alright babes. Blimey, you brush up well!"

"Thanks!" I turned my attention to the Carly. "Hey Carl". We hugged but it felt awkward. "How are you?"

Carly smiled sweetly but it was obvious she was nervous too. "I'm good thanks. *You* look well".

"Thank you, so do you".

There was a big pause but thankfully Pete filled the gap. "Can I get you two ladies a drink?"

Carly replied first, "Vodka and diet coke, please hon".

I smiled knowing we still liked the same drink but tonight I had a point to prove. "I'll just have a diet coke please, Pete". Carly looked at me like I'd just told her I'd taken up prostitution and I ignored it.

Pete wandered off to the bar and we were left alone for a few minutes. We turned to each other and started talking at the same time, both stopping to laugh. I then offered, "You first".

"I was just wondering what happened to NMT?" She meant 'Nicky Mean Time', my lateness was long reigning and infamous; so they had named it NMT, which was GMT + fifteen minutes.

"Ha! I was aiming to get here for quarter past seven, so it's *still* in effect".

Carly smiled, "Glad to hear it".

We made small talk about their journey, Pete's folks, where they were living and Carly's new surprising career as a restaurateur. I zoned out for a second when I realised that I'd never seen where or how they lived, I'd missed so much. Pete, the intermediary, was back to cover our silences. "So where's Marcus?"

I felt my heart sink to my stomach. "Err... he's at his dad's at the moment. You should give him a ring; he'd love to see you". I desperately hoped they didn't detect my badly packed emotional baggage.

"I did, he said he couldn't make it but didn't say why. Shame, *love* that geezer. So where you working now, Nic?"

I took a moment to wonder what Marcus was doing then forced my attention back to Pete. "I'm still in the same job. Six years now!" Carly and Pete both knowingly nodded, acknowledging my impressive record.

Carly and I joined the boys and we all stood together talking. Then Pete tapped his watch. "You ladies better get going or you'll miss your dinner".

We left and did the obligatory climb over all the smokers, who were now forced to stand outside. "Do you miss it?"

Carly was gesturing back towards the puffing crowd as we walked towards the restaurant. It had taken every ounce of willpower I had, to quit smoking and it was an achievement I was proud of. "Sometimes. Not on a cold night or when it's hoofing it down though, no! I still crave one after a good drink".

"That'll be every night then!" Carly was laughing and I joined her but at least it confirmed that she still thought I had a drink problem, my non-alcoholic choice earlier had been a wise one.

Not being able to find words was not usually an issue for me (however inappropriate some of the ones that did come out were) but now I was struggling. We filled the walk with chit-chat about Brighton and she told me she loved it there but that she missed the people here. We were doing OK, we were both trying to make it work and I just prayed that we would at least make it past the starters before it all went breasts up.

We were seated straight away and ordered a couple of drinks with another soft drink for me as we talked briefly about Emma, Alice and Jenna and what they'd been up to, only stopping to place our order, including extra water, which seemed to baffle my vodka swilling dinner partner.

It was a perfectly pleasant evening and so I surprised myself by being the one to raise it but it *had* been like a cloud over us and I didn't see the point in dragging it out any further, we needed to clear the air. "So?"

She looked apprehensive. "So".

I was tentative. I wasn't usually known for my subtlety but I really didn't want to put my foot in it tonight. I thought carefully about my next statement before I said it, "I guess we should talk about... the last time we saw each other".

"I guess so".

I paused for a moment to compose myself. "Your leaving do. I want to apologise to you and Pete for how drunk I got that night. It was... childish and inappropriate". I had been practising that apology all afternoon; I wanted to get the words out clearly and concisely. "When you said you were leaving, I was devastated and that's why I kind of knocked 'em back that night and also... I was a little jealous".

"*Jealous?*"

"We used to talk about leaving here, remember? Going off to some far flung place. Then suddenly you were going and I was left behind. You said you were sick of this place... and I thought that meant *me* too". Carly shook her head and went to speak; I cut her off quickly. "It's pretty mortifying saying this now because we've grown up since then but I felt I owed you an explanation for my behaviour at the time and I'm sorry".

"No, *I'm* sorry. I hadn't realised you'd taken it that way. I was just so frustrated, Nic. Honest mate, it was nothing to do with you and *everything* to do with my mum". Carly took a deep breath and explained. "She'd phone when we were out to say we'd left a light on and were wasting energy. Every time we had a party, she'd turn up the next day to say everyone had been talking about the noise, she'd pop in on her way to Bridge Club and start criticising the colour we painted the lounge and we came back from work one day to find her in the garden, because she felt we were neglecting our plants and *then* there was..." Carly looked around, as if she were on covert ops. "If I tell you this, please don't tell Pete I told you".

"Of *course* not". I was intrigued and leaned in, trying not to get my top in my dinner.

"Pete and I were in bed, you know..." She gestured something with her eyebrows. "We hear someone knock at the door but Pete's in the middle of some of his best work, so naturally, we didn't answer. The next thing we know, we hear the door go. She'd let herself in with the spare emergency key we'd given her and was calling up the stairs!"

"Nooo way!" I took a sharp intake of breath and held my hands up over my mouth.

Carly nodded wide-eyed. "I'm not shitting you Nic, Pete threw on some jogging bottoms and a t-shirt, unfortunately, he didn't realise until half-way down the stairs that he'd put on *my* jogging bottoms and they were a little tight round his nethers. He looked like an extra in Swan Lake". We both took a moment to have a little chuckle. "Anyway, my mum says she saw the car outside, so thought we must be in and obviously didn't hear her knocking. That was the final straw, it was *totally* humiliating".

I was shaking my head in astonishment. "I can't believe your mum *did* that, that's not just crossing the line, that's charging over it in a steam-roller".

"I *know!* We had to get out after that. Pete's firm had already announced that they were opening up a new office in Brighton and wanted to know if anyone was interested in moving down there to help set it up. They were offering a hefty relocation package, so it was a no-brainer".

I poured out some more water and offered some to Carly and she declined. She eyed me suspiciously again; searching my face for answers, sighed and then gave in, "OK, what's going on?"

"With what?"

"With the water and the diet cokes. Is there something up?" Carly looked from the water towards my stomach area. "Something you're not telling me?"

I laughed and nearly choked on my dinner. "*What?!* No! You've gotta be kidding!" I decided to tell her honestly, "When you left, you made it clear you thought I had a drink problem. I was merely demonstrating that I don't". I smiled a little sarcastically and looked back down towards my dinner.

"Drink problem? If anyone's got a drink problem it's Jenna, not you! Christ! I *never* said you had a drink problem!"

I looked around us, a few people had caught the end of that, so I lowered my voice to almost a whisper and repeated Carly's departing statement back to her about me apparently not seeing what was under my nose. She immediately stopped what she was doing, put down her knife and fork and put her head in her hands. What did I say?

Suddenly all the other noise from the restaurant just faded away and you could've heard a pin drop. I looked around again and a few people were now staring at me, obviously wondering what I'd said to cause this adverse reaction; I smiled back which made them quickly look away. I wanted to say something to Carly but I didn't know *what* and then finally, she spoke, "What do you remember about the night of our leaving do?"

I thought for a moment. "Well, I remember it was in the function room above Dribbler's, there was a punch up, you were yelling at Pete to stop him trying to kill Luke, which caused a barney with Jenna and then you told me I was stupid and didn't have a fucking clue and then we left". I tried smiling to take the edge off. It didn't work.

Carly was searching my face again. "Is that it?"

"Why? Did someone else pitch in or throw a punch?"

Best of Friends?

I was falsely chuckling, trying to make light but Carly's face was stony as she spoke quietly and precisely, "I didn't tell you, you were stupid but I did say you didn't have a clue. There's a *big* difference".

I sat back in my chair and tried to regain some composure but I was confused. So she wasn't mad at me because she thought I had a drink problem and Jenna told me that she and Carly had argued because a drunken Pete had tried to hit Luke for no reason. I just didn't understand why Carly was so upset now? I had this awful feeling of dread.

We sat there for a moment; neither of us saying anything but each one trying to read the other one's mind. Carly picked up her cutlery then said, "You want to finish up, get the bill and get out of here?"

I was surprised. Was *that* it? She didn't want to talk anymore? I don't even know what I'd said; I'd just answered her honestly. Fortunately, she saw my face and cut back in before I *really* went off on a tangent. "There's that pub over the road that was always a bit quieter, maybe we could talk properly in there?"

She looked around the room, indicating that our conversation was hardly private and I followed her gaze to see the stares and glares and quickly agreed. "Sounds like a plan, Stan". We smiled at each other, finished off our food in record time, got the bill and left.

Chapter 29

The dress was on, the hair was coiffed, the shoes were broken in and now I was just applying the finishing touches as tonight was the night we'd spent forever planning, the night I'd been dreading; the night of our big party.

It had been almost a week since I'd seen Marcus and up until this afternoon, there was *still* a strong possibility that he might not show. It was a text from Alice to double-check what I was wearing that also happened to mention she'd seen him in town and that he was looking forward to the party. It was a miraculous turn around, he was coming! It meant I had a chance to put things right and my reparation skills were in pretty good shape after last night's amends with Carly.

It had been a fruitful night, we'd managed to sort out some petty squabbles over dinner and then we left the restaurant and walked quickly to the pub opposite to tackle the main ones. We'd never gone in that pub before, as it was always deemed *far* too quiet for our crowd, so it had no nickname. Luckily, the possible naming of the venue took my mind away from the anticipation. Carly obviously had a good tale to tell but I wasn't sure it was one I'd enjoy. We walked in and it was like a scene from 'American Werewolf in London', the door creaked and all the regulars looked up quizzically from their ale at the unknowns that had entered their domain. I looked around to see if there was a pentagram etched on the wall and half expected the elderly barman to say in a heavy West Country accent, "You're not from round these parts". As it was, he seemed really nice. "What can I get you ladies?"

"Two vodka and diet cokes and a tequila, if you have some, please". Carly was smiling sweetly and the barman obliged.

I was impressed. "Tequila? You really *are* getting on one tonight!"

Carly waited until the barman had poured the Tequila and brought it back over to us before she answered, "It's not for me, it's for you. You've got some catching up to do". She placed it in front of me and I looked from Carly, to the tequila, to the barman, who shrugged his shoulders. I breathed out and took the tequila in my right hand and then made the Catholic sign of the cross with my left and downed the tequila. I was still wincing, while Carly paid, picked up our vodka's and gestured towards a table away from everyone else, in the corner. I followed, still reeling from my tequila, shaking my head as if I had a nervous tick.

We sat down and Carly took a big mouthful of her drink and then played with her glass, placing it symmetrically in the middle of the beer mat on the table. I was just watching her; I'd never seen her like this before. "The night of the party, you were pretty hammered".

"You don't have to tell me, mate. I spent almost all the next day talking to God on the porcelain phone". Maybe a little *too* much information.

Carly took another deep breath and I wondered if I needed to run out and get her an asthma pump. "It's fairly clear that a lot of what went on that night… was not *observed* by you".

Observed by me? She was being so careful with her words. I decided to clarify. "Is this the part where I '*didn't have a fucking clue*'?"

Carly grimaced at the replay of her own words back to her but then looked relieved that I understood her meaning. "Yes it is". Carly took another big mouthful of drink.

"Do you want me to get another round in?" I gestured towards her now near empty drink and went to stand up.

Carly grabbed my arm and pulled me back down again. "No!" Carly composed herself. "That night, you and Jenna were knocking some back at the bar. I heard Jenna telling you '*screw her; she obviously couldn't give a shit about you*". Carly mimicked Jenna's accent. "I *assumed* you were talking about me as you said something back to her about me being a crap mate".

"Carly, I…"

Carly cut straight back in, "I *know*, don't worry, you'd had a lot to drink and she was winding you up, I *know* that. It's just she was at the bar with you, pretending to be your best mate and all the time, she'd been…" Carly stopped and shook her head. "You and Luke, you'd always had this thing and for all I know you still are, and…"

Best of Friends?

I dived back in. "No. Trust me, that is *SO* over".

Carly closed her eyes. "I'm glad; because he was playing you".

Carly most definitely had my full attention as I mulled over her interesting choice of words. She looked up from her drink to hold my gaze then looked back down as she continued, "Our party, Luke told me he needed to talk about you. He'd been hitting on me since Primary School, so I normally would've stayed away but he said it was about you, so we went outside. Before I knew it, he'd cornered me in the Car Park and wouldn't let me leave". Carly's eyes welled up. "He said he had feelings for me, that it wasn't too late to change my mind about Pete". She was biting the inside of her mouth and trying not to cry but a few stray tears slowly made their way down her face. "He really frightened me that night; he wouldn't let me go, I tried to get past him and he forced me back and tried to kiss me. I kneed him in the groin but I obviously didn't catch him right and he just held me tighter, so I scraped my shoe down his shin as hard as I could, he let go and I ran back upstairs to the party".

My heart had fallen so deep in to my stomach, it needed a submersible and I had a sudden need for another tequila. Carly continued, "I wasn't gonna tell Pete anything, I knew he'd lose it but then Luke came strutting back in, trying to cover up a limp and then immediately started flirting with you again, buying you loads of drinks and trying to get you to leave with him. Pete saw my face, so I only told Pete that he'd drunkenly come on to me; *nothing* else but Pete was over to him before I could warn you. If anything, Pete was trying to protect *you*".

The 'big fight' now all made horrible sense as my head started to flood with memories. Pete had come storming over and shoved

Luke back hard towards the bar, which made Luke spill his drink on my shoes. Luke had managed to look shocked that Pete had just attacked him out of nowhere. "Whoa there, buddy, what's your problem?!"

Me, well on my way, chimed in for good measure. "Yeah, for fuck's sake Pete, these are new shoes!" What a lady. Pete looked at me like I was a Class A moron and now I know why. Pete had Luke by the scruff of his neck and told him to stay away from *all* of us. I cringed, as I remembered telling Pete to stay out of my business and I'll see who I want to see and then I believe I called him an arsehole. Carly came running over, astounded that I had stuck up for Luke and pulled Pete away. She then asked to speak to me, saying it was important and Jenna came over and told Carly to leave me alone, they argued about something or other and I went to walk away, that's when Carly told me I didn't have a clue and then Pete hit Luke for 'no reason', Jenna and I picked up an injured Luke and then we left the party.

I sat there, staring at the table. It was like a veil had been lifted and suddenly I realised, "What did Luke say to Pete that made him hit him?"

Carly looked pained. "He told Pete he could taste strawberries". I looked confused, so she enlightened me. "It was my lip gloss... Luke was letting Pete know that he'd kissed me".

I felt sick. Carly and Pete had given me every opportunity to see the truth and I'd ignored them; I'd just believed everything that Jenna and Luke had told me. It took a while for any words to come out and when they did, I kept repeating them. "Oh my God. Oh my God!" Carly didn't say anything; she just let me process it for a minute. "I didn't know Carly, I swear! I just... I thought you were pissed at me because I got tanked at your party, I had no idea".

"You thought I'd lose it over something like that? Shit Nic, we'd have fallen out at 14, when you first discovered the delights of alcohol!" She smiled at me and I managed a little chuckle.

I quickly reverted back to feeling like a prize idiot. My naivety throughout this whole mess had astounded me and I felt ashamed. I told her what had happened after they left, what Luke and Jenna had told me; everything I'd been led to believe.

Carly's eyes narrowed and then she nodded. "I realise now that you didn't know. For a long time, I thought you *had* to have known. You're a smart girl, you *had* to have seen what was going on but I think I'm beginning to get it. This wasn't just about you and Luke; you had someone *else* in your ear".

I got up and went to the bar and she let me leave this time, I think it gave us both a chance to soak it all in. I looked back towards Carly who was staring at the wall. I'd been feeling sorry for myself these last three years, wondering why one of my best mates would desert me and the whole time, she must've been thinking the same thing, except I'd deserted *her* when she needed me the most. I went back to the table and Carly thanked me for the drink, she looked apprehensive and I became anxious, letting out an involuntary laugh. "You're not going to tell me there's more are you?" I picked up my drink and took a massive gulp.

"I think we've had enough revelations for one night, don't *you?*"

"I've been joking with myself lately that I've been dropping IQ points but I don't think I've *ever* felt as stupid as I do right now". I smiled at Carly, "I should have seen. I was spectacularly shit-faced that night but it's *no* excuse, I should've been there for you. I won't ever forgive myself for that. You were my best friend Carl, you and Marcus". It was the first time I'd thought about him in hours and I felt my chest tighten. "I really know how to fuck up a friendship".

"It's not your fault, Nic. It looks like we've *all* been part of the game". She took a sip of her drink and said casually, "How *is* Marcus? I miss him. Actually, I'm surprised you haven't mentioned him more, you two are *usually* thick as thieves".

I glanced up but couldn't hold her gaze... Damn it! I suddenly realised what I'd just said and she knew, just from *one* look that probably lasted half of a second, she knew. "Oh my God! *Marcus?*"

I swallowed hard. "What if I told you that...?" Carly leaned in closer, looking wide-eyed. I could feel my mouth drying up and my voice begin to crack. "Well, let's just say that you had... 'relations' with someone that you shouldn't have".

It was like being back in Confession; but Carly was no Priest. "Relations? As in the horizontal mambo?"

I was looking at the table, I couldn't look her in the eye. "Yes". I heard Carly gasp. "Well, maybe a rumba with a tango thrown in".

"I can't dance, is that *good?*" Carly was biting her lip now, to stop herself from laughing and no doubt stop her jaw hitting the table again.

"Yes it is, it's *very* good, it's the best... *dancing* you've ever done. Probably because it's the first time your... *dance* partner has partnered... well, someone like you and he's taken the time to really... learn the steps, you know?"

Best of Friends?

I could see Carly was still trying to work it out. "I think so…"

I confessed everything about what happened the week before with Luke (which was extremely uncomfortable considering our earlier discussions), up to the night I told Luke his fortune, which she seemed to enjoy and then the *entire* Marcus saga. I told her how I had come to realise that I might have feelings for him, how I was going crazy not seeing him, my Edward Scissorhands impression and my trip to Confession and she quite rightly laughed her arse off. She asked so many questions, questions I'd asked myself and I was really glad I'd told her, I knew she would understand; she was the only person who could.

We spent the rest of the night swapping childhood stories about A-Team re-enactments with wheelbarrows and corrugated iron and our made up dances to 'Bucks Fizz'. Then we finally and aptly decided upon a name for our drinking venue; 'Confessions'. It may have been years that we hadn't seen each other but by the end of the night, it really only seemed like weeks and when time came to say goodnight, she gave me such a massive hug and said, "Christ, I've missed you". The feeling was totally mutual.

My reconciliation with Carly, had given me hope. Marcus was definitely coming to our birthday celebrations tonight and that meant I *finally* had a chance to talk to him. I took one last look in the mirror; I was ready. Well, as ready as I'll ever be.

Chapter 30

The Party - Nicky & Marcus

The place looked amazing; Mitchell and Daniel had done a fantastic job. The Gods were obviously smiling down on us as the sun was shining and we could open up the side doors and our guests could spill outside. The food was being laid out and looked like a feast fit for a King (assuming of course, that the King likes flan). I arrived an hour early, hoping to bump into Marcus but he wasn't here yet. I just needed to be patient, he'd definitely be here early, even if he did think I was the chosen one, prophesied to bring about the apocalypse; he could never bring himself to be late for anything.

I was wrong. The first guest's arrived and I dutifully welcomed them without really paying attention as I was fixated on the main doors. The next guest, then the next guests, then the next. I was now surrounded by people and they were all asking after Marcus but he was nowhere to be seen. Just moments later, there were hands on my waist and a whisper in my ear. "Hey babe, Happy

Birthday". I turned round quickly, really hoping it wasn't but it was; it was Luke and I'd accidentally spun into his hug. Those Gods were now having a laugh at my expense because it was of course, that *precise* moment that I saw over Luke's shoulder that not only had Marcus arrived, he'd seen me 'hugging' Luke and turned to walk outside. Great! That's just perfect.

I removed Luke's hands from me and with a single look, warned him to stay away. I tried to follow Marcus but got stopped at the first hurdle. "Nicky, Hi!" It was Jeremy and Helen. Jeremy or Jez as he was once known, used to be in our crowd and dated both Emma and Alice (at different times of course) but Helen didn't approve of drunken binges, nicknames and a close proximity to ex-girlfriends and he was no longer allowed out with us.

"Hi, it's great to see you". I was looking straight past them at Mitchell, Daniel and their flan outside talking to Marcus. He looked incredible; he was in a black suit and black shirt, with a white tie and white handkerchief in his top jacket pocket. "Thanks for coming. I hope the journey was OK". I was on autopilot, with the standard polite greetings and it showed; Jeremy and Helen only lived round the corner. Fortunately, they thought I was joking and they started to laugh, so I laughed too and sarcastically added, "In case you're weary from your trip, there's drinks at the bar or there's a potent punch over by the food, please help yourself". They laughed again; I smiled graciously and managed to get away quickly. I looked at the path, between me and Marcus, there were another six couples that I had not yet said hello to. I was mentally trying to work out if I could do an assault course round them, duck under a side table, swing on a light over the next, sniper crawl and roll across the floor, sidle along a window frame and then stepping stone it over the chairs. Could it be done? I really wasn't wearing the dress for it.

Luckily for me, the flan conversation was lengthy, so Marcus was still there. I finished up with my last door-blocking couple, Sarah and Michael. "...Ha ha, well if you're weary from your trip, there's drinks at the bar or there's a potent punch over by the food, please help yourself". I smiled and moved quickly towards the door. Just as I loomed, Mitchell and Daniel headed towards the catering tent and Marcus was alone. He turned to come back inside, saw me approaching, turned on his heels and went to walk the other way. Before I even knew what I was saying, I called out, "Marcus!"

He stopped and slowly turned around. It all happened so quickly that I had no plan of what to say, as if shouting his name wasn't embarrassing enough, I then only managed a pathetic, "Hi".

He was looking around for salvation; it was devastating, he couldn't bear to look at me. "Hey".

"So, how are you?" I searched his face, looking for my friend but I didn't find him.

"Fine, you?"

"I'm good, thanks". It was pretty obvious now, that he *did* blame me for what happened and he wanted the whole thing to go away; including me.

"A load more people have just arrived, I'd better go say hi".

Marcus went to walk past me and out of instinct, I grabbed his arm. "Marcus, we need to talk".

"I know". He looked solemn. "But for now, we should enjoy our party and go and greet our guests". He smiled but it was empty and then he took my hand as a token gesture and we walked back in together.

We welcomed the new arrivals, including a tipsy Jenna and a peeved David. I hadn't spoken to Jenna yet about the revelations from Carly, I hadn't wanted to ruin a good mood and now wasn't the time either but I definitely had one or two things I wanted to say to her. "Hi! Happy Birthdays!" Jenna winked at me and then kept *on* winking at me. She was as subtle as a gay parade and I hoped and prayed Marcus didn't see. She practically ran off to the bar, leaving behind an apologetic David. As soon as he went, Marcus let go of my hand and excused himself and as more guests arrived, all I could do was watch him walk away.

I looked around the room and now that it was filled with people in their black and white, it looked like something from a 1950's musical. When Mitchell and Daniel were finished monopolising Marcus, I would go and thank them again. I went to the bar to get a drink and got chatting to Sadie and Ash, who'd just arrived but was distracted by Luke's laughter resonating as he joked with Simon and next to them in the corner, Jenna was arguing with David. I guess nothing changes; Jenna and Luke still loved to be the centre of attention. I excused myself from my current group and made my way back in to the hall, dutifully making my way around the room talking to guests I hadn't seen arrive and it looked like Marcus was doing the same on the other side. Then just as the party was just gathering some momentum, the music stopped, the lights came on and Mitchell collected our group of friends for a photograph. Mitchell stood Marcus next to me but as he stared straight ahead, not making eye contact I was grateful to feel a friendly arm about my shoulder and turned to see that Carly and Pete had arrived. I grabbed her for a hug and didn't want to let her go; I was so relieved they were there. She seemed to be clinging on to me too; maybe she'd seen how cold Marcus was being? As soon as we all disbanded, Carly and I headed over to the buffet stand to talk but we were surrounded by people and constantly interrupted, so I found myself rambling about the food. Unfortunately, Daniel came and dragged me away as Mitchell was having a hissy fit with the caterers before I properly caught up with Carly.

The DJ was playing our list of favourite songs through the decades and as the night moved on without a hitch, I tried not to think about it or discuss it; I didn't want to put the mockers on it. I was talking to Pete and Craig in the bar when Greg came in looking a little frantic. "Hey Nic, have you seen Jenna anywhere?"

"Jenna? No, sorry... Why? Are you looking for someone to start off a limbo?"

Pete laughed and Craig said, "Miaow, saucer of milk for Thompson!"

Greg chuckled nervously, looked around the room again then left to go outside. Pete sighed, put his beer on the bar and said, "Shit. Excuse me Nicky". He chased after Greg, closely followed by Craig, they grabbed him in the foyer and swiftly marched him back in to the main hall.

I was stood on my own, totally flummoxed and muttering away, when Carly came in. "Talking to yourself again?"

"Yeah, I find I get a better class of answer".

"I hear ya". She was smiling at me and moving me in to a space at the bar away from earshot. "So, you talked to Marcus? I hear from Alice you two were holding hands, I take it *all* is well?" She looked hopeful and I hated to dampen the moment but I told her the hand holding had just been for show and relayed to her our conversation from outside. "Oh". Carly put her arm around me. "Come on, let's get you a drink".

Carly and I were laughing with some old school friends that had joined us when Carly suddenly made a bizarre announcement to excuse us from our present company and then pulled me to one side, out of earshot. "Right, if you put down that drink now, get out your lippy and freshen up, by the time you walk out towards the foyer, you'll get Marcus all to yourself".

I looked up and saw she was serious, didn't question her source and did as I was told. She was a genius and had timed it to perfection, as *just* as I walked out, Marcus came from the men's room across the foyer and it looked as though we'd run into each other by accident. "Hey".

"Hey". He was still looking around for help and sounded uncomfortable. "Been a good party, eh?"

"Yeah, Mitchell and Daniel did a great job, it looks amazing". I smiled at him but he turned away.

I almost didn't hear him as he said, "So do you, by the way". I don't think he meant to say it as he turned bright red.

He suddenly reached in his pocket for his phone, I had a sneaking suspicion he was about to pull a 'GOJF' text on me, so I spoke quickly. "Marcus, we need to talk about what happened".

Seconds felt like hours, before he put the phone away and placed both his hands in his pockets. He started rocking back and forth on his heels as he looked down at his shoes. Then he looked at me, for the first time since this all happened, held my gaze and waited for me to speak.

I steadied myself and obliged. "That night was…" The door opened and music came flooding out. One of our guests, came out of the hall towards the toilets, it was Simon. We both turned and smiled at him and waited for him to disappear. As soon as the door closed, he turned to back to face me and I continued on, "That night was kinda crazy, you know?"

The rocking returned. "I do".

I bent my head trying to see his face. "I'd never intentionally do anything to hurt you…"

My apology was cut short again as Jenna suddenly walked in through the front door, she must have been outside having a smoke. She looked dishevelled and surprised to see us. "Oh, hey? What ya doin' out here?" She started giggling; she was clearly hammered.

Marcus answered, "Nothing, we'll be in, in a minute". He smiled at her as she headed off with the one-legged walk towards the ladies. He looked at me then remembered, "Oh and Greg was looking for you". Jenna was fumbling and mumbling into her bag as she stumbled towards the loo.

Marcus turned back round only to stare at his shoes again. I was the only one doing the talking. "I would never disrespect you or your values, you know that, right?" I was worried it sounded like I'd practised this, probably because I had, a hundred times over. His rocking intensified and he now resembled a schizophrenic but I kept going, "We're friends Marcus, *best* friends. You mean the world to me; I would *never* want to ruin that. I…"

Simon was now exiting the men's room and heading back across the foyer towards the hall. We both turned to him and smiled, the door to the hall opened, the music came flooding out and we both waited impatiently for the door to close before we turned back to face one another. The next part was completely unplanned and just came out. "I *miss* you, please come home".

He looked up at me with a pained expression and breathed out with frustration. He was just about to speak when Luke walked in the front door.

Marcus looked at Luke and then looked back at me; there was no disguising he was upset. Luke however, was all smiles, probably because he was totally wasted. He came over and stood behind Marcus and put his hands on to his shoulders. Marcus turned his head to glare at one of Luke's hands and I was surprised the hand didn't melt right off. As Luke leaned in, Marcus tried to pull away but his grip was firm. "Heeey, alright buddy, talking to ya bird". He looked between us. We were staring directly at one another, both with a look of fear, wondering if he knew. We didn't have to wait long until we were put out of our misery. "S'alright, Jenna told me. Who'd 'ave fought it, eh? Sly ole dog". He was punching Marcus on the arm now, like he was his best pal. I looked from the arm punch back to Marcus; expressing my shock and horror. I shook my head, wanting to tell him that I'd only told Jenna because I needed to talk to *someone* but no words came out. Marcus just stood there, rigid, his face getting redder and redder, he was totally humiliated and it was all my fault.

"Luke, could you give us a minute". I spoke softly; it was the only volume I could find.

Luke looked up, swaying slightly. "Yeah, sure, you two probably wanna be alone, right?" He winked at me and went to punch Marcus in the arm again but Marcus saw it coming, moved and he missed, causing him to struggle to keep his balance. Luke tapped his nose like in the Monty Python sketch. "Say no more, eh?! Secrets safe with me". He bumbled off, laughing.

We both watched him leave, the music came flooding out again as he opened the door and a second before the door closed, I turned back first, desperate to get in my plea. "Marcus, I…"

Marcus held up his hands to stop me. "DON'T! Just don't!" as he stormed off towards the hall.

I stood in the foyer on my own for a moment and looked towards the ceiling. I needed a moment to regain my composure but it wasn't granted, as Jenna practically fell out of the toilet. Apart from Luke, she was the *last* person I wanted to see. I quickly walked back in before her; I was in no mood to deal with her and her crap.

When I walked back in, the lights were on and the music had stopped but before I could enquire what had happened to our party, the DJ suddenly welcomed me back into the room. "Here she is, the Birthday girl herself! Now we have them both". I looked over and saw Mitchell standing in the middle of the dancefloor with Marcus and he beckoned me to join them while the DJ spoke for him. "Come on Nicky, we need you and Marcus together". I wanted the ground to open up. I had intended to slink back into the room unnoticed and go and sit in a dark corner but now every pair of eyes in the room were on me. I rustled up my biggest and best fake smile and walked towards them, glancing at Marcus as I approached and he looked away. Mitchell waited until I was in range, then he got in the middle and put his arms our shoulders and nodded towards the DJ, who sounded like he doubled as a bingo caller. "This is a special treat tonight, put together by Mitchell, just for you". The lights went off and as an homage to our childhood in the 80's, 'If you Were There' by Wham started playing as amusing pictures of Marcus, myself and our friends throughout the years, were projected on to a big screen. It was a really sweet thing to do, the audience loved it and I had a few minutes in the dark and damn good excuse to have a silent release of tears.

Chapter 31

The Party - Carly & Pete

For Carly and Pete, walking in to that hall had been like stepping back in time. They immediately saw all their old friends and although it had been three years, it was as if they'd never left. They were late as anticipated; escaping Carly's mother had been *no* easy task but fortunately, the party was a pretty good excuse to eventually break free.

The second they arrived, Mitchell rushed them in, removed their coats and shepherded them towards the group for a photograph. Carly and Pete ran to the middle next to Nicky and Marcus and Carly became instantly worried about Nicky who almost crushed her with a welcome hug. Carly was smiling ready for the photo when she felt a hand on her shoulder and a sudden chill down her spine when she realised who it belonged to. As soon as it was over, Carly grabbed Nicky and moved as far away from Luke as possible, she really didn't want to make a scene. Carly and Nicky were desperate to talk but were constantly interrupted by birthday wishes for Nicky and welcome home's for Carly. Nicky, was obviously struggling for a neutral topic amongst their listeners and told them all about Mitchell's (now famous) flan before Daniel came and whisked her away, citing a shish kebab emergency.

Carly was hugging, kissing and respectfully answering questions about how they'd been, what they were up to and where they were living and smiling to herself, knowing that she would have to later concede to Pete that his suggestion of taping the answer to those very same questions on a Dictaphone and playing them on a loop had merit. She managed to escape for a moment and was happily tucking into a king prawn, when she looked up and saw Jenna arguing with David at the bar, he looked *seriously* pissed off, got up from his stool, handed Jenna some money and stormed out. Carly chuckled, wondering if Jenna had taken to charging her own husband; Pete was up at the bar getting the drinks in, so in the interests of some good gossip, she'd find out if he'd heard anything when he got back. At least that was the plan before Carly stood there in shock and amazement, wondering if her eyes deceived her; did she really just see Jenna grab Pete's arse? Pete had his hands full of drinks, so couldn't defend himself and she was about to storm over when saw Pete's face, he rounded on Jenna and obviously said something very unpleasant before he turned away and headed at speed, back towards Carly. He stopped in his tracks and breathed deeply when he saw that Carly had witnessed the exchange and approached with extreme caution. "I'm sorry about that".

"What the hell?!"

"She gets a bit full on when she's had a drink, is all. Just forget about it, babe". Pete looked worried that Carly was going to make a few introductions 'Jenna's face, pavement. Pavement, Jenna's face'.

Carly looked from Pete back to the bar, Jenna had moved on to poor Greg now. "So you're telling me she's done this before?" Pete looked really uncomfortable as he handed Carly her drink. Carly was trying to get him to look her in the eye. "Pete?"

It was at that moment that Alice arrived and was standing in front of Carly and Pete. "Hey, you two!" Carly thought it was typical of Alice, that she was completely unaware she'd walked in on a tense situation.

So Carly did the only thing you can do and pretended that there wasn't one. "Oh hi Alice!"

Pete was a little lost for words, so went in for a staple, "Nice dress". He frowned; worried his clothing tourette's was back.

Alice thanked him but seemed uncomfortable, Carly thought Alice was probably too bashful to take the compliment and she proved it by rapidly changing the subject. "So, how've you both been? What've you been up to? Where have you been living?"

Pete just smiled knowingly at Carly before excusing himself to return to the bar, where Jenna had left and Greg was now on his own.

Carly and Alice stood chatting for a while and she couldn't help but notice that Alice looked a little on edge and was avoiding talking about herself, quickly changing the subject to the birthday boy and girl and how sweet it was that they'd been holding hands earlier. Carly tried to hide her smiles. Pete was on his way back via the DJ stand as Craig literally dragged Alice on to the dancefloor.

Best of Friends?

Carly looked suspiciously at Pete. "Felt an overwhelming desire to get in a request, did you?"

"Something like that". Pete laughed and Carly didn't. They had unfinished business and she stood there with her arms folded and eyebrow raised until Pete started talking. "It was at our leaving do". Carly pursed her lips and nodded; Pete warily continued, "You'd gone off somewhere and Jenna came up to me at the bar. She said she needed to talk to me about you, so I went out on to the landing with her and then she massively came on to me. She was smashed though hon, so I told her to go home, drink some coffee and sleep it off and then I went back inside. Then you came back, looking really upset, Luke was all over Nicky and you told me that he'd hit on you... and well, you know the rest".

"So while Luke lured me outside telling me he wanted to talk about Nicky, Jenna lured you away to discuss me? At the *same* time?" Carly was trying to manage the information and there was only one obvious answer. She stared into space and voiced her thoughts out loud. "They tried to set us up".

"*What?* No, babe, I know Luke's an arse but even *he's* not got the stones for that. Besides, I really don't think he's clever enough to come up with more than one plan at a time".

"No, that's why they planned it together... and *trust* me babe, Luke has the stones".

Carly had been apprehensive but she knew it was a long time coming, so she confessed everything to Pete about the night of the leaving do. She'd never seen him so angry or indeed noticed just how many veins there were in his head before but she made him promise *faithfully*; that he wouldn't start anything tonight. They both knew that this promise was a one night only deal and that as soon as the party was over; anything goes. It was a relief to finally unburden and once she started, she couldn't stop. She told him about Nicky's reaction the night before and Pete mirrored her own thoughts, "So she probably doesn't know about Jenna, either?"

Carly shook her head. "No, she doesn't. I couldn't tell her Pete, she'd heard enough for one night. I *will* tell her though, when the time's right".

It seemed like half the night had passed before Carly finally saw Nicky on her own. She hurried over and they filled each other in on as much of an update as they could before a few old secondary school mates joined them at the bar. They were all stood laughing and reminiscing when Carly happened to look round and notice Marcus leaving the main hall towards the bathrooms, she quickly announced to their immediate crowd that she had a chicken fillet emergency and pulled Nicky to one side. She tidied Nicky's hair, helped her with her lipstick and sent her best friend off on a peace mission while she stood, protector of the doors and guarded the entrance from wanderers. Access would only be granted to those desperate to use the conveniences, like Simon, who was re-enacting Riverdance. Pete wandered over. "Have you seen Marcus and Nicky? Mitchell wants to start this little picture show thing". Carly didn't answer but over her shoulder, he could see them talking in the foyer, through the glass in the door. "Oh, *there* they are".

As he went to get them, Carly quickly grabbed his arm. "Wait!" Pete looked startled and she realised she needed to tone it down a notch. "Err, give them a minute, yeah? They haven't had a chance to chat all night".

Pete looked with confusion between his friends and Carly. "What about Mitchell?"

Carly noticed Mitchell fast approaching and headed him off; Pete dutifully took point in front of the glass. "Hey Mitchell".

Mitchell looked relieved to see her. "Carly darling, have you seen the birthday kids?" He sounded out of breath.

"Now that you mention it Mitchell, I *have*". She linked arms with him and turned him in the other direction. "The last I saw, they were heading for the catering tent".

Mitchell looked round baffled. "Why would they be in the catering tent?"

"I think I heard Marcus telling Nicky all about some marvellous flan someone had made and they went to find out when it was joining the rest of the food".

Mitchell suddenly calmed down for a second and looked immensely proud as he patted his chest. "That's my flan".

Carly was beckoning Pete behind Mitchell's back. "*Really?* Pete loves to cook; he said he'd love to see it as well". Carly grabbed Pete and pushed him towards Mitchell and then quickly took his place in front of the glass. They walked away with Pete smiling and nodding as enthusiastically as he could as Mitchell explained the delicate process of flan making. Pete turned his head back to her, pulling a face and Carly winced and mouthed, "Sorry!"

Carly was still guarding the main doors when Emma walked past her. "Hey Em". Emma didn't even turn her head and carried on walking towards the buffet table. Carly had given Marcus and Nicky a good head-start, so left her post and followed her over. Emma was eating a sandwich, staring in to space, when Carly picked up a plate and sidled up next to her. She was about to make a joke about the prawn ring when she noticed Emma had tears in her eyes.

Chapter 32

The Party - Emma and Justin

Emma and Justin arrived early, they had to; Emma *had* to get out of the house, the kids were driving her mad and she had a mammoth headache brewing. As they walked in, Emma noticed how beautifully the hall had been decorated with black and white sashes, fairy lights and flower arrangements. She knew it must have taken Mitchell and Daniel all day to do it and would only take her children minutes to destroy it. They were still bringing out the food when Abigail nearly skidded into one of the server's carrying a platter full of pastries. Emma rubbed her forehead and asked Justin to pick her up from under the buffet table while she escaped to Nicky, who was over by the DJ stand. "Hi Nic, you look fantastic!"

"Thank you. So do you". She knew Nicky was just being polite; her hair was a mess where Jessica had grabbed it on her way out of the car seat and there was a water mark on the bottom of her dress where she'd tried to remove the evidence of Abigail's strawberry lolly.

"Where's Marcus?" Emma instantly realised it was the wrong thing to ask as Nicky looked intensely uncomfortable, so she quickly changed the subject and thanked Nicky for Thursday; they both agreed they should do it more often.

A few people had started to arrive and Nicky had to meet and greet, so Emma went to fix her hair in the toilets. She was only gone a few minutes but by the time she'd returned, her brood were running riot in and out of everyone's legs while Justin stood oblivious with a pint. She threw him a look and headed outside for some air, hiding round the corner and nursing her now *stonking* headache. She only intended to be a few minutes but a couple of guests had come out for a sneaky cigarette and she could hear them gossiping, so she moved closer to the edge so she could hear. Sarah, who they'd known since kindergarten, was commenting on the floor show being put on by Emma's children, telling the others that both kids were a nightmare and that Emma wasn't welcome anywhere anymore because of it. Emma was devastated.

She sat on her own round the corner, waiting for them to leave and trying not to cry. She knew she needed to rejoin the party and so managed to regain at least *some* composure and stood up. The intention was to go back in, grab her children and leave but suddenly, she heard more voices. Mitchell was instantly recognisable and she could make out Daniel as well but they were talking to someone else. "What's going on with you two?" Emma could *only* just hear what Mitchell said, so she moved nearer to the edge again and snuck a look around the building, they were with Marcus.

"Nothing". Marcus looked annoyed as Daniel was trying to straighten his tie.

"Horse poop. Something's happened and I want to know what".

"Mitchell, nothing has happened, please drop it". Marcus seemed angry now and held his hands up to stop Daniel trying to dress him.

"Fine, I'll ask Nicky then".

"No!" Marcus sounded panicked, knowing Mitchell was used to getting his own way, "Don't do that. She and I have just had a little disagreement is all".

"Well, I suggest you two stop being so selfish and put it aside for the evening, we've put a lot of work into this". Emma had to cover her mouth so that they wouldn't hear her laugh.

"I know and I thank you. Everything looks amazing guys, really".

Mitchell pointed to the creation he was delicately holding. "Did I mention my flan...?"

Mitchell then went on and on talking about his flan and some cooking course and as much as she wanted to ask a few culinary questions, Emma couldn't very well come round now, they would know she'd heard their conversation about Nicky. She knew something was up on Thursday and earlier Nicky had tensed at the very mention of his name; this wasn't just a 'disagreement' this was much, much more.

Finally, Mitchell and Daniel walked away and she was just about to re-surface when she heard Nicky shout Marcus' name. Christ, at this rate she'd be there overnight but at least she might find out what had been going on, so she listened in intently. They hadn't been talking but apparently and they needed to talk about what happened? They annoyingly walked back inside without revealing what that was, so now Emma's curiosity was at intrigue level; there was no *way* she was leaving now, she was on a mission. She tip-toed in a few seconds behind them and by that point Abigail had one of the sashes off the wall and was running round like a rhythmic gymnast; fortunately Mitchell hadn't seen. Justin had a new pint but was back by the buffet table, discussing the finer points of Top Gear, so she took away the sash and hid it under one of the tables which drew screams from her child and more disapproving looks from the other guests. Emma knew it was going to be a *long* night.

A whole chunk of the evening went past in a blur for Emma. They'd all had their picture taken but you could cut the atmosphere with a knife and then she spent the next hour or so running around after her children while her husband did nothing. She'd had a couple of glasses of wine on top of some headache pills and an empty stomach and she started to feel dazed, so she made her way over to the buffet table. Everything that Sarah had said about her kids was true, they *were* uncontrollable and becoming unbearable and she was slowly drowning. She was trying to eat as her eyes welled up and she wondered if she should follow his advice when her thoughts were interrupted. "Hey, what's the matter?" It was Carly.

Emma wanted to lie but she'd been caught at a vulnerable moment. Carly tried to comfort her and she managed to get control of her tears (which was a first) and ravenously ate another sandwich. She turned to Carly, "I just wanted kids so badly, I never stopped to think about how they'd turn out".

Emma was now staring at her children running amok again and Carly followed her gaze and grimaced when she saw Abigail hitting Jessica with the flowers from the table (luckily she'd taken them out of the vase first). "They're just spirited, that's all".

Emma laughed. "Spirited? That's one way of putting it, thanks". Emma put down her plate. "I'm on my own. Justin works late all the time and when he *is* around, he doesn't help, he's a bigger kid than *all* of them... but then that's partly my fault. I made sure I organised everything for him, so now he's practically incapable of tying his own shoes without me". Carly looked over towards Justin who was standing there cradling another pint, neglectfully chatting with the other dad's while Jessica tried to shove a chicken goujon up Abigail's nose; she could see her point. "Not to mention the fact that unless I dressed up like Jeremy Clarkson and hung 'new car smell' magic trees round my neck, he wouldn't even notice *me*".

"Do you really...?"

Emma cut her off. "No, I *don't* dress up like Jeremy Clarkson. I was being ironic". Emma shook her head and briefly smiled at Carly, before continuing her tale of woe. "His parents just feed them sweets all the time and let them get away with murder, so by the time they come back, they're actually worse. My own mum can't handle them; she had a total breakdown years ago and now I think I'm heading the same way". Carly tried some soothing comments but Emma shrugged them off. "It's true Carl. Did Nicky tell you what happened last week? I just dropped the kids with them and *seriously* thought about not coming back. I went down to the river and sat there for hours trying to get my head straight. I'd been to see my doctor that day, he put me on anti-depressants last year and *now* he's suggesting that I take a break for a week or two. I was actually just standing here debating whether I should... but how do you leave your family?" Emma's eyes filled with tears again.

They talked some more until Emma started staring again but this time she was smiling, Carly tried to follow her line of sight. "What? Who are you looking at?"

"Oh, I was just thinking that guy over there would be a nice match with Nicky, don't you think?"

Emma was digging. She knew Carly and Nicky had made up and if Nicky told anyone about 'what happened' with Marcus, it would be Carly. Carly was oblivious to Emma's inquisition but fully aware of her efforts over the years to set Nicky up, so she put her arm around Emma, turned her around, patted her on the back and said, "I think Nic's off men for a little while. Let's go get a drink". Emma knew she was on to something.

They walked past Alice and Greg at the other end of the buffet table, who looked like they'd had an argument; they weren't talking and just staring down at their food. Emma and Carly shared a look and were about to ask Alice to join them but before they reached her, Carly stopped in her tracks and looked worriedly around the hall as Marcus came back through the main doors with a face like thunder, the lights came on and the DJ called him into the middle of the room. They were now looking for Nicky and surprise, surprise, a minute later she came through the doors, only they must have had another 'disagreement' as she too looked *really* upset; she just hoped their frost would melt when they saw what Mitchell had planned. Emma had provided him with most of the pictures, so she'd been looking forward to this all day and wasn't disappointed.

As childhood pictures filled the screen, Emma and Carly laughed all the way through, remembering a time when everything seemed simpler. When the lights came back on, Carly nudged her and pointed over towards Jenna, who'd practically fell through the door and was fumbling with her bag by the side of the dancefloor but before anyone could even reset the lights to disco level, Alice was marching across the hall towards Jenna. Carly and Emma took one look at each other and ran but they were too late to stop Alice grabbing Jenna by the arm and swinging her round to confront her.

Chapter 33

The Party - Jenna and David… and Luke

They'd been arguing while they got ready and they were *still* arguing on the drive over. "I think you should drive back tonight, at least *then* you can't get steaming drunk and show yourself up".

Jenna had been down Stumpy's all afternoon with some friends from work, so was in no state to drive but she *was* feeling like her old self, more and more each day. "They're *my* friends, *you* should drive".

"I warned you Jenna, I'm not gonna put up with this crap for much longer". David was removing his coat and straightening his tie.

Jenna produced a sinister smile. "You promise?"

David was just about to reply when they saw the birthday duo in the hall and were suddenly all smiles. "Hi! Happy Birthday's!" Jenna noticed Nicky and Marcus were holding hands, so she subtly winked at Nicky but she didn't think Nicky noticed, so she did it again. Anyway, who cared, they were wasting valuable drinking time. "Right. Let's get one in then". Jenna was off and left her boring husband with them.

Much to David's embarrassment, Jenna carried on the bickering at the bar. She was just starting to warm up and enjoy herself when some idiot turned on the lights and told them all to go into the main hall for a group photo.

"Some arsehole better not nick my stool".

David looked around in shame, hoping no one heard. "I'll look after your stool, if you tone down your language. Go on, I don't want to be in it".

"Oh for fuck's sake David, get a life. Stay here then". David noticed that Jenna usually lost her patience and her manners, somewhere between her fourth and fifth glass of wine and he was less than impressed.

"Keep your voice down!"

Jenna ignored him and joined on the end of the group, cosying up to Greg, just to annoy David some more. Greg whispered to her, "Please don't touch me". What a wuss! Jenna smiled for the picture then sauntered back to the bar, shouting, "Whatever".

David was sat on her stool and Jenna stood there with a face like a smacked arse until he moved. Luke was laughing loudly next to them with some old mates, about how many of the local girls he'd 'nailed' and David shook his head in disgust.

"What's your problem? You can't spend a night with my friends?"

David sighed and looked around again and lowered his voice. "I'm not going to argue with you in public Jenna, so stop trying".

Jenna downed her drink and said loudly. "I'm just trying to talk to my husband, where's the crime? Gonna lock me up for that are ya?"

"D'ya know what Jen? Do what you like". He pulled out his wallet and took out a £20 note. "There's some money for a cab. I'm gonna stay at a mates tonight but I suggest tomorrow you get your things together and find somewhere else to go. I don't see any point in carrying this shit on". And just like that, after only one hour (and five years) David had left the building. Jenna thought about it, was she free at last? She smiled, David was gone. Now the party can *really* get started.

Jenna's way of dealing with life's issues obviously hadn't changed much over the years. She saw Pete at the bar and went up to talk to him, she was only trying to be friendly and he rudely told her to keep her hands to herself; the bastard. Greg was also on her case tonight about a load of old crap from the past, he even tried to threaten her, so she thought she'd make it interesting and warned him it was about time this town *knew* what went on under their own noses. You know what they say, an ear for an ear; or whatever it was. Jenna laughed as he went a sort of grey colour when she told him she planned to take to the stage later and tell them all everything. She loved playing with Greg, he was *so* easy to wind up but there was someone else at the bar that caught Jenna's eye who was even *more* fun to play with. Luke had *never* turned down a sure thing and he wasn't about to start now; Jenna gave him the nod, left a distraught Greg at the bar and waited for Luke at the front of the building.

Best of Friends?

She came back in, trying to straighten her dress out, from her rendezvous in the car park and was surprised to see Nicky and Marcus were in the Foyer. "Oh, hey?" She was glad she'd suggested to Luke that he wait a few minutes before he came back in. "What ya doin' out here?" Then she remembered they were probably talking about their dalliance last week. She had a little chuckle to herself then Marcus said something back about "just being a minute". He smiled but it was obvious that he wanted rid of her. Bloody charming. She headed towards the loos to go and freshen up but as she was looking for her lipstick in her handbag, Marcus shouted out. "Oh and Greg was looking for you".

Jenna mumbled to herself, "Fucking typical, can't even have a wazz without the fucking party Police".

Her hair was a mess, her mascara had run a bit and her lipstick was smeared, she laughed as she realised she looked like Robert Smith of the Cure. She was re-touching her make-up when she noticed the dark circles under her eyes, she tried to cover them up but make up appliance was proving difficult as she was having a job standing. It was those damn heels, she'd nearly gone over a few times, she might send back to the online shop next week, they were obviously faulty. She tried to fix her hair, put on yet another coat of lippy and took a quick snort from the vial Luke had given her. When she came out of the Ladies, Marcus had gone and Nicky was going back inside, she was about to follow her, when she saw the lights were on and it looked like some lame ass present thing. When the slideshow started up, Jenna aired her thoughts, "Fuck this", as she made her way back outside for a fag.

She breathed in the cool night air and *two* cigarettes worth of smoke, making sure they had time to finish faffing about with photos before she headed back in. She saw Luke on the other side of the hall leering at her and she ignored him as she tried to get her fags back in to the stupid clutch bag; so she didn't notice Alice until she grabbed her arm and nearly pulled her over. Alice was totally in her face, going on about something. 'How long' what? Who knew and who fucking cared. Who the fuck did Alice think she was anyway? Jenna planned to take her down a peg or two, it was about time to remind little Alice that she wasn't the perfect angel she pretended to be.

Chapter 34

The Party - Alice & Greg

Alice was bored. It was a perfectly good party but she'd just spent the last half hour on her own as Greg was talking to the lads, she'd only spent about three minutes with Nicky and even less with Marcus, Emma had her hands full, Carly and Pete were late and then instantly occupied and Jenna looked like she'd already had a skinful.

It was about an hour into the evening when Alice saw Carly on her own and made her way over. She got stopped on-route by Craig who was very complementary about her appearance and by the time she made it over to Carly, Pete had rejoined her and they were clearly having a disagreement. She hadn't *meant* to intrude but it was too late to walk away, so she pretended not to notice. "Hey, you two!"

"Oh hi Alice!" Carly thankfully played along. Pete then complimented her dress and Alice made a mental note to revive it for another social occasion, it was obviously a winner. Alice briefly glanced up and caught sight of Greg talking animatedly to Jenna at the bar, her heart sank to her stomach and she quickly looked back to Carly and Pete and fired out some generic questions about their home life in Brighton. She desperately hoped they wouldn't notice how distraught she was.

Greg was on his own at the bar; tornado Jenna had hit and run and he had no clue as to what he was going to do.

"What's going on mate?" Greg looked up to see Pete stood over him.

Greg knocked back his drink like he'd been stuck in a desert for a month. "Nothin, I'm cool".

"Dude, you're so *far* from being cool, you're as warm as a... warm thing". Pete was laughing at his own lack of imagination, hoping Greg would join but he was just staring into his drink. Pete sat himself down. "What's the deal with you and Jenna now? Saw you two talking before; looked pretty intense".

Greg looked around him to make sure no one was listening. "David's told her to leave". Greg waited while Pete nodded the obligatory 'bout time' head bob. "She's stuck a few away". Greg waited while Pete pulled the 'no shit' facial expression. "And she's decided that she's had enough of all the secrets and lies and as a special birthday treat to Nicky and Marcus, she's going to take the microphone later this evening and tell everyone about all the affairs that have been going on". Greg waited while Pete picked his jaw off the floor. "Then she left, I don't know where she's gone". Greg took a deep breath and then looked over at Alice. "She looks stunning tonight, doesn't she?"

Best of Friends?

"She does mate, got yourself a beaut, there". Pete slapped Greg on the arm. "From now on, don't screw it up, yeah?" Pete smiled, "I tell you what, I'll go tell the DJ not to let Glenn Close get hold of the mic, how's that?" Greg nodded and Pete headed back towards Carly and Alice via the DJ stand.

Alice was sneakily trying to find out from Carly what was going on between Nicky and Marcus. She'd seen Marcus earlier that day and he'd been very touchy when she'd asked after Nicky and despite an earlier display of fake hand-holding, it was obvious they weren't talking. She was still probing when Craig came over and asked her to dance, she politely declined but he wasn't taking no for an answer, he grabbed her hand and dragged her on to the dancefloor.

Greg headed back into the hall to find Jenna, he looked everywhere for her, making his way round every inch of the hall, getting stopped by old friends along the way, it took ages but he didn't want to arouse suspicion by blowing them off. He'd been out the back, looking round the sides and even in the catering tent, he was starting to consider looking under tables. He asked Pete, Nicky and Craig if they'd seen her and then realised he hadn't checked out front. He was on his way when Pete and Craig stopped him in the lobby. "Come on mate". Pete had his arm around him. "Let's go get some food in you". The boys took him over to the buffet table, where Alice joined them, seeming angry; Pete and Craig left them to it.

"I haven't seen you all night, what's going on?"

"Nothing". Greg felt like he was back at school, being caught doing something he shouldn't. Alice eyed him for a moment; he looked like he was having an anxiety attack. He managed to steady himself, smile and repeat more calmly. "Really babe, it's nothing".

"I need a drink. You coming?" Alice was daring him for the wrong answer.

He gave it. "I... err, need some air. I'll catch up with you in a minute".

"Fine, then I'll come with you".

His sudden need for more oxygen dissipated. "Let's just get some more food, first". Greg loaded up his plate and they both sat down and started to eat in silence.

Alice had been watching him all night and had seen him running around asking after Jenna. She'd witnessed their heated discussion at the bar and now she was watching him scour the room every few minutes with his eyes. Emma was at the other end of the buffet table and looked upset but fortunately Carly came to her aid. Alice would have normally been there for Emma like a shot but she wasn't about to give Greg an excuse to run off after Jenna. He looked up every time the main hall doors opened but this time it was Marcus. As soon as he walked in, the lights came on and the DJ called him to the middle of the floor and Alice noticed Greg took the opportunity to do a full visual scout around the illuminated room. The DJ was looking for Nicky who wasn't far behind and as she joined Mitchell and Marcus, the lights went out and what sounded like 'Wham' started playing to old pictures of them all together as kids. As the song progressed, so did their age, until it finished with the photo taken of them all earlier in the evening. The picture showed Jenna with her arm around Greg, kissing his cheek; Greg swallowed hard and Alice was quietly seething.

When the lights came back on, the DJ asked the guests to applaud Mitchell and Daniel on the presentation and decorations and that's when Jenna walked (or rather stumbled) back into the room and Greg's face lit up; he'd found her. He was putting down his food and getting ready to make his excuse to Alice but Alice had anticipated his move. "Don't! You'll just embarrass yourself even further".

"What do you mean?" Greg tried to look baffled but his voice was shaky and immediately gave him away.

Alice didn't need to say anything as she looked with hurt towards Jenna and then back at Greg, narrowing her eyes and shaking her head. Greg let out a nervous laugh. "*What?!* Don't be ridiculous!"

"*Ridiculous?* I'll show you ridiculous". As she marched over towards an unsuspecting Jenna.

Alice grabbed Jenna by the arm and spun her round. "How long?"

"What?!" Jenna was slurring and fiddling with her bag.

"I *asked* you how long?!" Alice shouted. People stopped what they were doing and looked over, no-one was used to Alice raising her voice, no-one was used to even noticing Alice.

"What the fuck you on about, Alice?"

"How long have you been screwing Greg?" There was a silence that passed over the room like a mini shockwave.

Mitchell tried desperately to turn off the lights and was frantically giving hand signals to the DJ trying to get him to play another song. The DJ fumbled and in his bingo caller voice said, "Errr... where, err... where were we? What ye... Ahh yes, 2005. Here's a classic by... errm, that fella in the hat..." He let out a nervous giggle and then practically shouted when he remembered, "Jamiroquai!" The DJ sat down breathing heavily.

Alice suddenly noticed that Carly and Emma were by her side and Nicky had just run from the other direction and joined them. Alice grabbed Jenna's arm again. "I *asked* you a question. How long have you two been going behind my back?"

"Aren't you one to talk about cheating, eh?!" Jenna raised her eyebrow at Alice and dared her to continue. That ironically, is when Luke decided to wander over to find out what all the fuss was about.

Alice had *finally* had enough of Jenna holding her to emotional ransom. "Yes, that's right Jenna; I am because *I* slept with Luke". Alice raised her hands in the air in a dramatic gesture. "There! I said it". Silence fell over all of us that were in earshot and Carly, Emma and Nicky looked over at Alice, all *utterly* stunned. Alice remained unmoved and looked over at Luke with pure hatred, then back at Jenna with defiance and then at Greg with remorse.

Greg looked like he'd been hit by a train and barely managed to get the words out. "*What?*"

Chapter 35

I knew it! I *knew* that it was a total impossibility for the night to go without incident. What I didn't know was that it was about to make the 'big fight' look like a light slap.

The four of them were stood in a diamond shaped holding pattern, looking from one to the other, waiting for someone to make a move, with the rest of us just standing round the edges. Marcus had now joined the crowd and was standing next to Pete, still avoiding eye contact with me. Greg now looked like he was going to cry and was the first one to finally speak, he looked over at Alice. "You slept with Luke?"

Alice kept her composure, took a deep breath and simply answered, "Yes".

Greg was shaking his head. "You slept with Luke".

Jenna's drunken drawl now filled the room. "Yes, genius, I think we fucking got that".

Greg looked over and shouted. "Stay out of it, Jen!"

It was at this point, that Luke made the mistake of breathing, let alone talking. "Calm down mate, yeah?"

"What did you say?" Greg rounded on Luke. "Did you *seriously* just tell me to calm down?" Greg's face was getting redder and more contorted by the second. "You were *supposed* to be my best mate! How long've you been with Alice?"

Alice answered for Luke. "It was one time, about five years ago, about the time I imagine you started sleeping with *her*". Alice was pointing towards Jenna, who'd stopped paying attention.

Greg looked from Alice, to Jenna, to Luke. Luke shrugged and then made a fatal mistake... he smiled. Greg's key had slowly been wound all night and now he was ready to be let go. He lunged towards Luke so quickly and hit Luke with everything he had. Suddenly everyone ran forward, except Jenna, who was still trying to fasten her bag. Greg and Luke were rolling on the floor like two scrapping boys in a playground, trying to get punches in but failing so just pulling at each other's clothes and pushing at each other's faces. The rest of the boys were desperately trying to pull them apart but it was Pete who finally managed to drag Greg off of Luke. Mitchell was flapping like a headless chicken and was trying to get people up to dance and avert their eyes away from the nasty brawling at his lovely party but he was proving about as popular as a Traffic Warden; they wanted to watch the show.

When the fighting was over, Greg tried to talk to Alice but Pete and Marcus walked him outside, urging him to leave and sort it out in the morning. Once he was sure Greg had left, Pete then accompanied Luke out front but before Luke could thank him for his help, Pete landed one right on his nose, sending him to the floor again. We caught Marcus happily applauding when Carly and I escorted Jenna out to the taxi we'd ordered, to take them as far away as possible. Jenna was off with the fairies and had *no* clue what had happened and even smiled and said, "I'll call you tomorrow", as the cab drove off.

We all moved back into the bar, quietly stunned when Emma noticed Alice was about to leave the party. We ran out in to the foyer after her. "Oh no, you don't". Carly had Alice by the arm and the DJ had now caught up to 2008, ironically playing 'Shut Up & Let Me Go'.

Alice tried to protest as she looked down at Carly's arm lock and then back at me. I was shaking my head. "No way hon, I'm with her; you're staying!"

There was only one thing for it, as us girls took Alice to the bar, where we spent the next forty minutes, laughing and drinking, *not* talking about what happened and just being there for our mate. Emma had sent 'That' Justin home with the kids and apparently told him not to wait up and she'd also secured Alice a bed for as long as she needed one. Other guests had started to filter out (they'd obviously had enough fun for one night), Mitchell was being comforted by Daniel and the rest of the boys were propping up the bar, so I asked the DJ for his finest slice of cheese and then Carly, Emma, Alice and I danced the rest of the night away.

Chapter 36

The doorbell rang and rang and then my mobile started up, followed by the home phone and I heard Sadie moan from her room. Luckily, I'd been up for an hour or so, already showered and changed and had been looking after Sadie. Carly and Pete were standing in the doorway. "C'mon, we're off to Ruth's. Figured you ladies could use a hearty breakfast!"

"Come in, come in. I just need to check on Sade". I had been checking on Sadie every ten minutes since I got up, she was *not* in a good way. I came back out simultaneously slipping on my trainers and putting on my coat. "Errm, Sadie won't be joining us this morning, I'm afraid". Pete and Carly winced in sympathy and we made our way over to Ruth's.

Pete was looking round fondly at our favourite café. "I think it's fair to say, your party even out-did our leaving do".

I grimaced, "Have I apologised for that in the last twenty four hours?"

Best of Friends?

Carly laughed and then thought better of it and rubbed her forehead. I chuckled, "How you doin' there, Carl?"

"Not good babe, not good". She was smiling but listing to starboard.

Pete looked over at her affectionately. "Lightweight. Never could handle her drink". Carly just mumbled and waited for her side order of toast. I couldn't help but smile, it was normally me that had my head *that* close to the table and holding a brew like I'd just been rescued from a mine.

Carly started the after-party analysis. "So last night was quite the stand-off. How're you feeling?"

I smiled. "Honestly? I feel like I got off the mountain, just before the avalanche".

Pete responded. "Me and Marcus were talking about it last night. Gotta say I'm glad you did".

Pete was adding another sugar to his tea, so didn't see the exchange of looks between Carly and myself. Carly spoke on my behalf, "Yeah? What did *he* have to say about it all?"

She was anxiously looking over at me but Pete was oblivious. "Oh, we were just chatting at the bar and I mentioned it was a good thing you'd biffed off matey boy last week on your *own* terms. Hope you don't mind but Carly did tell me you'd told Luke to take a hike?" I sat there silently shaking my head, so Pete continued, "And he said 'ah huh' and then I said I'd have loved to have seen Luke's face when you called him a wanker, nice work by the way, and he said 'ah huh' and... that was pretty much it".

Carly's sarcasm surfaced with a hangover. "So what you're saying is, you did all the talking and he just said 'ah huh' a lot. Are you sure he was conscious?"

Pete looked up from his breakfast. "*Yes*, thank you. I don't suppose he wanted to talk about it, he's not exactly Luke's biggest fan".

I acknowledged his statement with a nod and quickly changed the subject. "Has anyone heard from Greg?"

Pete put down his brew. "I spoke to him this morning. He's not in a good way. For all his faults, he does think the world of that girl, you know".

We all nodded. It was at that moment that Alice and Emma came through the door and we all got up and exchanged hugs. Pete had phoned to invite them, I congratulated him on a job well done and we moved up to make to room for them, while Alice went up to the counter to order their food.

I turned to Emma. "So I take it you two got home OK last night?"

"Yeah, we sat up chatting for a while when we got in. Needless to say, I made Justin get up for the kids this morning and take them round to his mum's". Emma smiled at Carly and nicked a slice of my toast.

"Did she say much else?" Carly was still struggling to keep her head up.

"Just that she'd known he fooled about with other girls but didn't think he'd ever go behind her back with one of her friends. She started to suspect something last year but never had any proof. The *good* news is, she's going to stay with me for a while until she figures things out".

Everyone changed the conversation quickly as Alice was on her way back. She looked different this morning, like a weight had been lifted. "You don't have to stop talking about the party because *I'm* here, you know". She was smiling. "How's Sadie? She looked a little worse for wear last night, I saw her asleep in the corner".

"She's a bit rough, mate. Apparently she was upset that her fella Long Arms, sorry Ash, left early so she drank herself into a stupor".

Emma commented that she'd seen Carly and I pick her up and put her in our shared cab and I told them how I'd struggled to get her on to her bed but I refused to undress her as friendship only goes so far. I relayed her fragile state this morning and concluded, "I'll take her something back with me... a new intestine, maybe".

They were all laughing except Carly, who looked like she might barf. "Poor Sade".

I nodded with a knowing look. "Yeah, poor Sade indeed. Apparently Luke approached her at the buffet table last night and asked her if she wanted to play 'hide the sausage'".

Pete spat out a bit of tea and Carly sat with mouth agape, "*What?!*"

"Yeah, apparently our Sadie didn't quite get his meaning, laughed and then hid some chipolatas under the sandwiches". I winced and rubbed my forehead in vicarious shame, trying not to laugh.

Pete was not so subtle, laughing out loud. "Pete!" Carly slapped him on the arm.

Alice was struggling to contain herself and once she caught sight of Carly and me, she was ready to blow. It wasn't until Emma said, "I don't get it?" that we all burst out laughing.

It took a while for our respiratory systems to get back to normal; we wiped our eyes and did the obligatory after-laugh sighs and then the conversation inevitably turned to Jenna. We were trying to work out just how many people she'd been seeing and Carly involuntarily giggled when she heard about Barry. That's my girl.

It was Alice that offered, "She must have been eating her veggies to keep up the stamina for all three!" Alice laughed but Carly, Pete, Emma and I all just looked at her, we weren't used to hearing her speak, let alone crack a funny. Most girls would be forgiven for lying face down in their porridge sobbing their hearts out but for Alice, last night had been the sledge hammer that smashed the shell she'd been hiding in.

I replied, "You're not wrong mate. She told me all about *what's-his-face* and that she felt terrible about it. She obviously didn't count Greg or Luke as cheating". I took a moment to be bitter. "Must be wonderful to live in her world".

Alice shook her head. "I'm not so sure about that. I wouldn't want to be her right now".

Alice then told us the story of her and Luke. How it was Jenna that told her Greg was regularly stepping out and that he wouldn't be doing that if he was happy at home. She'd managed to convince an insecure and paranoid Alice that what she really needed was more experience. Cue Luke. It also gave Jenna an excuse to make a play for Greg. Jenna had been holding it over her head for years but now Alice was finally free of it.

It was Carly's turn to astonish us with her discoveries about what happened on the night of the 'big fight' (which had now been downgraded to the 'small scrap'). It was a tangled web that Jenna and Luke had woven but what no-one could understand was *why* they'd done it. I sat there quietly feeling sick to my stomach as I found out that for half of the years I'd been with Luke, Jenna had also been seeing him. Carly had held on to that bomb and I didn't blame her for not dropping it. I took a deep breath and made a *choice* not to react, instead I took a leaf out of Alice's book, if she can sit there with her head held high this morning, then so can I. It was a day of reflections *and* unanswered phone calls. Jenna had left me three or four messages begging me to call, Greg was ringing Alice every half an hour, Emma had gotten texts all morning from 'That' Justin, asking if it's safe to come home yet and Carly and Pete had countless messages from Carly's mother, asking them to stop by before they leave. *None* of us intended to reply today.

We all hugged and kissed and said our goodbyes outside of Ruth's and then Carly, Pete and I walked back to mine. Carly linked my arm and I thanked her for her support at the party. She had been behind me all night, getting me drinks and making sure I didn't tuck my dress in the back of my undercrackers, she'd been my rock and I don't know how I would have coped without her.

Pete was now linking Carly's other arm, helping to hold her up. "So how come Marcus went home with Samuel and Neil last night? Have you two had a fight or something?"

I looked at Carly then at Pete. "I wish it *was* just a fight".

Pete nodded wide-eyed as if it all suddenly made sense. Carly rested her head on my shoulder. "What are you going to do about it?"

"Well, the way I see it, I have a choice. I can sit around moping all day *or* I can do something productive".

Carly patted my arm. "Good for you".

"*Well*, I haven't quite decided yet..." Carly looked up with her eyebrow raised and I laughed.

It was then that Pete suddenly cut in. "You *need* to do something about it. We've all lost enough mates over the last few years. I mean, Christ! If there's any more parties, we'll *all* end up Billy no mates". Carly and I laughed. "Seriously though Nic, get round to his Dad's house, you're not backwards in coming forwards mate, *sort* it out!"

Carly looked at me. "He's right my friend, you need to go round there. The sooner, the better".

We arrived back at the house and I hugged Carly and Pete like I wasn't ever going to let them go. I promised that I would go down to visit in Brighton next month and I *meant* it. I went back in to the house and Sadie was still in bed. "Hey babes, you OK? You need any more tablets?" Sadie was lying on the bed with her head propped by a pillow, so that her face was positioned over the side of the bed in front of the bucket I had put there, with her arm hanging limply down the side. I went and got her some water and an Alka Seltzer; it was do or die time. She lay perfectly still and mumbled some inaudible noise that sounded like it could have been a badgers mating call; bless her, she did look *really* rough. I climbed up on to the bed and stroked her hair; it was something

Carly always used to do for me, whenever I felt like Lucifer had come to collect my soul after consuming my own body weight of the devils broth.

We stayed like that for ages before I asked, "So what *happened* with Ash last night?" I hadn't probed earlier, despite the fact that she couldn't talk properly, she'd skated around it but my superior detective skills suspected Ash's early departure from the party and Sadie's resultant state had stemmed from an argument of some kind.

"He said he had to get up early today. Load of old shite if you ask me". Sadie was barely moving her mouth, she was obviously in pain and it wouldn't be long now before the bucket collected it's dues.

"You don't believe him?"

She let out a sigh, which was followed by a grimace. I think she would have cried if there'd been any moisture left in her body. "He told me I was... *nice*".

OK, I wasn't expecting that. "Wow, you want me to go round there and kick his arse?"

Sadie's breathing was laboured and she didn't answer, she didn't need to, I understood. Of all the insipid words he could have used, that was numero uno. I didn't however, feel that this was the end to this budding relationship, just a sign that young Ash needed a thesaurus. I was about to reply when Sadie's breathing got heavier and she managed to move herself further over the bucket. Oh dear. The target was acquired, the bay doors were open and she clearly was ready to drop.

Chapter 37

Marcus stared at the phone, he was in torment; the last few weeks had been hell. Things hadn't been right with Nicky since he bumped into Luke in the kitchen that morning and things had just spiralled dramatically out of control from there. If truth be told, things hadn't been right with Nicky since he knocked Luke on his arse in Club Vom's.

Now his only option to start making things right was the phone in front of him. He picked it up for the fourth time, punched in the first two numbers and then put it down again. Well, at least he'd dialled some numbers this time. He threw his head back and breathed deeply in frustration. He wanted to phone her but what could he say? To explain why he'd stayed away for so long, he would have to tell her the truth; he'd have to tell her *everything*. He knew if he did that, their friendship would probably be over. Then again, after last night, their relationship was pretty much in the can anyway. If he'd just stayed that morning, they could have at least *tried* to sort it out but he didn't, he ran...

Best of Friends?

That dreaded morning, Marcus pulled up at his dads' house in an unrecognisable state. Neil answered the door and immediately saw something was wrong. He ushered Marcus in the living room, sat him down and called up the stairs, "Samuel! Samuel! *Quickly!*"

Samuel came running down the stairs, half expecting to see a performing elephant or at least catch a burglar in the act. "What the hell's going on?"

"It's Marcus! I've put him in the lounge".

Samuel ran into the front room and fell to his knees in front of his son. "Marcus!" Samuel lifted his head to look at him and was trying to check his body for blood. "You OK? What's wrong? Are you hurt?"

Marcus sullenly shook his head. "No, I'm fine, dad, honest".

Samuel's shoulders dropped and he breathed a huge sigh of relief and then he shot Neil a look for his dramatic over-reaction that suggested he'd deal with him later. He bowed his head trying to look in Marcus in the eye. "Problem is, you may be in one piece but you don't *look* fine, boy. What say I stick the kettle on, eh?"

Samuel came back in the room, with a tray full of tea and biscuits and Neil was sat at the other end of the sofa, biting his nails. Neil had never missed an event in Marcus' life, he'd been there, front row and centre for all of them but he *always* left the pep talks to Samuel. Samuel sat himself down across from Marcus, who was looking down and shaking his head. Samuel and Neil looked worriedly at each other but neither of them said a word, waiting patiently for Marcus to open up. "I slept with Nicky".

"Oh". Neil and Samuel exchanged rather different glances this time. Neil knew opened mouth before engaging brain in a sudden outburst. "I knew it! I told you Samuel, I said so but oooh no, you wouldn't have it!"

Samuel shot Neil a warning glance. "I seem to have forgotten the Custard Creams Neil; would you be so kind as to get them for us all?" Neil looked over at Marcus who now had his head in his hands and nodded at Samuel. Samuel smiled sweetly in return and mouthed, "Thank you". He waited for Neil to leave the room and spoke softly, "When did this happen?"

"Last night".

"Last night? Wow, that's errr, that's new". Samuel had prepared himself for many moments of parenthood but this one was a curve ball. "I know that you two have always been close but I thought it was more of a brother/sister thing. Do you have *feelings* for this girl?" Marcus looked briefly at Samuel and didn't need to answer the question. "Is there any reason *why* you didn't tell us that you had these feelings?" Marcus knew Samuel was upset and didn't know how to reply. Samuel put down his tea. "Marcus, we brought you up to be liberal minded, not to label or to judge. Why on earth would you think that we would do that *now?*"

"I'm sorry dad. I know you did. I just…" Marcus breathed deeply. "I guess, I just thought you'd be… disappointed". Marcus' head returned to his hands. "I don't know what I thought. It just came on so gradually that I didn't even know myself and then when I hit Luke that night, it hit *me* and I wanted to run and keep on running. I didn't know what to do".

"When did you hit Luke? Last night?"

Marcus shook his head. "No, about five years ago".

"Five *years?!*" Neil had shouted from the kitchen doorway but by the time Samuel had turned to look at him, he was just staring with his mouth agape, Samuel suspected he'd gone catatonic.

"Errr... Neil, why don't you go get us some cookies to go with those Custard Creams". Neil walked in a trance back in to the kitchen and Samuel patted Marcus on the back. "So come on, tell me what happened. Why are you so upset *now?* Did you tell her how you felt and she didn't feel the same way? The errr... the other thing... wasn't erm... *good?* It wasn't what you expected? *What?*"

Marcus looked embarrassed and let out a nervous laugh. "No, that was all fine. *More* than fine, it was..." Marcus looked up and was too embarrassed to finish the sentence, "That definitely wasn't the problem". Silence passed for a moment again and Samuel waited patiently for him to speak. "She's ashamed, dad".

Samuel looked at Marcus in disbelief. "*What?!* Why?"

Marcus relayed his side of the story and Samuel sat attentive as he told him how Nicky had snuck in quietly, which wasn't like her and Samuel knew enough of Nicky to nod in acknowledgement. He told him how he'd heard her crying and went in to comfort her. "She cried her heart out and then fell asleep on me. When she woke up, I don't know, she seemed... I don't know but *something* was different and we ended up... *you know*". Samuel nodded, he knew alright. Marcus went on, "And then afterwards I couldn't sleep, I spent most of the night thinking about what this meant for me and for her... for *us*". Marcus stopped for a second to smile. "Then I just watched her sleep. I finally dozed off this morning and we were like, hugging and she took my hand and I thought, she's cool about it, you know, this'll work, this is *gonna* work". Marcus shifted uncomfortably in his seat. "Then she turned around". He bit the side of his mouth and briefly glanced at Samuel. "And she realised it was me". He looked down at his feet again. "She must've been drunk last night but she didn't seem it, otherwise I *never* would have…" He took a deep breath and continued, "So this morning, she sees me and jumps up out of bed, grabs her clothes and tries to cover herself up, so I wouldn't see her again. Then I heard the front door close, our room-mate was home and she was so embarrassed that Sadie might actually see us together, that she practically threw my clothes at me and threw me out of the room".

Samuel placed a comforting arm around Marcus's shoulder. "Are you sure you didn't misread it? She was probably just as thrown as you; you two have known each other since the year dot. It may just have been a knee-jerk reaction. Did she *say* anything?"

"She didn't have to. She was hiding out in the bathroom forever, so I asked Sadie about what happened the night before, I thought she might be able to shed some light on *why* she was so upset". Marcus wiped his eyes with the back of his hand. "So Sadie tells me, Nicky's on/off bloke was there and she was chatting to him at the bar". Samuel looked confused, so Marcus explained. "Whenever she runs into this arsehole, it's the same thing every time; she gets upset, gets drunk and grabs the first bloke that comes along. This time, that bloke was *me*".

"I don't know what to say. You two are great friends, you *can* get past this. You just need to talk to her and tell her how you feel".

"I can't do that. Not *now*. Not now I know she's embarrassed about what happened".

"But you don't *know* that she's embarrassed. You *need* to talk to her Marcus, clear the air".

"What else *can* it be? It's a pattern dad, she does it every time. As soon as I found out about Luke, the *arsehole*, I left and came round here. I can't see her dad, I can't face her".

Samuel hugged him. "You can stay here as long as you need, son, you know that". Neil saw them hugging and ran into the room to join in.

That was exactly a week ago and they hadn't made things right, they'd made them worse and now Marcus was seriously confused. At the party he hadn't wanted to talk to Nicky at the start of the night, for the same reason he'd avoided her all week; he was delaying the inevitable, where Nicky would tell him it was all a terrible mistake. Instead she came out with an obviously practised pc spiel about respecting him, best friends, blah blah... but then she looked so genuine when she said she missed him. That had thrown him. He was about to tell her everything and confess how he felt but it was at that moment the arsehole walked in and he found out she'd told half the town about them. Only problem was, he'd noticed that last night Nicky had been avoiding Jenna like the plague and she'd looked happy when she threw her out and then Pete said something about Nicky telling Luke where to go, so he wasn't sure what had happened. Had she regretted telling them? It didn't take away the fact that she had. Did *everyone* at the party know? Had they all been having a good laugh at his expense? He was angry again now and he wanted to tell her that but he also needed to know. If only he could lift that phone and dial the number.

Chapter 38

It was the last day of August, Carly and I were like best pals again, my friendship with Jenna was over, my long affair with Luke had ended, my distance from Emma had been bridged, Alice had come back to us and due to a night of bad judgement, I had landed my friendship with Marcus in serious trouble. It had been *quite* a month!

I paced the floor almost wearing out the carpet; Sadie had finally finished emptying her innards and was now sound asleep. I had been surprised, for such a small person, she really held a lot of liquids. I put the TV on, then turned it off again, put on some music, then turned it off again, I tried to read a book but who was I kidding? I couldn't concentrate on anything. Carly and Pete were right, I needed to sort this out once and for all; I needed to go and see Marcus. Before I knew it, I had grabbed my coat and keys and started walking up the road. Marcus' family lived about a mile away and my normal mantra that 'God wouldn't have made cars, if he intended us to walk', was out the window and I didn't care; I was on a mission.

I wondered what was wrong with me, maybe it was an age thing but lately I had disturbingly found walking therapeutic. Today, it gave me the chance to organise my thoughts, so I wouldn't shout a load of gibberish when he opened the door. I arrived in record time (or maybe I'd just been chatting to myself so much, I hadn't realised where the time had gone) and Samuel answered the door, looking *very* surprised to see me. "Oh, hi Nicky".

I felt like a schoolgirl again, asking if Marcus could come out to play. "Hi Mr Benjamin, err, Samuel". I went bright red. "I was wondering if Marcus was here?"

"Err... *yes*, he is. I'll just get him for you". Samuel then called up the stairs. "Marcus! You have a visitor".

Samuel invited me in and Neil came out from the kitchen to find out who it was, he looked heartily disappointed when he saw it was me. Samuel, obviously sensing unease, turned back to me. "I'm sorry we didn't say goodbye last night, our cab turned up early, so we had to leave quickly before someone else jumped in. Great party though. Mitchell and Daniel really went to town on those dec's, eh?" Before I could respond, he was grabbing his and Neil's coats off the banister. "I'm afraid we must excuse ourselves, we were *just* on our way out". Samuel handed a baffled Neil his coat. "I hope to see you again soon". Samuel guided Neil out of the door and then turned back to hug me and kiss me on the cheek, he smiled and pulled the door to. Samuel had never hugged me before; it was really sweet, I must have looked like I needed it. As the door closed, I turned round to see Marcus halfway down the stairs.

He looked up the stairs, probably wondering whether to run back up and lock himself in his room because he did *not* look happy to see me. He walked down and went into the kitchen to get a bottle of water and I followed his every step. "Why are you here?"

"You con't make wy talls". OK, what was that?! I'd over-practised and now I was panicking. I breathed deeply and tried again. "You won't take my calls. I didn't know what else to do?"

"Not answering my phone is a pretty good indication that I don't want to talk, wouldn't you say?" He walked into the lounge and I followed like a wounded dog.

"But we *need* to talk about this. Haven't I at least earned the right to defend myself?"

He looked directly at me. "I don't know. *Have* you?"

Ouch, that one stung. My voice gave away my lack of composure. "I believe that I have. I happen to think that we have a friendship worth salvaging".

"That's why you're here? You want to salvage our *friendship*?"

"Don't *you?*"

I'd asked the question but I wasn't sure I wanted to know the answer. He looked down at his feet. "I don't know".

As my heart sank down to my stomach, the quivvel bottom lip set in. "Wow. You *really* hate me. I knew you were ashamed but this is just..." I couldn't finish the sentence; I had tears in my eyes and was trying to control them. I hated crying at the best of times and I'd cried enough lately in front of Marcus.

"*Ashamed?! I'm* not the one who was ashamed! You were the one who spent nearly an hour in the shower trying to scrub off any memory of me". I'd never known Marcus to shout like that before but he was doing a pretty good job for a first timer.

"*What?!* When?"

"You *know* what I'm talking about, don't patronise me by pretending you don't, it totally fucking belittle's us both".

"I'm not trying to patronise you Marcus, I genuinely don't know to what you're referring". I was going to throw in a whence and wherefore in the spirit of using an extended vocabulary, as Marcus was so eloquently doing but felt that maybe it wasn't the right time.

"The next morning, you threw me out of your room and then took the world's longest shower; probably trying to scrub off any memory of me. You just couldn't wait to get rid of me! I know you think it was a mistake Nic but *that* was just humiliating".

Whoa! Hang on! "I didn't *throw* you out of my room, Sadie was back and would've seen us, I didn't think that's what *you* would've wanted and yes, I recall the shower the next day, it was a particularly *nice* shower where I had some pretty fabulous flashbacks from the night before". I was talking so fast that I had no control over the content. "As for 'mistake', you're right, it *was*. It ruined our friendship but if I had the chance to go back and do it all again, then I wouldn't change a *thing* about that night". I hadn't meant to shout and I definitely hadn't planned on telling him *that*. I felt my cheeks fill with heat and I wanted the ground to open up and swallow me. It was time to leave.

I couldn't look at him and went to walk away but he moved towards me and blocked my exit. I backed off quickly, the last thing I wanted from him, was a condescending hug.

"Why did you do that?" Marcus was speaking so softly, it was almost a whisper.

"Do *what?*"

"Move away like that".

"I don't need your pity".

"Actually, I was going to kiss you".

I couldn't hide the surprise but quickly tried to act cool. "You were?" I failed miserably.

"I *was*".

"But… you're not now?"

"I'm deciding".

My nerves were audible. "And what are you leaning towards?"

He continued to stare at me for a couple of seconds before he said, "That I'm *still* going to kiss you".

My stomach flipped. "Right". I went bright red again and had to work hard to keep my voice at a normal pitch. "So, what kind of kiss had you got planned?" Marcus raised an eyebrow and I smiled back. "A peck on the cheek, perhaps?"

He shook his head and laughed. "No". His gaze never left me which made me unsteady as he walked closer.

I tried to hide my anxious smile but it was pointless now. "Maybe a chaste kiss on the forehead then?"

He smirked and gained more ground. "Hadn't planned on it".

He was standing right in front of me but I suddenly felt too shy to make the first move, after all, this would change *everything*. It was a lot to take in, which might explain why I was now seeing things, I looked again through the window and there was nothing there, I could have sworn I saw Neil's head behind the privet hedge. Luckily, Marcus took the initiative; otherwise we'd have been standing there all day.

Chapter 39

The fallout from the party was bigger than most of us expected. It was no surprise that Jenna and Luke had become the social lepers of the community but the past few weeks had been an eye-opener, more and more stories about them surfaced and once the truth started to come out, it was like a surgeon hitting an artery, it just wouldn't stop. I'd known them nearly all of my life but it would appear I didn't *know* them at all. None of us could fathom why they had done what they'd done but at least now, I had stopped wearing the voltaged underpants and razorblade flip flops and stopped punishing myself for being so gullible and naïve.

Jenna kept on phoning, asking for me to call back but we had rallied together to support Alice and our shield was now impenetrable. On the quiet, I had tended to my own wounds; after all, I'd been a victim too. Carly had been right when she called it a game, we all must have been a constant source of amusement to them. Even if I managed to disregard everything else she had done, the one thing that would ensure that I would never forgive Jenna was her involvement with Carly and I. She lied to me about the night of 'the small scrap' and as soon as Carly left she'd done her best to widen the gap. I don't know why I was so surprised, I had known that Jenna would sell her own grandmother to get what she wanted, but I guess because my friends meant so much to *me*, I couldn't understand why anyone else would take it all for granted. It was Alice that was surprisingly philosophical about Jenna's behaviour, she observed that it was Jenna's *own* insecurities that had driven her to be so manipulative, if Alice cheated on *her* partner, then Jenna wouldn't feel so bad about her *own* indiscretions. I was impressed at Alice's assessment, she'd clearly been reading self help books but it was fantastic to see that she felt so healthy about the whole thing. And she was right; when Jenna's marriage began to show cracks (I believe it was when they got back from their honeymoon), she had tried to divide us *all* the only way she knew how. She had gone after Luke, Greg *and* Pete. It's maybe just as well that she didn't know about Marcus sooner...

Alice had been living with Emma for the last six weeks but came to stay with us frequently. It turned out Greg really *did* love Alice, proven by his constant gift-bearing visits to Emma's as often as she'd allow but he wasn't her only attentive gentleman caller. It turned out Craig had been harbouring a secret crush on Alice for years and according to our spies (that would be Emma), that's why he and Luke had fought at our 25th birthday party; Luke had bragged of his night with Alice and Craig had gallantly defended her honour. She received their attentions with smiles but was in no rush to make up her mind, as according to Alice, any relationship she entered into now, would be on *her* terms.

The longer Alice stayed, the happier Emma was. Alice was there to lend a hand with the dinner and the housework and play with the kids, it gave Emma the help and company she desperately needed and it gave the kids the attention that they craved. It also gave her the time to get out of the house and appreciate the wonder of a childless hour here and there. 'That' Justin initially complained but once he saw the difference in his wife, he *happily* sat down and shut up.

Luke is officially the most hated man in a ten mile radius and bearing in mind he never leaves the area, his life pretty much sucks right about now. As the gossip machine went into overdrive, the world had crumbled around him; his friends disowned him and all the girls gave him an extremely wide berth. It turned out Lyndsey's friend *did* see Luke in Vom's that night and a mate of Big Ears was chatting to some girls that were standing nearby, who heard the whole thing and so on and so on; it didn't take long for things to get around town. I'm only surprised from the way it dominated every conversation, that I hadn't had a phone call from my mother, where she'd read it in the local parish newsletter. Lyndsey royally dumped Luke of course and made sure that everyone knew he was a liar and a cheat. Oh, and she also told anyone who would listen that he had a small penis and gonorrhoea; nowt like a woman scorned! I bumped in to her on a night out in town and we chatted about everything that had happened, consoling each other's stupidity for getting involved with a... now what did she call him? Oh yeah, a twat, like Luke. Needless to say, she and I have become really great friends.

Talking of great friends, Carly and I are in constant contact now. They returned to their much quieter life down in Brighton and Carly confessed that she missed all the fireworks here; so Pete told her he'd happily start a fight in the restaurant to cheer her up. Marcus and I have plans to head down there for the weekend next month for her birthday and Pete confided in Marcus that he intends to propose. I can't wait!

As for Marcus and me? After we finally kissed and made up; he came back home. We told our friends one by one and enjoyed the mirth of a few of their jaws hitting the floor (although not as many as we'd suspected). We took the massive step of sharing a room like a proper couple and it's him I cuddle up to now when we're 'forced' to watch the Antiques Roadshow on a Sunday. It had taken a few weeks to get used to our new status and we'd avoided talking about 'the big fight' and 'the small scrap' at first but now everything is out in the open and we've been slowly checking off the things we promised to do before our silent period. Like for example, we managed a Sunday roast at Smokey Joes and we'd *finally* decided on our holiday destination; Las Vegas. The second he mentioned it, my eyes lit up and we knew we'd reached a compromise, only we decided that this kind of holiday would need back up... so we've invited our best friends to join us. Emma said she's going to take her doctor's advice and take a well earned break away from her family, Carly and Pete have already booked the time off work and Alice, well we knew she'd love wonderland. We've decided to go for a week in December for *Alice's* birthday, as we all agreed, it was about time she started celebrating her existence.

Marcus and I have already discussed it and I'm pleased to report that we'll be resisting the urge to do a Britney and we will return happily *unmarried*. It's not that the thought of marriage sends me running for the hills like a vegan from an egg custard anymore (far from it) but I think even the very mention of it, might *just* be a step too far for my mum and Neil. For now at least.

I was feeling pretty mature; maybe I didn't need a twelve step programme after all... I just needed a Marcus. I had gone from single to technically living with my boyfriend in just a few weeks and so far, I hadn't wigged once. Not even when he won the coin toss and got the right side of the bed, nor when he suggested we change the colour of my bedroom to something more neutral or when he continually left his underpants on the floor. Nope, I'd been cool, calm and collected; well, *almost*. The truth was, it was *us!* We annoyed the hell out of each other and constantly mocked each other; we were most definitely back to normal. Except this time, it was much more fun making up.

I'm still only 30 years old, so I don't know all there is to know about life, I'm still learning every single day but this I do know; almost every memory, every step of my life has been aided and abetted by my friends, the people that I *chose* to spend my life with have altered my course on countless occasions and whether good or bad, I thank them for it. See, life can suck, just when you think everything's going great it can turn but if you've got friends, *good* friends, the *best of friends*, you'll cope with anything life throws at you. There's a saying 'If life deals you lemons, you make lemonade' - personally, I always thought that could use a little Jenna on it; I think if life deals you lemons, you ask your best mates to pass the salt and hand you the tequila.

The past few months had been a journey. It hadn't started out as one and so I hadn't been prepared but now I had learnt my lesson that you *always* need to pack for any occasion... and thanks to my co-conspirators, I now know two *very* important things;

1) Growing old is inevitable but growing up is optional

 and

2) I know who my best friends are.

About the Author

Hayley Coulson grew up in Essex under the cloud of stiletto jokes, knowing that the only way to make it through life was to laugh at it.

After a year and a half of living in Portugal, she has been residing in Cambridgeshire for the last six years, travelling back to Essex as frequently as the border control and quarantine would let her through, to spend quality time with family and friends whom she adores.

Working in Communications for a big, multi-national company, Hayley learnt the importance of reaching an audience and sharing stories, so it was no surprise that when Hayley became redundant in the credit crunch of 2008, she chose writing as her new career. 'Best of Friends?' is Hayley's first novel but with a whole host of other ideas in the pipeline, she knows that there's so many more stories yet to tell.

Oh, and she's never once danced round her handbag...

Printed in the United Kingdom by
Lightning Source UK Ltd., Milton Keynes
141914UK00001BA/4/P